PRAISE FOR DHARMA KELLEHER

"Dharma Kelleher packs a lot of punch into a couple lines, and once you're snared, hang on, cause it just gets better and better."
Book Review Crew, Authors on the Air

"Kelleher's characterizations and voice are fresh and new, the action comes fast and furious."
Greg Herren, author of *Baton Rouge Bingo*

"Dharma Kelleher is a top-notch storyteller."
Kristen Lepionka, author of the Roxane Weary series

"Dharma is on my shortlist of favorite LGBTQIA authors."
PopCultureBeast.com

A PLAGUE OF GRACKLES

Carol,

Enjoy!

—Dharma Kelleher

6·19·24

A PLAGUE OF GRACKLES

AVERY BYRNE GOTH VIGILANTE
BOOK 3

DHARMA KELLEHER

A PLAGUE OF GRACKLES

AVERY BYRNE GOTH VIGILANTE SERIES

BOOK 3

Ebook ISBN: 978-1-952128-38-7

Paperback ISBN: 978-1-952128-39-4

Hardcover ISBN: 978-1-952128-40-0

For Eileen, who has seen me through many incarnations.
These twenty-five years have been the greatest blessing of my life.
You taught me what true love is. You showed me its depths.
You helped heal my deepest wounds.
Thank you for sharing this journey with me.

CHAPTER 1
DATE NIGHT

SOPHIA BITSUI GAZED DEEPLY into Étienne François's dark eyes aglow with candlelight. The aroma of cologne with a hint of shea butter made her senses tingle. Étienne leaned closer and trailed a line of kisses down her throat.

Her body reacted as if awakening for the first time. A deep need grew in her core. She craved him in a way she'd never felt with anyone before. The kisses continued along her chest, teasing the buds of her nipples, making her gasp.

Dialogue from the half-watched movie murmured softly, its meaning drowned out by the thunder of their synchronized heartbeats. Wrapped in this magnificent man's embrace, Sophia allowed herself to let down her shield and be in the moment—a respite from the hatred and vitriol of the white man's world that preferred women like her to disappear without a trace.

Étienne's touch was gentle, strong, and reassuring, pushing her ecstasy to heights she'd never thought possible. She moaned hungrily when at last he entered her. He was so big yet still a perfect fit.

Faster and harder he thrust until, at last, pleasure overwhelmed the circuitry in her brain. The orgasm rippled through every cell of her body. She cried out and laughed, her heart fluttering.

"Oh my God, oh my God, oh my God..."

When the waves of rapture subsided, Sophia floated on a cloud of euphoria. "That was... better than I ever dreamed possible. I haven't had an orgasm since..."

He chuckled. "Well, it was about time, then."

Étienne's deep and resonant voice sent shivers through her body. His spellbinding accent danced around each syllable.

"You... you're so amazing," she said.

"As are you. For many years, I dreamed of meeting a woman as lovely and enchanting as you."

Sophia flushed. "I don't know why you say that. I'm nothing special."

"*Okontrè, cheri mwen,*" Étienne replied in Haitian Creole, his eyes sparkling. "You are a woman so rare."

"I think the word you're looking for is *freak.*"

"Non, non, non. Rare like *yon bijou presye,* a precious jewel."

"Why? Because I'm trans? Or because I'm Navajo?"

"Both have shaped you into the woman you are—brilliant, beautiful, fearless, and strong. The struggles you've overcome to be your authentic self—they've amplified your radiance. Your vibrant, courageous soul enchants me like a siren's song."

"You've faced far worse struggles than I have."

He nodded. "*Wi,* I have survived many tragedies. Hurricanes, earthquakes, disease, government corruption, loss of my family."

"You did more than survive. You thrived. To become a doctor after all of that? You did your family proud, baby."

"*Wi,* but my proudest moment was finding Mademoiselle Sophia Bitsui of Phoenix, Arizona."

Étienne kissed her deeply again. She felt their souls intertwine. *Bliss* was the only word to describe it.

Without warning, he broke off the embrace, his eyes alert with alarm. "What was that sound?"

"What sound?" She'd noticed nothing over the thunder of their heartbeats. But when she concentrated, she heard it too—a muffled clomping of footsteps and tinny, distorted voices.

"It's just the TV," she assured him, not wanting to interrupt their second round of lovemaking.

Étienne sat up and snatched the remote from the coffee table then muted the television. The sounds were getting louder. The front door burst open, and a group of men dressed in combat gear stormed into the house, their assault weapons trained on Étienne.

"Police! Get on the floor! Do it now!"

Étienne sprang to his feet, his naked body shielding Sophia's. "Who are you?" he demanded, brandishing the remote. "How dare you break into this house! Get out this instant!"

Terror coiled around Sophia's heart as she sat up, her blood chilling to ice. She sensed the impending doom but was powerless to stop it. Time slowed, each second stretching into eternity.

In an instant, deafening gunfire filled the air. Bullets tore Étienne's body apart in a grotesque tableau of death. His once sturdy frame collapsed to the floor.

"Nooo!" She reached for him, and searing pain bit into her own shoulder.

Her ears rang with an otherworldly silence. Her body felt detached from her spirit, even as her shoulder burned with hellfire. Consciousness faded as the hungry void pulled her into merciful oblivion.

CHAPTER 2
MIDNIGHT MOVIE

SWEAT BEADED on my forehead as I stood in line outside Tempe's Mill Avenue Theater for the midnight showing of *The Rocky Horror Picture Show*. Even at this late hour, the desert heat held steady at nearly ninety degrees, despite it being early October.

The growing crowd filled the air with excited conversation and snippets of songs from the movie. It had been more than a year since I'd last seen the cult classic, and I couldn't wait.

My outfit, a slinky black negligee, showed off the tapestry of tattoos on my arms and chest, much of it my own work. The frizzy wig I wore to emulate Magenta felt like a fur coat fastened to my scalp and had me craving the cool air-conditioning that waited inside.

I yearned for autumn's reprieve after yet another record-breaking summer. To step outside during the day without feeling as if my eyeballs were boiling in my skull would be an overdue change.

Roz Fein, my girlfriend, stood beside me, sparkling in her Columbia ensemble—sequined outfit, top hat, and tap shoes clattering softly. "Wow, that's exciting, Mom!" she exclaimed into the phone. "Sounds like an Israeli version of Coachella. Have fun, and give my love to Jude, Talia, and the kids."

When she ended the call, I asked, "What was that about Coachella?"

"They're going to the Supernova, a huge music festival celebrating the end of Sukkot. It's near my brother's kibbutz," she explained. "I think my mom's looking forward to reliving her riot grrrl days."

"I hope they have a blast."

A shout from a familiar voice interrupted our exchange. "Avery Byrne, you look hot as fuck!"

Kimiko Sato, my best friend, was dressed as the demure Janet Weiss. The white cardigan and knee-length pink dress with a Peter Pan collar were a stark departure from her usual sugar-skulled La Calavera Catrina stage persona as the front woman and upright bass player for the psychobilly band Damaged Souls.

"Slut!" I responded in true *Rocky Horror* tradition.

"That's me."

"You look great," I told her. "Better than the original Janet."

"Wow!" Chupa Melendez, Kimi's hulk of a husband, looked as if he were about to drool over my revealing outfit. He wore a full-length trench coat and flip-flops.

"Eyes up here, big guy," I teased, pointing to my face. "We're both taken."

"Sorry." His tan face turned bright red.

"I figured you would dress as Frankie like you did in Las Cruces, Avery," Kimi said.

"Magenta's more my style," I assured her. "Besides, we remember what happened in Las Cruces."

Chupa winced and placed a hand on his belly. "Don't remind me. I still have a scar from the gunshot wound."

I gave him a sympathetic look. That bullet had been meant for me.

"Aren't you hot in that trench coat, big guy?" Roz teased, tugging at Chupa's sleeve.

He blushed. "It's a little cold out."

"Cold?" I asked, grateful for a change in subject. "It's ninety fucking degrees."

"He's shy!" Kimi said. "He's got a costume on under there."

"Come on, Chup. Let's see." I had a good idea what he was wearing.

Chupa undid the tie and opened the coat to reveal a gold lamé bikini bottom and nothing else.

"Oh, Rocky!" Roz said. "Wow. If I didn't play for the all-girls team, I'd be all over you."

Kimi cleared her throat. "Back off, slut! He's all mine." She mimed protecting her husband.

"Here comes the rest of the crew."

The arrival of Omar "Torch" Shaheen—dressed dramatically in corset, fishnets, and heels—and McCobb as a hump-backed Riff Raff added to our eclectic group. A tattoo of the sonogram of Torch's son peeked out from above his corset.

"Nice legs, Frankie!" I said to Torch.

He strutted and twirled, showing off his muscular legs. "What can I say? If you got it, flaunt it!"

As we shared a laugh, Kimi revealed her stash of props for the night—water pistols, toast, rice, confetti, and noise-makers. "I was supposed to cook the rice, right?"

I looked at her incredulously. "Um, no?"

She burst out laughing. "Just kidding. By the way, we've got a virgin joining us tonight."

"Who?" I asked.

Kimi pointed toward a middle-aged man in a tweed suit wheeling toward us in his electric wheelchair. Scott Murray, the band's manager, had been struck this past summer by a wrong-way driver. The trauma to his back left him only able to walk short distances.

"Great Scott," said Roz. "Is that…?"

"It is," Kimi assured us.

"Evening, young people," Scott said.

"Evening, Scott," I said. "I never took you for a *Rocky Horror* fan."

"Not my usual taste in cinema. But I figured it would be an opportunity to promote the band's upcoming release of *Graveyard Groove*." He held up a handful of postcards featuring the band's new album cover on one side. "These rather… uh, colorful people are very much our demographic."

"I think you're right. And might I say, you look rather dapper as Dr. Scott."

Just as the line began to move, my phone rang. The caller ID told me it was Theo Carter, a trans masculine member of the Phoenix Gender Alliance. *Why the hell's he calling so late?*

"What's up, Theo?"

"Avery, thank God you answered." He sounded panicked. "Sophia's been shot. Her boyfriend too."

"By who?"

"The cops! They busted into our house and shot them."

"Fuck! Are they okay? Are you okay?" I asked.

"I'm… I'm okay. I wasn't there when it happened. But Sophia… she's in surgery. And her boyfriend, Étienne… he's dead."

"Shit. Where are you?"

"The emergency room at Scottsdale Osborn."

"I'm in Tempe. I can be there in twenty minutes." I hung up. "Sorry, folks, but I gotta go. A friend's been shot."

Roz's eyes widened. "Who?"

"Sophia Bitsui, the chair of Phoenix Gender Alliance. That was her housemate, Theo."

Roz gave my hand a squeeze of support. "Let's go."

"You want us to come too?" Kimi offered.

I hugged her. "No, y'all have fun. Help Dr. Scott, here, promote your album release."

"I'm sorry about your friend."

"Thanks."

"DM me and let me know how she's doing."

"Will do."

We hurried to the parking lot, and I hopped behind the wheel of the Gothmobile, my restored 1957 Cadillac. Roz slid into the passenger seat, and we raced north to the hospital.

"Motherfuckers!" I growled, taking a corner faster than I meant to and clipped the curb.

"Easy, babe," Roz replied. "Let's try to get there in one piece."

"It's just that last year, the cops accused members of the Phoenix Gender Alliance of being members of a criminal gang. The year before that they tried to frame me for Sam's murder. Now they're busting into our homes and shooting us."

The Phoenix Gender Alliance was a support group for the valley's trans and gender-questioning community. Sophia was the chairperson; I was the vice chair. Before Roz and I started dating, the Desert Mafia had killed my girlfriend, Samantha Ferguson. The horror of discovering her brutalized body still haunted me.

"We don't know what happened."

"Yes, we do. The whole fucking world's trying to wipe us out, including the cops. Between the rash of anti-trans laws and the increasing violence, they just may succeed."

I cut in front of a slow-moving pickup truck, whose driver laid on the horn and flashed his high beams in retaliation.

"Ave, if you don't slow down and take it easy, you just may wipe us out first."

Goth, I hated when she was right. Which she was. A lot. I took a deep breath to calm myself. It didn't help.

I shivered when we stepped through the double set of automatic doors into the ER waiting room. The cold, sterile air smelled strongly of disinfectant. Just inside the entrance, a cluster of uniformed cops quietly chatted and joked. Their hushed laughter left me wondering if they had been the ones who shot Sophia and her boyfriend.

We found Theo asleep in the waiting room, hunched over in a chair, his muscular arms wrapped around his chest. His black curly hair was clipped short, accentuating his high cheekbones. He wore faded jeans and a tan shirt that complemented his dark-brown skin.

Gently waking him, I braced myself for the news that awaited.

CHAPTER 3
CHOSEN FAMILY

THE OCCASIONAL MURMUR of hushed conversations and the distant sound of medical equipment punctuated the silence, adding to the surreal, time-warped feeling of the emergency room at night.

Theo looked up, his eyes flickering with a mix of worry and bemusement. "Um, did I interrupt some kinky sex?" His attempt at humor interrupted the somber silence of the late-night ER waiting room. "I mean, I know you're goth, but..."

"What? Oh, the costumes. No, you didn't interrupt anything," I quickly clarified, as Roz and I settled beside him. "We were about to see *Rocky Horror* at the midnight show."

"Sorry to ruin your fun."

"No need to apologize. You're family. How's Sophia?"

Theo's voice wavered. "She's in recovery now and will be taken to a room shortly."

"So, what the hell happened?"

His eyes narrowed with concern, glistening with tears. "I was out with friends when it happened, so I don't know all the details. Sophia and Étienne were having a date night at the house. I got into the neighborhood around ten thirty and found the street blocked off. I told the police who I was, and they questioned me for, like, an hour."

"About what?"

"If we kept any guns in the house, which we don't. They asked what I knew about Étienne, which wasn't much. He and Sophia had only been dating a couple of weeks. They also wanted to know if he was ever violent with Sophia, which he hadn't been as far as I know."

"Why were the cops there in the first place? Was Étienne wanted for something?"

"I asked, but they wouldn't tell me nada. But there was a SWAT truck parked in front of our house."

"Sounds like someone may have swatted her."

"Swatted?" Theo looked horrified. "I know Sophia's a gamer, but damn. Swatting someone is seriously messed up."

"It's not just gamers who get swatted these days," Roz said. "These jerks are doing it to politicians and anyone they don't like."

"That means whoever did this knows where we live."

A young man in scrubs walked into the waiting area. "Family of Sophia Bitsui?"

I stiffened, but Roz and I followed Theo over to where the man was standing.

"Yes?" Theo said.

"I'm Jake, one of the assisting nurses. Sophia is in her room. She's groggy but stable."

"Oh, thank God. Can we see her?"

Jake eyed Roz and me suspiciously. "You're her family?"

"Yes," I said, daring him to refuse me. "Chosen family."

"Very well. I'll take you to her."

Just as Jake started down the corridor, a voice called, "Hold up!"

A woman in a crisp navy-blue suit, slightly worn at the edges, strode toward us with a presence that commanded

attention. She wore her gray-streaked auburn hair in a prac-
tical short style. Fine lines marked the sun-damaged skin of
her face. Two uniformed officers trailed her.

The suit flashed a badge. "I'm Detective Rutherford. Is
Sophia Bitsui out of surgery? I need to ask her some
questions."

Anger and suspicion surged within me. "Haven't you
people done enough? You shoot her and kill her boyfriend.
Now you want to interrogate her while she's recovering
from surgery for bullet wounds you inflicted?"

Rutherford cocked her head. "And who are you?"

"Avery Byrne. Sophia's my friend. And you're not
talking to her without a lawyer."

I expected the detective to push back, but her hazel eyes
softened. "Fair enough. How soon can her attorney be here?
We need her to answer some questions about what
happened tonight."

You're not the only one, lady. "I'll call her now. She'll get
here when she gets here. Until then, you vultures keep your
fucking distance."

Rutherford held up her hands in a pacifying gesture. "We
will."

I turned back to Jake the nurse. "Take us to her room."

Our footsteps echoed in the hallway on the awkward
walk into the bowels of the hospital. After a brief elevator
ride brought us to the fourth floor, I called Kirsten Pasternak,
a lawyer and member of the Phoenix Gender Alliance. The
phone rang four times before a sleepy voice answered.

"Kirsten, it's Avery. Sorry to wake you up, but a bunch of
trigger-happy cops shot Sophia Bitsui and her boyfriend,
and now they want to interrogate her. We need your help."

"Okay, okay. Where are you?"

"Scottsdale Osborn."

The nurse stopped at a room with Sophia's name written
on a dry-erase board by the door. "She's in room 437."

"Be there as quick as I can."

As I tried to enter the room, Rutherford blocked our path. "No one talks to her before me, except her attorney."

"She's on her way. Until then, Sophia needs her friends."

"I'm sorry, but I can't allow that."

"Why not?" I argued, my anger boiling over. "Afraid we might learn the truth?"

"Why won't you tell us what really happened?" Theo demanded, tears again forming in her eyes. "Why'd you shoot them? They've done nothing wrong."

"I'm afraid I can't discuss that at this time."

"Just all full of secrets, aren't you?" I said. "So afraid everyone will learn that Phoenix PD is nothing but a bunch of transphobic Nazis. Last year, you arrested a bunch of us, including Sophia, for being part of a so-called criminal gang. I guess this year, you're not even bothering with arrests. You just bust into our homes and shoot us on sight. Well, Sieg heil, you fascist bitch!"

Rutherford's stern expression softened. "I understand you're angry. If I can be honest…"

"That would be a refreshing change."

"My brother is trans. He transitioned a few years ago."

I studied the woman's face and recognized a familiarity in her features. "Chris Rutherford's your brother?"

"He is. And I support him one hundred percent."

"And yet you still work for the cops? After all they've done?"

"I'm trying to change things for the better. When members of the Phoenix Gender Alliance were arrested at the rally, I protested loudly to my superiors. All the way to the Chief Williams herself. We've initiated new protocols to be more sensitive to the needs of the trans community."

I'd heard it all before and didn't buy it. Promises of progress, committees formed, initiatives proposed, but nothing ever changed.

"I don't know exactly what happened earlier this evening," she continued, "but I promise you all, I will get to the truth. And when I do, those responsible will be held accountable."

My animosity toward Rutherford faded, but my skepticism lingered. "Fine," I said. "We'll wait."

The weight of the situation hung heavily in the air as we waited in the sterile, dimly lit hospital corridor. Forty minutes later, Kirsten Pasternak strode in, her presence commanding as always. Towering a few inches above six feet, she was the epitome of poise in her light-gray tailored suit and lavender top.

"Sorry for the late call, Kirsten." I glanced at my watch, which showed it was almost one in the morning.

She embraced me, her assurance palpable. "Not a problem. Comes with the job." Her deep voice, carefully modulated to blend femininity with assertiveness, had a musical quality.

"Don't let them jam her up."

"I promise I'll do everything I can to protect her." She turned to Rutherford. "Detective."

After a brief negotiation with Rutherford, Kirsten entered Sophia's room, leaving us in a corridor rife with tension and whispered fears.

CHAPTER 4
SOLIDARITY

TEN MINUTES LATER, Rutherford knocked then walked into Sophia's hospital room and shut the door.

"Why would someone target Sophia like this?" Theo's voice trembled with anger. "She's the sweetest person I know."

"Maybe because she's a female gamer," Roz suggested. "A lot of toxic masculinity going on in that world. Mediocre players who get pissed when a girl is better than them."

"Or someone found out she's trans," I added. "She's listed as the chair on the Phoenix Gender Alliance website."

"If they know where we live, what could they do next?"

"You can stay with us for a while," I said, glancing over at Roz, who nodded her approval. "At least until this blows over."

"I can't impose on you like that."

"You're not imposing," I said. "We're offering."

He seemed to consider it then nodded. "Thanks. Just for a night."

I hugged him. "No problem. We're all family, right?"

"You know, Sophia getting sidelined makes you acting chair," Theo noted.

I hadn't realized it until just then. When the vice chair position had come open a year earlier, my foster father, Bobby Jeong, had encouraged me to take it despite my reticence.

"I'm not the leader type, *Appa*," I'd told him, using the Korean word for father. "I'm more a 'lurk in the shadows' kinda gal."

"As vice chair, you would be in charge of the Hatchlings group." The Hatchlings was the Phoenix Gender Alliance's youth group, where I had started several years earlier. "The kids in the Hatchlings group need your experience and guidance. After all the support you received from them when you were their age, it's time to step up and pay it forward."

I remembered all the shit that had happened after my bio dad discovered my stash of girl clothes when I was thirteen. He'd kicked me out onto the streets, where I'd been sexually harassed by a teen shelter manager, hassled by dirty cops, and jumped by junkies.

By the time Bobby and his wife, Melissa, took me in, three years later, I'd been through hell so many times I'd lost count. Bobby was right that I could make a difference for these kids and help them make better choices than I had. So in the end, I'd told Sophia yes to being vice chair of the Hatchlings.

With her in the hospital, I now shouldered her responsibilities as well as mine. I suddenly felt out of my depth. "We had the monthly meeting earlier this month. I'll be chairing the Hatchlings' meeting on Wednesday and hosting the Halloween party. What all was Sophia working on?"

"She and Danielle were coordinating the Trans March and the schedule for manning the booth at the Pride Festival this coming Saturday. You think it's still safe to march?"

I considered the question. All the violence we'd been witnessing over the past few years had one objective—to erase us. I would not let that happen.

"Whether it's safe or not, we need to represent now more than ever," I said firmly. "The march isn't just a parade; it's a stand of defiance, a statement that we will not be silenced."

Kirsten and Detective Rutherford emerged from Sophia's room. "Thanks for your help, Detective."

They shook hands, then Rutherford handed each of us a business card. "If any of you hear anything that might help us find who did this, call me. You all have a good night."

As she disappeared down the corridor, I crumpled the business card. There wasn't a trash can nearby, so I dropped it in my purse.

"You thanked her for her help?" I asked Kirsten. "They fucking shot her."

"Strange as it sounds, I believe she's on our side in this."

I scoffed.

"What happened?" Theo asked. "Why'd they shoot her?"

"From what Detective Rutherford explained, someone called 911 claiming to be Lionel Robertson."

"Who the hell's Lionel Robertson?"

"He's an enforcer for a local drug gang and the primary suspect for multiple brutal murders in the Valley. The caller claimed to be holding several people hostage and would shoot any cop who approached the house. So Phoenix PD sent in SWAT team."

"Fuck," I said.

"When SWAT entered, they mistook Étienne for Robertson. He refused their orders to get on the ground and allegedly pointed a weapon at them. That's when they shot him."

"What weapon?" Roz asked. "She and Étienne were on a date. Why would he have a gun on him?"

"That's what Detective Robertson is investigating."

"Yeah, right. What's going to happen to the cops who shot them?"

"I don't know. Rutherford is part of the Professional Standards Bureau. She investigates officer-involved shootings."

I wasn't so easily mollified, even if Rutherford had a trans brother. "Cops protect their own. We've seen it over and over again. The thin blue line. Odds of those trigger-happy assholes going to jail are nil. We saw what happened when cops murdered Breonna Taylor. Nothing."

"We'll have to see. Detective Rutherford is an ally to the community, so we have that going for us. For now, I think we should all go home and get some rest."

"I'd like to go in and see her for a minute," Theo said. "After that interrogation, she needs to know we're here for her."

"I think she'd like that," Kirsten replied. "Good night, all."

"Thanks for coming out," I said.

"Any time." Kirsten gave us all hugs. "I'll talk to you soon."

When Kirsten left, Roz and I accompanied Theo into the room, which was suffused with the muted glow of the room's lights and the screen of the vitals monitor. The persistent, rhythmic beep of the heart monitor merged with the faint hum of the air-conditioning system. The room felt suspended in a hushed tension, as if the walls were holding their breath.

Sophia lay there, a pale shadow of herself under the hospital lights. A stark white cast encased her shoulder and arm, bright against her skin. Lines of discomfort and fatigue were etched in her face. Her breathing was shallow and measured, the effort evident each time her chest rose and fell.

"Hola, chica," Theo said. "I'm so sorry this happened."

"Yeah." Sophia's drowsy dark eyes fluttered open, seeming to search for answers. Her voice was a ragged whisper. "How's Étienne? The detective wouldn't say."

I felt a tightness in my chest. No one had told her. "He didn't make it."

Her reaction, a mix of pain and disbelief, tore at my heart. Theo grasped her free hand.

"Why?" Sophia asked. "Why'd they do this?"

"I think someone swatted you. Cops are looking into who made the call," I told her, though I wasn't all that hopeful.

"We should let you get some rest," Roz piped in, putting an arm around my shoulder.

"Yeah. Get some sleep, girl," I said. "Theo's gonna stay with us until this mess gets sorted out."

"We'll stop by tomorrow morning and check on you," he added.

Sophia managed a weak smile. "Thanks."

As we left her to rest, the heaviness of the situation hung over us. The night air in the corridor felt colder, in contrast to the warmth of our shared resolve to stand by Sophia and each other.

CHAPTER 5
A GATHERING STORM

THE MORNING LIGHT filtered through a half-open window, casting a warm golden hue across the painted purple walls of the kitchen. Mismatched mugs—treasures from Roz's garage-sale excursions—hung from brass hooks below the worn wooden cabinets. I sipped my coffee, scouring local news sites on my phone for any mention of Sophia's swatting incident.

Roz shuffled in, wearing black fleece pajamas, her shoulders hunched. Fear and panic flickered in deep-set hazel eyes. Her dark-brown hair, usually styled in a spiky, side-shaved look, was disheveled.

I jumped up from the table and put an arm around her then guided her to her chair. "Sweetie, what's wrong?"

Her eyes brimmed with tears. "T-Torch texted me. Hamas attacked the Supernova festival. Fired thousands of rockets into Israel."

"Oh goth!"

"I… I can't get ahold of my mom, my brother, or Talia. I don't know if they're alive or…" Her husky voice trembled with vulnerability. In our eighteen months together, I'd never seen her so shaken.

"Oh shit." I wrapped her in my arms, feeling her body shake. "I'm so sorry, sweetie."

I wanted to assure her that her mother, her brother, and his wife would be all right, but I knew such guarantees were bullshit.

"What's Israel doing about the attack?"

"According to the news, IDF sent jet fighters to bomb Gaza. Torch hasn't been able to reach his grandparents or other family members in Gaza City. None of them have anything to do with Hamas. What the fuck is happening to this world?"

I kissed her temple, trying to send her some of my strength and resilience. "Beats the hell outta me. Things have been bad ever since that orange turd got elected. And lately, the hate and violence toward minorities feel ramped up tenfold."

We held each other in silence for a long time. I could feel her pulse racing, her breath shallow and quick.

"Theo still asleep?" I asked in a whisper.

"Door was still closed when I walked past."

"So fucking tired of this shit." Frustration and anger erupted inside of me. "This is the fourth attack on the trans community in as many months," I grumbled.

Three Black trans women had been murdered and a Latinx nonbinary person assaulted. Each attack felt like a knife in my chest. These people were my found family.

"Maybe you should cancel the Trans March next Saturday."

I sat up and looked at her. "Are you kidding? We can't back down now. That would only embolden the fascists. We've got to send a message that we will not be bullied. We will not be silenced. We will not go away just because our existence exposes what a sad joke the patriarchy is."

"Maybe you're right. I'm just worried something will happen to you too."

"Nothing's going to happen at Pride, aside from a bunch of pathetic Jesus freaks waving their little signs near the festival entrance. Nobody pays them any attention. Let me pour you some coffee."

I filled a mug, added a spoonful of sugar, and placed it in front of her. She sipped it tentatively.

"Any news about Sophia and Étienne getting swatted?" she asked.

I turned to the article still on my phone. "It says, 'Two people were shot in an officer-involved shooting late Saturday night near Fifty-Sixth Street and Thomas in Phoenix. One man was killed. A woman is listed in stable condition. Phoenix police have not released the identities of the victims nor any details on what led to the shooting, since this is an ongoing investigation.' That's it. No mention that Sophia was trans. Not sure if that's good or bad."

"Police are playing things close to the vest. I suppose shooting innocent unarmed civilians is never a good look for them."

"Question is, will the press publish the truth once it does come out? Will they misgender Sophia or try to blame the attack on her being trans?"

"Why would they do that?" Roz asked. "I thought the press had gotten better about not misgendering trans people."

"They had. But lately, it's a toss-up. The *New York Times* has been publishing transphobic hit pieces. Even the ones that don't outright misgender us still take a 'both sides' approach to anything to do with transgender issues. As if our basic civil rights and the fascists' blatant bigotry and lies are on par with each other."

Roz placed a hand in mine. In this fucked-up world, at least I had someone like her by my side.

Theo walked in, dark circles under his eyes, wearing the

same wrinkled clothes from the night before. "I thought I smelled coffee."

"Morning, Theo." A hospitable smile blossomed on Roz's face despite her anguish. "Have a seat. We'll fix you a cup."

"How do you like it?" I asked.

"A little cream if you have it." He sat down.

"Coming up."

Roz placed a hand on Theo's arm. "You get any sleep?"

"A bit. Worried about Sophia. I feel violated, even though she's the one who got shot."

"Why wouldn't you?" I set the mug down in front of her and took my seat. "The cops turned your home into a crime scene."

"As did whoever swatted them." Roz added, ever the voice of reason.

Theo sighed. "Why do some guys have to be such dicks? Makes the rest of us look bad."

"Who knows? Testosterone poisoning?" I gave him a gentle elbow to the ribs.

I stood up, ready to shift gears. "Let's get breakfast going, and then we can check on Sophia."

A couple of hours later, we found Sophia in her room, looking sullen and clumsily manipulating her phone with her good hand. On the plus side, she seemed to have regained some color in her cheeks. Roz set down a vase of flowers we'd picked up from the gift shop.

"Hey, girl," Theo said. "How're you feeling?"

"Miserable." Sophia stared at the sheets covering her. "I finally found a man who loved me, and they murdered him."

"I've been there," I clasped her hand.

Roz put an arm over my shoulder. "You in a lot of pain?"

"Feels like a buffalo perched on my shoulder. Doctor said the bullet shattered my clavicle. Had to put in a bunch of pins and rods to piece it back together."

"Do you remember what happened?" Theo asked.

Sophia hesitated, her face contorting with pain. "Étienne and I were making out on the sofa in the living room. Next thing I know, these men in riot gear busted into the house, brandishing assault rifles, and yelling. I was terrified. And Étienne…" Her voice faltered.

I placed a hand on her uninjured arm.

"Étienne stood up and demanded they leave. They shouted at him to get on the floor. When he refused, they opened fire. Murdered him right in front of my eyes. Shot me too. I don't remember anything after that until I woke up here. I couldn't understand why they were there, but that detective thinks someone swatted me."

"Have any of the people you game with been threatening you?" I asked her.

"There's always trolls—pathetic guys who don't like getting beat by a woman. Lately, a player named AlphaNinja45 has been giving me shit me during *League of Legends*. He found out I'm trans and has been misgendering me and calling me a pervert. Said he knew where I lived and that he'd fuck me up. I brushed it off as an empty threat. Maybe I was wrong to ignore it."

A dormant, vengeful part of me stirred to life, hungry for justice and violence. "Is this AlphaNinja45 guy local?"

"No idea. He could be overseas and spoofed his location so that the 911 call got routed to Phoenix. The detective mentioned coordinating with the feds to locate him."

"I'm sure they'll do everything they can," Theo told her. "You just focus on getting better."

"I wish Étienne were here with me. He was such a good man."

"I know it's hard," I said. "I struggled after Sam was killed."

"I'll never meet someone as kind and understanding as Étienne. He was so loving. And didn't care that I was trans."

"I felt the same way. But then I met Roz. As much as I loved Sam, I've never been happier than I am now."

Roz kissed my cheek. "Just focus on healing, Sophia. There are plenty of people out there who would love to be with you."

Sophia sobbed while the rest of us sat, offering silent support. When she gained control of her emotions, she wiped the tears from her face. "The Pride festival and the Trans March are next weekend. I'd been working with Danielle, but she hasn't returned my calls in weeks. Emails come back as undeliverable. I'm worried something happened to her."

Danielle Kirkpatrick had been a member of Phoenix Gender Alliance for a few years, starting out in the Hatchlings like me. This news of her sudden disappearance worried me. I hoped she hadn't become yet another casualty in the far right's war on trans people.

"Isn't Danielle a sophomore at ASU?" I asked. "Maybe she's busy with her studies."

"She mentioned having problems financially," Theo said. "Something to do with her scholarship."

"I remember. I donated to her GoFundMe. Didn't she get that sorted out?" I asked.

"She ghosted before I heard one way or the other," Sophia replied.

"Let me try to get a hold of her. I'll let you know what I find out."

Sophia squeezed my hand. "Thanks, Avery. If you can't reach her, would you mind coordinating the Trans March and the Phoenix Gender Alliance's booth at the festival?"

I hesitated. Leading the Hatchlings group was one thing. But taking over the march and our booth at Pride was something else. I wasn't an event planner.

Theo spoke up before I could say no. "She and I can do it together, Soph. Avery, if you could pick up the banner and signs we ordered at the Office Oasis, I will manage our booth."

"I can handle that," I said, not wanting to disappoint.

The conversation shifted to lighter subjects, but after a while, our visit was taking a visible toll on Sophia. Her eyelids drooped, and the emotion in her voice became palpable.

"We should let you get some rest," I told her. "Hang in there, okay?"

"We'll see you soon, chica," Theo said.

We all hugged her and walked to the elevators.

"I should head home and assess the damage those damned cops did to our place," Theo muttered bitterly as she pressed the call button.

"Do you need us to come with you?" I offered.

"Would you mind? I don't think I can handle it by myself."

"Of course. We're free, right?" I glanced at Roz for confirmation.

"Absolutely. Family first," Roz affirmed with a supportive smile. "We'll be right behind you."

CHAPTER 6
CRIME SCENE

TWENTY MINUTES LATER, we pulled up to their house near Fifty-Sixth Street and Thomas. The front door was shut, but the frame was shattered.

"Damn cops." Theo easily pushed open the unsecured door.

A peculiar odor greeted us—a blend of spent gunpowder and stale blood. A reddish-brown stain tarnished the living room carpet. Similar stains streaked the sofa while bullet holes scarred the opposite wall.

"Shit," I said as broken glass crunched underfoot.

My nostrils filled with the smell as the memory of my late girlfriend's tortured body rose like a leviathan from the depths of my trauma. The deafening thunder of gunfire and the acrid stench of gunpowder had filled the air as Sam's killers came after me. A cop had been involved then too. A dirty cop. A now-dead dirty cop.

"Ave, you all right?" Roz's concerned voice pulled me back to the present.

"Yeah, I'm okay," I assured her, shaking off the haunting recollections.

"Damn," Theo said. "What am I going to do about all this?"

"Contact your insurance," Roz advised. "They'll know professionals for crime scene cleanup, especially the blood."

"You should sue the fucking cops responsible," I added. "Let them foot the bill for this mess. Maybe Kirsten can recommend someone."

"The front door should be a priority," Roz said. "You don't want anyone walking in and robbing the place."

"Call Jinx Ballou." I touched the wall where a slug had punched a quarter-sized hole.

Theo frowned. "Isn't Jinx a bounty hunter? Why would she help?"

"Her brother is a contractor who restores and flips houses. He could fix the doorframe in no time."

He nodded. "Thanks."

"You going to be okay here?" Roz asked.

After composing himself, Theo said, "I'll be all right. I'm not letting those gun-thug cops drive me from my home."

As we drove off in the Gothmobile, my mind was awash with a million concerns. The safety of Roz's family was foremost, but I was also concerned for Sophia and Theo, especially with the swatter still at large. Danielle's inexplicable silence also worried me. *Has someone attacked her too?*

Ten years had passed since my tumultuous coming out. I'd survived the streets, but the other Lost Kids who'd squatted in the vacant house with me had not. We'd dubbed ourselves the Lost Kids after the Lost Boys in *Peter Pan*. A terrorist bomb killed my foster mother, Melissa Jeong, a few years later. Then Sam was murdered. I worried that anyone who got close to me was destined for disaster. For the past eighteen months, Roz had brought stability into my life. Yet I couldn't shake a feeling of impending doom, especially amid the rising tide of transphobic violence.

"You okay?" Roz's voice broke through my ruminations.

"Worried."

"About Theo?"

"About everything. The escalating bigotry, the violence... It's terrifying."

"Yeah." From the haunted look on her own face, I knew her family's situation was foremost in her mind. She'd been putting on a brave face all morning, but she had to be going out of her mind with worry. I sure as hell would be.

"I wish... I wish I knew what to say about your family. That they'll be all right. But I know I can't promise that."

"No, you can't."

"But your mom is strong and smart. She's a survivor. I'm sure your brother and his family are too."

"None of that can stop bullets or a terrorist rocket."

Suddenly, the taste of metal and the stench of burned flesh filled my senses as the memory of the explosion that killed my foster mother overwhelmed me. Even sitting in the safety of the Gothmobile, I choked and gasped for breath. I rallied to stay in the present moment.

"No matter what," I told her, "you've got me. I know that's not much, but..."

"It means everything to me." She wrapped her hand around mine. "Right now, you're my lifeline, babe."

"And you mine."

Roz took a deep breath and let it out. "Hopefully, Detective Rutherford can figure out who swatted Sophia."

"Maybe. I'm not holding my breath. Rutherford's a cop. I don't trust cops."

"You have reason not to, given your history. But still, I think she wants justice for what happened."

"She could start by arresting the officers who shot Sophia and her boyfriend. That was inexcusable."

"I agree."

"In the meantime, I need to find out what's happened to Danielle. Her disappearance right before Pride is alarming."

"Do you know where she lives?"

"Her address is in my phone."

Roz pulled my phone from my purse. "What's her last name?"

"Kirkpatrick."

"Here it is. Maple Avenue. Looks like it's just south of Eleventh Street, near Mill Avenue."

We found the address—a duplex with an empty carport and old newspapers in the driveway. It appeared deserted. A heavyset man in a white tank top was trimming bushes next door.

"Doesn't look like anyone's home," Roz said as we approached the house.

I checked the date on a newspaper, a neighborhood weekly. It was a couple of weeks old. "I think you're right."

No one answered the door when I rang the bell, and I couldn't see anything through the window. "Maybe we should go inside and look around."

"I believe that's called breaking and entering."

"I call it a safety check," I said.

"People generally call the police for that."

"Yeah, the police that just shot Sophia and murdered her boyfriend. No thanks."

"Can I help you, ladies?" called the man from next door.

"Yeah," I said, turning to him. "I'm looking for the woman who lives here."

"Haven't seen her in a while. Good riddance, ya ask me."

I felt my hackles raise. "Oh? And why's that?"

"Playing loud music at all hours. Freaky-looking people wandering through my yard, trampling my lantana. Figured she was a whore or a drug dealer."

"For your information, she was none of those things. She was just a student. When was the last time you saw her?"

"Dunno. Labor Day, maybe? Saw a guy packing boxes into a truck a week or so ago. Figured she moved out."

"What'd this guy look like?" I pressed.

The man shrugged. "Just a guy. Didn't get a real good look at him."

I wanted to press him for more information, but clearly, this knucklehead didn't know shit. "Let's go," I told Roz.

As we drove back home, I kept ruminating about it. Something wasn't right.

"Maybe she's on vacation," Roz suggested, taking my hand as I drove. "She's a college student. They do impulsive things."

"In the middle of the semester? Doubt it. When she was in the Hatchlings, all she talked about was becoming a doctor. Theo said she was having problems with her scholarship, but that doesn't explain why she's disappeared."

"Maybe she really did move."

I considered it. "Seems the most logical explanation. But where?"

"Back with her family?"

"Definitely not. She hated them. They're a bunch of right-wing evangelical wackos."

"Maybe she found a room to rent," Roz suggested.

I wasn't so sure. Danielle's radio silence, coupled with her neighbor's account of a man packing boxes into a truck, troubled me.

"I'm sure she'll show up," Roz reassured me.

"Maybe. I didn't get that kind of vibe off the neighbor."

"You think he was lying about someone putting boxes in a truck?"

"He clearly hated her. He seemed glad she's gone."

"You could call the police and report her as missing."

I harrumphed. "The cops? After what they did to Sophia and her boyfriend?"

"I hear you. But if you're really worried, that might be the best solution."

"I'll think about it."

CHAPTER 7
EMPTY

ON THE WAY HOME, we stopped by a few garage sales and thrift stores. I'd hoped it would help get her mind off of things, but Roz didn't see anything she liked. Back at the apartment, we watched horror movies on Shudder while I cooked a pot of chili for dinner. Periodically, Roz called her mother and brother but without success.

After a rather quiet dinner, Roz insisted on running to the grocery store since we were out of eggs, milk, and other staples.

"Okay, let me grab my purse," I told her.

"No. I think I need some alone time. Besides, you made dinner."

"You sure?" I feared I'd upset her. Maybe I'd been too clingy and hovering while we were garage saling?

"I'm sure. You just relax. I won't be long."

"Okay."

After she left, I found myself doomscrolling through social media and news sites, each headline fueling my growing anger. Endless stories about right-wing politicians pushing laws to strip basic rights from trans people. Laws mandating restroom use based on sex assigned at birth, banning changes to gender markers on official documents, outlawing drag, and even prohibiting gender-affirming medical care for trans kids and adults.

Apartment complexes could now deny housing to queer individuals based on the manager's religious beliefs. Opinion pieces in major outlets, masquerading as news, spewed venomous transphobic rhetoric, falsely accusing the trans community of grooming children.

My thoughts drifted back to Danielle. The possibility of her being attacked—or worse, murdered—gnawed at me. Images of her lying injured or lifeless, undiscovered in her home, haunted my mind.

I texted Roz before speeding off in the Gothmobile.

ME:

Going to Danielle's. Will B back soon.

The street was desolate when I parked in front of the duplex engulfed in darkness. After ensuring that no one was around, I slipped around to the back.

From my purse, I retrieved nitrile gloves and a set of lockpicks. I'd become a crack lock picker when I was a homeless teen. Breaking into places and stealing shit to hock was more lucrative and less degrading than hooking. The first time I met Bobby was when he caught me breaking into his old tattoo studio on Roosevelt Row, leading to our eventual foster relationship.

In under a minute, the tumblers aligned, the knob turned, and I was inside. I stepped into a house heavy with stale air, dust, and a faint whiff of mold—fortunately, no trace of death. This eased my worst fears but left me with questions about Danielle's whereabouts and well-being.

I pulled out a small red-lensed flashlight I'd bought in Roz's shop, Spy Gal. Its discreet red glow pierced the darkness but was less visible from the street.

The Arizona room where I'd entered held a barren desk

without any clutter of papers and electronics. The wicker basket beside it revealed a crumpled doctor's appointment reminder, a torn photo of Danielle, and a letter from the Quinn Fund Scholarship For Women, threatening legal action if Danielle did not immediately return the seventy-five grand the Quinn Fund had given her for her previous year's tuition and living expenses. They had revoked her scholarship, accusing her of committing fraud for "pretending to be a woman."

"Fuckers," I muttered. I still had no idea where she was, but I had a better picture of her financial situation.

The kitchen was a scene of neglect—moldy food in the fridge, a cloud of tiny flies swarming around overripe bananas and rotten avocados on the counter. I covered my nose and mouth with the collar of my shirt, afraid of breathing in spores or tiny insects.

The master bedroom was nearly empty. The bed had been stripped, and the closet emptied except for a few dresses. Two large garbage bags filled with clothes hinted at a hasty departure or, more disturbingly, a clearing out. I dug through a bag and pulled out a blouse with a large reddish-brown stain that matched one I'd found on the bare mattress. *Is it blood?* I couldn't be sure.

In the bathroom, discarded makeup and a half-empty box of estrogen patches filled the wastebasket. I pocketed the patches, thinking someone in the Alliance could use them.

A chilling thought occurred to me. *Has Danielle been murdered? Was her killer simply disposing of evidence? And who was the killer? The surly neighbor? A relative?* I tried not to let my mind wander down that path, but the evidence of a violent end was mounting.

My phone pinged. Roz had sent me a text.

ROZ:

U OK? U want me there?

I was about to reply when a car pulled into the driveway, its high beams shining through the windows.

"Shit." I rushed back through the house and ran out the back door without locking it behind me. Around the side of the house, I spotted a tall figure approaching the front door. I couldn't see a face, but he had short-cropped hair and wore a button-down shirt and slacks.

Is this the guy the neighbor saw? Part of me wanted to confront this man and demand that he tell me where Danielle was. At the same time, I preferred not risking arrest for breaking and entering.

The man unlocked the front door and disappeared inside then called out in a muffled voice, "Hello? Anyone in here? I'm calling the police."

That was my cue to leave. The Gothmobile's engine roared as I raced out of the neighborhood.

My heart thundered in my chest, panic triggering fits of hysterical laughter. The humor faded as I reflected on what I'd found. I now had more questions and fewer answers. But none of them looked promising for Danielle.

I was halfway home before I remembered Roz's text. At the next red light, I quickly called her.

"Shit, girl," Roz's voice shook with concern. "I was worried. You find Danielle?"

"No. Looks like someone cleared out most of her stuff. Makeup, clothes and shit. And I found a letter from her college scholarship fund. They were demanding their money back and threatening to sue."

"Oh, how awful! Why?"

"Apparently because she's trans, and the scholarship is only for cis women."

"Poor girl."

"It gets worse. There was a bloody shirt in a garbage bag next to a bloody mattress. I think someone may have killed her, Roz."

"Oh my goth! Ave, I don't know what to say. Did you call the police?"

"And tell them what? That I broke into her house and found evidence she'd been killed? I'd rather not go to jail over this."

A truck with a MAGA sticker on the back cut me off, igniting a brief, fiery urge to retaliate.

"When will you be home?" Roz asked.

"About ten minutes."

"Drive carefully. Try not to run any fascists off the road."

"No promises."

CHAPTER 8
MISSING

OVER THE NEXT FEW DAYS, I left a couple more voicemails for Danielle. Roz still could not reach her mother or brother. On Monday, she called the US Embassy in Jerusalem, which took down her information and promised to contact her when they knew something. I left an additional voicemail message for Danielle, but by that point had little hope she would return it.

We kissed goodbye, and Roz headed off to the Spy Gal shop while I drove to Seoul Fire Tattoo. Diving into art usually helped my mental state when my life was in the shitter. But between the attack on Sofia, Danielle's inexplicable disappearance, and Roz's family being in peril, I struggled to focus on my work.

Early Wednesday morning, I was making us breakfast when Roz got a call back from the embassy. She sat at the kitchen table, listening intently to what the caller was telling her. I turned off the stove and sat beside her, my arm over her shoulder. I feared the worst when she clapped a hand over her mouth and tears streaked down her face.

She nodded, mumbled, "Thank you, sir," and hung up.

"What'd they say?"

She struggled to speak, emotion getting the best of her. I felt so out of my depth trying to comfort her. I wished Bobby were here. He always knew what to say in situations like this.

Finally, Roz said, "That was Aiden Goldstein, a consular officer at the embassy. They are still trying to identify all the bodies killed in the attack. Death toll from the festival alone is well over a hundred. They estimate a thousand more were killed elsewhere across Israel. But so far, my family isn't among the ones they've identified."

"Well, that's good news, at least."

She shrugged. "Hamas has also taken a lot of hostages, including a few dozen from the festival. Mr. Goldstein doesn't know if my family is among them or not."

"Oh shit." I hugged her, remembering when Melissa and Sam were killed.

Bobby always said there was no preparation for the unimaginable. Grief just had to be felt. But the gnawing uncertainty was nothing short of a mind fuck.

"I'm here for you, babe," I said.

She pressed her head against mine. "Thank you."

"I'll make us some breakfast," I said.

"Not really hungry."

"I'm not either, to be honest, but we need to eat. Want some Ben & Jerry's for breakfast?"

She managed a half smile. "Why the hell not?"

After we split a pint of Cherry Garcia, I called Danielle one last time. "Shit." I slapped my phone down on the kitchen table next to my bowl.

Roz glanced up, her eyes red-rimmed, her own breakfast barely touched. "What's wrong?"

"Danielle's number is no longer in service. Something seriously fucked-up's going on."

"Call the police. Report her missing."

"Maybe later. Right now, I just can't deal with talking to a cop."

"But the longer you wait…"

"She's been missing for over a month, Roz," I snapped. "A few hours won't make a fuck of difference."

The hurt on her face made me immediately regret my words. I gripped her trembling hand. "I'm sorry, babe. I didn't mean to snap at you. I'm just…"

"I know. We're both on edge."

"That's no excuse for me. I'm an idiot."

"It's okay," she whispered.

"I wonder how Sophia's doing," I said, desperate for a change in subject.

"You should call her."

It was only seven o'clock. Too early for a phone call, especially someone recovering from a gunshot wound. So instead I sent a text.

ME:

Hey, girl. How U feeling?

To my surprise, a reply came a moment later.

SOPHIA:

Better but sore. Off the fun drugs. 😵 Hospital food sucks. 🤢 Theo bringing bfast from Abuela's Cocina.

ME:

Glad ur better. When will they let u go home?

SOPHIA:

Dunno. Maybe tomorrow.

ME:

Any word from Det Rutherford?

SOPHIA:

Not so far.

ME:

Went by Danielle's place. Neighbor saw
man packing boxes into truck. I'm worried
something happened 2 her.

SOPHIA:

Mierda

ME:

I'll report her missing to the cops.

SOPHIA:

Let me know wht U find out

AVERY:

Will do. Feel better. Enjoy bfast.

SOPHIA:

"I'll be right back," I told Roz, giving her hand another quick squeeze before I dashed into the bedroom. I dug Rutherford's crumpled business card out of my purse and called the number.

"Phoenix police. Detective Rutherford speaking. How may I help you?"

"This is Avery Byrne. I met you a few days ago after your people shot my friend Sophia Bitsui and killed her boyfriend, Étienne."

"Good morning, Ms. Byrne. We're still looking into the matter."

"It's been four days. And you don't know who shot her?"

"We know who discharged their weapons. But we are still investigating the circumstances to determine if the shooting was justified. We're also still searching for whoever made the 911 call."

"Sophia and her boyfriend were unarmed, for goth's sake. They hadn't committed any crimes. How could shooting them possibly be justified?"

"Unfortunately, I can't comment on an ongoing investigation."

"That's what I figured. You people gun down two unarmed innocent civilians, but no one gets held accountable."

"If any of our officers acted with reckless disregard, we will hold them accountable. That I promise you." She let out an exasperated breath. "Is there anything else I can help you with, Ms. Byrne?"

"Yeah, you can find out what happened to my friend Danielle Kirkpatrick."

"I'm sorry. I'm not familiar with the name."

"She's disappeared. I think something bad happened to her." I wanted to tell Rutherford about what I'd found at Danielle's house, but that would be confessing to breaking and entering. "None of her friends have heard from her in over a month, and now her number's disconnected."

"Have you reported her missing?"

"That's what I'm doing. You're a cop. I'm telling you she's missing. My community is under attack, Rutherford. If you truly care about your brother Chris, you'll look into this. He could be next."

"I don't handle missing persons cases, but I can certainly take down the information and have someone look into it."

"Not someone. You need to look into it! You claim to care about our community, but so far, all I've gotten is lip service. Do your fucking job and start protecting innocent people."

"I'll tell you what, Avery. I will look into this. Personally. Believe it or not, the safety of your community is important to me, just as my brother is important to me. Give me what information you have on her."

I gave her Danielle's phone number, email address, and street address but held out little hope that Rutherford would do anything to help or that Danielle would be found safe.

"And let me know what you find out about who swatted Sophia."

"As soon as I have information that I can release, I promise to reach out to you."

I returned to the kitchen and found Roz staring blankly at a cup of coffee. "You filed a missing person report?" she asked.

"I called Detective Rutherford. She says she'll look into it."

"Good." Roz put a hand on mine. "Maybe we can get some good news for a change."

"Maybe."

"In the meantime, I have to open up the shop, and you have to go make tattoo art."

"I wish there was more that I could do for both you and Danielle," I said.

"Babe, you've done everything you can and then some. All we can do now is wait."

"Waiting sucks."

Later, we walked hand in hand to our cars in the Stonewall Apartments parking lot, a queer-friendly haven in these increasingly hostile times.

"I'll see you tonight," Roz said, her voice a comforting murmur, as we reached the Gothmobile and her newly purchased Hyundai Santa Fe.

We embraced and gave each other soft kisses. Goth, how I loved this woman. After Sam's death, I never imagined finding love again, not with all of my baggage and my tumultuous past. Roz had embraced my true self, my history, and my quest for justice. After eighteen months, she remained my unwavering rock, guiding me through healing and showing me the profound depths of real love.

"By the way, I have to chair the Hatchlings meeting tonight," I said, feeling a hint of melancholy.

"Oh, right. I forgot about that."

"Maybe I should cancel. With all that's going on…"

"No, don't cancel, babe," Roz insisted. "Those kids need you, especially now. They need to know that someone will be there for them."

I considered that. I knew what it was like not to have anyone. When my bio dad kicked me out, I was fucking terrified. Joining the Hatchlings a few years later felt like coming home to the family I always dreamed of—one that understood me and had my back.

"You're right," I said. "I should be home around eight thirty."

"See you then, gorgeous." Her unexpected smile was like sunlight breaking through clouds. The love in her eyes felt like an injection of endorphins—joy, gratitude, and love all mixed together, which still seemed so unfamiliar to my scarred goth heart.

When I arrived at Seoul Fire Tattoo, Bobby Jeong—my foster dad and the shop's owner—greeted me with his usual warm embrace. He was a stocky man in his fifties. His jet-black hair was streaked with gray. His T-shirt, depicting Darth Vader with his extended hand in a force-choke gesture, read, "Talk to the hand," a nod to his love of all things *Star Wars*.

"Morning, Appa," I said, using the Korean term for father.

I wasn't Korean, but he and Melissa had taught me some words and phrases. While to the rest of the world, he was Bobby J., he would always be Appa to me.

"Good morning, kiddo. Any updates on Roz's family?"

I shook my head. "Not really. She talked to a consular officer at the embassy. They're still identifying the dead. But Hamas has also taken a bunch of people hostage."

"I hope they're safe. Please let her know I'm thinking of her."

"I will, Appa."

"How about Sophia and Danielle?"

"Sophia hopes to be released soon. As for Danielle, I'm really worried. I asked the detective investigating Sophia's swatting to look for her."

Bobby nodded. "Hopefully, she'll turn up."

I wasn't so confident. "Gotta prep my station. I've got a client arriving in fifteen."

Bobby kissed my forehead. "Sounds good."

"Morning, Frisco," I said to the thin redhead whose station was next to mine. She was ten years older than me.

"Hey, you. I like your Halloween decorations."

In celebration of the season, I'd decorated my station with several figurines, including Jack Skellington, a goth girl holding a cat, and a vampire jack-o'-lantern and fake cobwebs stretched across the top of the mirror. But rather than the usual feeling of joy, I felt depressed looking at them.

"Thanks," I said solemnly. "No one celebrates Halloween like a goth."

"Ain't that the truth."

I acknowledged Butcher, the taciturn tattoo artist across the aisle, with a simple "Morning." His silent nod was typical of his reserved nature.

A tapping on the studio's glass front door drew my attention. Outside stood a male grackle, his glossy black feathers shining in the morning sun. He'd started showing up each morning a couple of weeks earlier, reminding me of Poe's "The Raven."

"Morning, George," I said despite my sullen mood.

"I wonder why he does that every morning?" Frisco mused. "It's not like we feed him."

"Probably sees his reflection in the glass and thinks it's another bird," Bobby said.

I looked over at Butcher. "What do you think, Butch?"

He shrugged. "Maybe wants a tattoo."

That got a few chuckles from everyone.

By the time I'd finished prepping my station, my client Becky arrived. She wore a spaghetti-strap top and jeans. I shifted into professional mode and set up a privacy screen around my station. Her Wicca-inspired back piece, a detailed mandala of the Goddess crowned with a triple moon bordered by intricate Celtic knotwork, was coming along beautifully.

"How's it feel?" I asked as she removed her top.

"Good. I'm just glad you finished coloring around my spine last week. That really hurt."

"Yeah, that's always a tender spot," I said, donning a pair of black nitrile gloves. "The good news is the worst is over. Let's get started."

Yet even as I shifted into creative mode, worries about Roz's family, Sophia, and Danielle lingered in the back of my mind.

CHAPTER 9
HATCHLINGS

SEVERAL YEARS EARLIER, Bobby and Melissa had encouraged me to join the Phoenix Gender Alliance's Hatchlings group. Meeting so many other transgender kids, each at a different stage of their transition, was eye-opening. Some had been rejected by their families as I had. A few had been forced into abusive conversion therapy. But many others had found acceptance from at least one, if not both, of their parents.

I had aged out of the Hatchlings years ago, but the memories lingered, reminding me of the Lost Kids, my family of homeless teens before Bobby took me in—young, innocent kids living in a world that more often than not treated them like garbage.

As the only survivor of the Lost Kids, I felt fiercely protective of the Hatchlings. At five-foot-six, I wasn't all that imposing. But my years on the street had taught me how to survive. I had faced off with dirty cops, abusive pimps, and murderous gangsters. And when the situation called for it, I had killed to protect those I loved.

I arrived at the Phoenix Library's Javelina branch, on Missouri and Twelfth Avenue, a little before seven o'clock.

The summer heat had finally broken, giving way to highs in the upper eighties. Compared to the triple-digit temperatures from the previous week, it was a relief.

Easton St. Claire, the Hatchlings' cochair, met me at the entrance. Their freckled arms peeked out from under the sleeves of a striped short-sleeved shirt, their long blond bangs partly hiding expressive blue eyes.

Easton was the first nonbinary person I had known. Their gregarious personality and skills at leading discussions had helped so many of the young people in the group come out of their shells. Being a dyed-in-the-wool introvert, I couldn't have run the group without them.

"How's it going?" Easton asked with a radiant smile when we opened the Rose Mofford meeting room. "Aren't you loving this weather?"

Inside, we pushed aside the tables to make room for a circle of chairs. Sophia believed the tables acted as barriers to honest conversation. Our job as leaders was to create a safe space for members to be their authentic selves.

"It's nice. You hear about Sophia and her boyfriend?"

Their smile faded. "The swatting? I heard. I can't believe somebody would do that to her. She's one of the sweetest people I know. How's she feeling?"

"Going stir-crazy in the hospital. She's hoping to go home soon."

"Well, give her my best when you see her. Did the cops find whoever made the 911 call?"

I shook my head. "Not that I've heard."

A boy of seventeen and a man in his forties approached. I recognized them as Shaun Martell and his father, Tequan. Shaun had joined the group several months earlier. In that short time, I'd witnessed his voice cracking and dropping as the testosterone therapy he was on did its magic.

"Hey, guys," I said. "How are y'all doing?"

Shaun shrugged, but his shoulders slumped. "Okay."

"Something wrong?" I asked. *Has he heard about Sophia?*

"School."

Tequan wrapped his arm protectively around his son. "One of his teachers refuses to acknowledge his name change or let him try out for basketball—not for the boys' or the girls' team."

"It's not fair," Shaun said.

"No," I agreed. "It's not. They should let you play."

"We've contacted Lambda Legal," Tequan added. "Waiting to hear back."

I struggled for what to say. I wanted to tell him it would all work out okay. But it might not. "I know it's hard. It was for me too. But at least you have a supportive dad. It makes a difference."

"We heard about Miss Sophia on the news." Tequan's expression turned grim. "Just don't know what this world's coming to. All this fancy technology, and we can't keep from killing each other. Might as well be living in the Stone Age."

"We should head on in," Easton said as more members trickled in.

When the meeting began, our circle comprised Easton, me, Tequan, one other parent, and twenty kids ranging in age from seven to seventeen.

"Before we get started, I wanted to make you aware of something that happened last weekend." I shared a brief account of the swatting incident.

The news visibly upset many in the group. Several of the younger kids started crying.

"Why would someone do that?" Leia Ripley wiped the tears from her face.

I offered her a tissue from my purse. "I don't know. The police are looking for the caller."

"Why'd the cops shoot her if they weren't doing anything wrong?" Zoë Hildebrandt, a fourteen-year-old girl, asked.

"'Cause that's what cops do," Shaun replied before I could answer. "They shoot first and ask questions later. Especially if the people aren't white."

"We don't know exactly what happened," Easton explained. "Clearly, the cops were wrong to shoot Sophia and her boyfriend. I understand the police are looking into that too."

Shaun snorted derisively. I didn't blame him. The number of cases of cops killing unarmed Black men was disgustingly high and the percentage of rogue cops held accountable disturbingly low.

"I don't normally trust cops either, Shaun. Had a lot of bad dealings with them. But the detective I spoke with is the sister of Chris Rutherford, a member of the main group. So I'm willing to give her the benefit of the doubt that she'll do the right thing." I could scarcely believe the words coming out of my mouth, but they were true. I trusted Rutherford and hoped my confidence wasn't misplaced.

"One important lesson to take away from this," Easton said to the group, "is to be careful with the information you share online. Especially on social media. Avoid sharing personal details like your phone number, address, or even your city. Keep private the names of family members, your school, your doctor, or even your pet—anything that could lead you to being identified."

"What about in the Hatchlings' chat group?" a nonbinary kid named Taylor asked.

Easton nodded. "That should be okay."

"No, not even there," I interjected.

This statement drew surprised looks from everyone.

"I know the volunteers screen the group, but even chat groups can be infiltrated or hacked. Given the current climate, it's best not to take any chances."

A heavy silence fell over the room. I could sense their fear, and it pained me. But the alternative, as I had seen so often, was far worse. Too many adults took great pleasure in causing harm to trans kids.

"On a more positive note," Easton said, "a little bird told me someone has a birthday in a few days."

Oh no, I thought. *Please don't.*

Easton turned to me and grinned like a Cheshire cat. "It's Friday the thirteenth, isn't it, Avery?"

I blushed. "Yes."

"I won't ask how old you'll be, but I think we should all sing her 'Happy Birthday.'"

And as embarrassing as it was to be the center of attention, a part of me appreciated the love.

When they finished singing, Easton said, "Why don't we talk about Saturday's Trans March and the upcoming Halloween party?"

We discussed the details of where and when to meet for the start of the parade, as well as a few openings we still had for help manning the booth at the Pride Festival. Many members of the group were excited to attend their first Pride. The topic brought a flood of memories of my first time at the parade a few years earlier—cheering crowds and the rhythmic beat of synth-pop, Pride flags waving everywhere, and the euphoric sense of safety and acceptance.

The conversation then shifted to costumes, music, and refreshments for the Halloween party, which Roz and I were hosting at our apartment complex's community room. Still, in the back of my mind, Danielle's disappearance and Sophia's swatting haunted me. I would give the cops their bite at the apple. But when they failed, as I suspected they would, I would step in. Avery the avenger would set things right.

Bobby believed that if the police didn't bring such people to justice, karma would eventually deal with them. But karma—if there was such a thing—was too damn slow.

Sometimes, karma needed a little push. That's where I came in.

As the meeting neared its end at eight o'clock, Easton and I initiated our traditional closing circle. We stood arm in arm, each offering an affirmation.

"I love my siblings, and I wish you peace," Easton said. The rest of us repeated it.

Zoë added, "I love my siblings, and I wish you to feel comfortable in your bodies."

Again, the group echoed the statement.

"I love my siblings, and I wish you safety," said Shaun.

One by one, the affirmations continued until it was my turn. "I love my siblings, and I wish you courage. And I will see you at the Halloween party."

The circle broke into a series of heartfelt hugs. Not one for physical contact, especially with strangers, I nevertheless found comfort in these embraces. These people were more than acquaintances; they were family.

After restoring the room to its original state, we all headed toward the library's atrium. The energy among the waiting family members was tense and filled with concern.

Zoë's mother, Marilyn, approached me. "There's a crowd of protesters outside. Some of them are dressed in military gear. They're just chanting things like 'protect the kids' and 'stop the groomers.' I informed the librarian, but she said there's nothing they can do unless things turn violent. I have a feeling they just might."

"How did they even know we were meeting here?" I asked.

"The library puts the meeting on the public online calendar," Easton explained. "These protesters must have discovered it."

"Don't worry. I'll go deal with them," I said, taking a step toward the entrance.

Easton held my arm. "Hold up, Ave. Maybe there's a back exit we can use. No point in starting a riot."

"There may be a back exit, but the parking lot's out front. If the librarian won't call the police, then we have to make sure these kids have safe passage out of here."

"Best if we just ignore them and wait them out," Tequan suggested. "Maybe they'll go away."

"The library closes in thirty minutes. They never go away until we make them go away," I insisted. "Tell the librarian to call the cops. I'll deal with the protesters."

I headed out the doors, ignoring Tequan and Easton's pleas for caution. Instantly, the mob of idiots surrounded me, shouting the usual litany of slurs.

"Groomer!"

"Freak!"

"Pedophile!"

"Pervert!"

"Faggot!"

I guessed their number to be about thirty. All white. Some of them dressed up like army Rangers. Several had guns strapped to their hips or assault rifles slung over their backs. But they didn't scare me—a bunch of posers like the idiots on January 6.

"No one's grooming these kids!" I shouted back. "Go home and leave these kids the fuck alone."

"You're a goddamn liar! God's gonna punish you for molesting those poor kids," said a woman wearing a shirt that read, "Take your kids to church, not drag queen story hour." A gold cross dangled from her thin neck, and she wore her hair in a tightly wound bun.

"Why do both the evangelicals and the Catholics keep having major sex scandals? Over and over again. Thousands of kids molested."

Church Lady got in my face. "Liar!"

"Just last week, a preacher at that Scottsdale megachurch

got busted for child porn. You wanna keep kids safe? Keep them away from the 'pedophiles for Jesus.'"

Her open hand connected with my cheek, the sharp sound of skin meeting skin ringing in my ears. The sting lingered. I felt a mix of pain and surprise.

"Fucking bitch!" I yelled.

She reared back to hit me again, and I grabbed her wrist. She swung with her other fist, but I kicked her feet out from under her and pinned her face down on the pavement with my knee in her back.

Before I could catch my breath, someone clocked the side of my head. Unseen hands hauled me off the woman. A barrage of punches and kicks came at me from all sides. I swung and kicked and bit anyone in reach, but my body became a blur of pain and fury.

CHAPTER 10
ARRESTED

I'D SEEN countless movies where the dauntless hero fought multiple opponents at once. Somehow, they knew when and where each blow was coming and how to counter it. Or the bad guys politely took turns. A bunch of Hollywood bullshit.

I was a pretty good fighter, having spent three years living on the street. A homeless vet named Clancy had taught me the basics. "Surviving a real fight comes down to a few things," she'd explained, "especially when you're a woman up against men. For starters, fight dirty. Rules are for sports, not combat. Use anything in reach as a weapon—a rock, a pen, a frying pan, dirt, whatever. Staying upright is also important, especially if you're smaller than your opponent. If someone pins you, you're in trouble. Lastly, fight like your life depends on it. Kill if you must."

Even as the blood trickled down my face and the pain in my body intensified, I refused to back down against this horde of self-righteous suburban Nazis—until someone from behind slammed me face-first onto the pavement.

Before I could move, the bite of the handcuffs clamped onto one wrist, then another. In the turmoil of emotions, I couldn't decide if I was more angry or relieved. Soon after, I was roughly shoved into the back of a patrol car, the hard seat barely registering through my daze. The police station was a blur of procedure. I was booked and then left in a holding cell.

My cellmates, two women sleeping off a bender, fortunately left me to lick my wounds in silence. I slumped against the cold, unforgiving wall of the cell. The adrenaline from the fight had long since dissipated, leaving me acutely aware of my aching body.

With shaky hands, I gingerly touched a tender swelling above my eyebrow, the skin stretched tight and warm to the touch, a souvenir from a particularly harsh blow. I winced, feeling the sharp sting of a split lip, the metallic taste of blood still lingering in my mouth.

My fingers trailed down to my jaw, probing cautiously. It ached dully, a constant throbbing pain that flared with each attempt to open my mouth. I suspected it wasn't broken, just badly bruised. Tomorrow, it would blossom into a kaleidoscope of purples and yellows.

More bruises were forming across my arms and torso, each touch bringing a new realization of pain. My right arm had borne the brunt of it, feeling stiff and sore from where I'd used it to shield myself. When I twisted slightly, a sharp pain shot through my ribs, not crippling but enough to make me catch my breath.

Despite the physical pain, it was the emotional toll that weighed heaviest on me. My mind replayed the chaotic flashes of the mob's anger, the fear, and the adrenaline-fueled desperation. I leaned my head back against the wall, eyes closed, trying to steady my uneven breathing, and braced myself for whatever came next. I'd been an idiot to ignore Easton's and Tequan's advice. I could only hope the kids were safe.

After an endless stretch of time, Kirsten Pasternak

arrived, likely called by Easton. A uniformed officer ushered us into a small, stark interrogation room for a private conversation.

"Jesus Christ, Avery. Do you need medical care?"

I shrugged it off. "I'll live."

"Very well. What happened tonight?"

I gave her an account of what happened after the Hatchlings meeting, and after a brief discussion, she brought in a Detective Griffiths, a white guy who looked barely older than I was.

"Ms. Byrne, we're charging you with assault and disorderly conduct," he said, setting what I guessed was the case folder on the table between us.

"That's bullshit. They attacked me."

"We considered charging you with aggravated assault because of the pocketknife in your purse, but we're holding off until we learn more."

"Look, asshole…"

"Avery…" Kirsten cautioned.

"Look, Detective," I corrected. "I defended myself and the transgender kids in my care against a mob of violent bigots. What was I supposed to do—hide in the library all night? They were going to be closing soon. Even if we'd snuck out the back, those people would have spotted me. I don't exactly blend in."

"Who struck the first blow?"

"Some bitch in a 'Take your kids to church' T-shirt. She got in my face, spewing all kinds of that 'Jesus hates trans people' bullshit. Accusing us of preying on kids, which is a fucking lie."

"And she struck you first?"

"Yeah." My memory was actually a little fuzzy after everything, but I was pretty sure that was how it had gone down. "All I did was try to subdue her so she couldn't hit me again. That's when the rest of them fuckers attacked me."

"Did you get any of it on video?"

"Are you serious? I was fighting for my life, not filming a documentary."

"Clearly, she was in fear for her life, Detective," Kirsten added.

"You bet I was. Some of them had assault rifles and body armor. I was terrified."

"Well, you can certainly tell that to the judge at the hearing tomorrow morning."

"Hearing? What hearing?"

"Like I said, you're being charged with assault and disorderly conduct. The good news is you're being released on your own recognizance. Unless you give me reason to hold you."

"Detective, I don't think that will be necessary," Kirsten assured him. "She will be there."

"Your hearing is at ten tomorrow morning at the courthouse," Griffiths said. "You'll be provided with the details when you're released."

It was after eleven by the time my belongings were returned. As Kirsten drove me back to the library, I saw that Roz had left several messages, each more desperate than the last.

I called her back. "Hey."

"Oh my goth! Avery, where the hell have you been? Why didn't you answer?"

I gave her the rundown. "Should be home soon."

"Thank goth! After everything that's happened lately, I was going out of my mind."

As much as I hated causing her distress, especially with her family in jeopardy, her concern was an odd sort of comfort. "Sorry to worry you. I'm on my way."

Roz's reaction upon seeing my battered state was heart-wrenching. Through tears and shock, she insisted on tending to my wounds. The pain was a numb buzz but flared sharply as she gently cleaned the blood from my face and helped me out of my shirt.

"Jesus, Avery! These bruises look bad. Maybe we should take you to the ER."

"No. Just want to sleep."

"You could have internal bleeding, a bruised kidney, or even a concussion."

Yeah, the same things I was thinking when I was sitting in the holding cell. But now that I was home, I didn't care. I just wanted to take a couple of ibuprofens and sleep.

"I'm all right," I reassured her, downplaying my injuries. "Just want to go to bed."

"Have you eaten? We've got some leftover soup."

I clasped her hand. "I love you. Never thought I'd have someone who cared for me the way that you do. But for the love of goth, please stop being a Jewish mother."

As soon as I said the words, I could have kicked myself. Roz's family was still in danger overseas. Or worse, dead. "Any word from Mr. Goldstein at the embassy?"

"No, not yet."

"I'm sorry."

She held my hand, the only part of my body that didn't hurt. "That's why I was so terrified of losing you. And why I think you should at least get looked at."

"I'm okay. Really. I look worse than I am. And to be honest, I gave at least as good as I got."

She helped me into bed. "Of that, I have no doubt."

CHAPTER 11
NO COMMENT

SOMEWHERE IN THE VOID, a buzzer pierced my slumber like a thousand needles stabbing my brain

"Cut that shit out!" I yelled into the abyss.

The noise persisted, rattling every nerve in my skull. When I squeezed open my eyes, razor-sharp daggers of light assaulted my vision. I recoiled, eyes snapping shut again, and flailed my hand to silence the offending sound.

My fingers, guided by muscle memory, wrapped around the slick surface of my phone and brought it to my ear. But it wasn't my phone that was ringing.

I heard it again and realized it was our door buzzer. "Fuck. Who rings someone's doorbell at six in the morning?"

When I sat up, the room spun wildly, forcing me to fight back a wave of nausea. Everything hurt. My reflection in the dresser mirror looked like a cross between the Elephant Man and a rotten eggplant. *What the fuck was I thinking, taking on that crowd of psycho bigots?*

The door buzzer continued to rattle my nerves.

"Fuck." I pulled on a robe and shuffled through the apartment to the front door.

A man in a suit holding a digital recorder stood on the stoop.

"Who the fuck are you, and why the fuck are you ringing my goddamn bell?"

"Spence O'Neill. I'm a reporter for the *Arizona Republic*. I'm doing a story on the riot last night at the Juniper Public Library. My sources tell me you started the riot. Is that true?"

I wanted to tell him and his sources to fuck off. Part of me also wanted to set this joker straight. But Kirsten had told me not to talk to the press.

"No comment." I started to shut the door, but the douchebag caught it.

"Weren't you a person of interest a few years ago for the murder of Samantha Ferguson?"

"Let go of my door or lose your fingers, asshole."

"Are transsexuals a threat to the safety of women and children?"

I slammed the door closed. The asshole journalist barely escaped having to type one-handed for the rest of his pathetic career.

In the bedroom, my phone started ringing. "Goddammit!"

I hustled back as a half-asleep Roz began stirring and mumbling my name.

"What?" I yelled into the phone as quietly as I could and hustled back out to the kitchen.

"Avery Byrne?"

"Who the fuck is this?"

"Maddie Gillespie, anchor for *Channel 7 News*. I have some quest—"

I ended the call and started making coffee. While I waited for it to brew, I checked my voicemail. Seventeen messages, all from unknown numbers. And it wasn't even seven o'clock. *Jesus fucking Christ.*

Just as the sacred dark liquid began dribbling into the

pot, my phone rang again. I was about to send it to voice-mail when I noticed it was Easton calling.

"Hey, Easton. What's up?"

"I just wanted to check on you. Make sure you were okay."

"Okay. Um, well. Other than every cell in my body hurting and the fucking press showing up on my door, I'm peachy. Oh, and of course, getting arrested. That's the icing on the cake. How are you?"

"I'm really sorry. I wish you'd never gone out there."

"Easton St. Claire, if you tell me 'I told you so,' goth help me, I will—"

"No, I don't mean it like that. I just hate seeing you hurt. It's all over the news. 'Trans youth leader attacks protesters.' That's one of the milder headlines. They get worse. Right-wing groups are claiming the Hatchlings are part of a child-trafficking ring. That's what's making headlines. Even the *Phoenix Living* website is giving more coverage to the lunatics than us."

Phoenix Living was an alternative weekly that prided itself on exposing corruption, as well as covering local cultural events. But even they had been taking a "both sides" approach to trans civil rights, going so far as publishing so-called opinion articles that were little more than transphobic hit pieces. Their latest edition was due out this morning.

"So no one's bothering to report our side of things? Like the actual fucking truth?" My voice rose in anger, which didn't help my aching head.

"I fielded some calls but didn't comment. Wasn't sure what to say. I've never handled anything like this. Since you're the acting chair while Sophia's recovering, I figured you should respond. Has anyone from the press called you?"

"I'll deal with it after the hearing this morning."

"So they arrested you?"

"Assault and disorderly conduct. I'm hoping Kirsten can get the charges tossed."

"Well, good luck."

"Easton, I'm sorry for ignoring your advice. You *were* right. I shouldn't have gone out there like that. It's just... hearing those bastards saying that shit when we're just trying to protect those kids..."

"I get it. But we have to be smart about it. Those jerks aren't worth your freedom or your life."

"You're right. Well, I need to get ready."

"Good luck in court this morning. I'll talk to you later."

"Morning, sweetie." Roz shuffled into the kitchen, her face etched with concern. "Shit, your face looks even worse this morning. Those assholes did a number on you. Does it still hurt?"

"Not as much."

"I called Polly. She'll open up Spy Gal for me so I can be with you at the hearing."

"Thanks." I kissed her gently. "I'm so lucky to have you."

"We're lucky to have each other." She stared down at the floor and sighed. "Mr. Goldstein from the embassy called. Mom, Jude, and Talia were among those taken hostage. Fortunately, Jude and Talia's daughters, Rebecca and Esther, were staying with a friend at the kibbutz. When the attack happened, they escaped and are safe in Be'er-Sheva. Or as safe as anyone can be over there."

"Well, at least they're alive. What's being done to get the hostages released?"

"Mr. Goldstein assured me they're working to get them released, but he wasn't able to give me any specifics due to the volatile nature of the negotiations. I just have to wait."

I hugged her, feeling utterly useless to ease her fears and sorrow.

Despite Roz's offer to help me conceal the swelling and bruising on my face, I wore no makeup. I wanted everyone to see what those fuckers had done to me. Instead of my usual goth attire, I wore a white button-down top and a navy skirt and blazer, all of which I borrowed from Roz.

While she drove us to the courthouse downtown, I sent Bobby a brief text letting him know I was okay but had a court date. I'd fill him in later. I then listened to several of the voicemail messages. Most were from media organizations, both local and elsewhere, asking me for my side of what had happened. Some messages were from randos accusing me of being everything from a child sex trafficker to a radicalized transsexual terrorist. I didn't reply to any of them.

We met Kirsten outside the courtroom at nine thirty. "How are you feeling this morning?" she asked.

Until that point, I hadn't given a lot of thought to what might happen in court. *Will I be acquitted? Given a fine? Probation? Jail time?* Suddenly, it was all hitting me. I struggled to keep from shivering.

"Not one of my better days. Then again, not my worst." I told her about the voicemail messages.

"Don't reply to any of them. At least, not yet. My investigator, Tabby Winters, is scouring the web for footage of the confrontation to show you acted in self-defense. Then we'll deal with the media."

"You can get the charges dismissed today, right?"

"No, this is just the arraignment. We'll enter a plea, and I can hopefully get you released on your own recognizance. Later, I will file a motion to dismiss."

After my sordid history with the legal system, I wasn't so optimistic.

"Don't worry, babe." Roz squeezed my hand. "You've got this."

I spotted Church Lady standing on the far side of the courtroom door. She was sporting a shiner, but looked a hell of a lot better than I did. She stood with a group that exuded an evangelical air—stern, composed, sanctimonious.

I wanted to beat them bloody all over again. But that kind of impulse had gotten me here. Though in this case, I'd acted in self-defense, I had done much worse things other times in my life. Was this karma? Hell if I knew.

Five minutes before the hour, the bailiff opened the courtroom doors, and we filed in.

CHAPTER 12
ARRAIGNED

PROMPTLY AT TEN, the bailiff announced, "All rise for the Honorable Judge Nathan Stevens."

The room collectively stood as a tall white man with a receding hairline strode in, his robe billowing slightly with each step. I sighed. An old cis-het white man was the last person I wanted judging me.

The court clerk began calling cases. "Faith Anderson."

The bitch who'd slapped me stood alongside her attorney. "Ethan Harrow, representing Ms. Anderson, Your Honor."

"Ms. Anderson, you are charged with assault and disorderly conduct. If found guilty, you could be sentenced up to six months in jail, up to five years' probation, and fines totaling twenty-five hundred dollars plus surcharges. How do you plead?"

"Not guilty," the bitch said.

Judge Stevens turned to the prosecutor. "Mr. Lewis, bail recommendation?"

"Ms. Anderson has no priors. The county attorney sees no issue with releasing her on her own recognizance."

After setting a trial date for November, Stevens banged his gavel to call the next case.

Kirsten and I stood up. "Kirsten Pasternak, representing Ms. Byrne."

"Ms. Byrne, you are also charged with assault and disorderly conduct. If found guilty, you could be sentenced to up to six months in jail, up to five years' probation, and pay fines of twenty-five hundred dollars plus surcharges. How do you plead?"

"Not guilty."

"Mr. Lewis, your bail recommendation?"

"Mr. Byrne has a list of prior arrests as long as my arm. Starting with solicitation and shoplifting when he was a teenager and graduating to first-degree murder and aggravated assault on a police officer. He also has a history of fleeing prosecution. The county requests he be remanded until trial."

I nearly shouted, "What the fuck?" but Kirsten gripped my arm and stopped me from speaking.

"Your Honor," Kirsten said sharply, "before we proceed, I must object to the prosecution's deliberate misgendering of my client. My client is a woman, and referring to her as 'Mr.' disrespects not only her but also the court. We request she be addressed properly as Ms. Byrne."

"Mr. Stevens, as public servants, it is imperative that we treat all those who appear in this court with civility and respect," the judge said. "Therefore, I am instructing you to use the defendant's indicated pronouns of *she* and *her* and the designated salutation of Ms. Do I make myself clear?"

"Yes, Your Honor."

"Thank you, Your Honor," Kirsten continued. "Additionally, there is no reason for my client to be remanded. She has no criminal convictions. All previous charges were dropped. She is neither a danger to herself or others, nor is she a flight risk. She is a local business owner with strong personal ties to the community."

"I disagree, Your Honor," Lewis shot in. "Last year, the defendant fled the state when police considered her the prime suspect in the brutal and gruesome murder of the defendant's own girlfriend."

"For which she was cleared," Kirsten insisted. "On the contrary, Ms. Byrne worked closely with the Phoenix PD to solve that case. In fact, further investigation revealed that the lieutenant supervising that very case was conspiring with the actual murderers."

A rather dramatic gasp rose from the people in the gallery.

"My client is similarly the victim in this case. As the video evidence will show, Faith Anderson and a mob of armed assailants assembled outside the library last evening intending to harass members of the Phoenix Gender Alliance youth group that my client led that evening. Ms. Byrne attempted to provide safe passage out of the library for the kids and their parents but was instead viciously attacked. Grossly outnumbered, she did what she could to defend herself while in fear for her life."

"Your honor, I object." Ethan Harrow, the bitch's attorney, stood. "My client was not armed."

"No, but many in that mob were," Kirsten insisted. "Mr. Lewis is biased against the transgender community, as demonstrated by his misgendering of my client. Worse, he is attempting to railroad my client, demanding she be remanded while the perpetrator has been released. I ask, Your Honor, at the very least, that my client be given the same consideration he so generously gave Ms. Anderson."

"Objection! Your Honor, I resent any implication that I or any other member of the Maricopa County Attorney's Office is in any way biased against the transgender community!" Doug Lewis shouted over Kirsten's defense.

Kirsten simply spoke more forcefully, trying to drown out both Lewis and Harrow. "Your Honor, the county attorney's office has been placed under federal oversight for attempting to frame members of the Phoenix Gender Alliance as a criminal gang. We are asking Your Honor to prevent a repeat of that outrageous miscarriage of justice."

The judge banged his gavel. "All right! That's enough out of both of you. Mr. Stevens, any other reason you feel Ms. Byrne should be remanded?"

"No, Your Honor. I think I made the county's case quite clear."

"Very well. Ms. Byrne, I am releasing you for now. But I caution you to stay out of trouble, and do not attempt to flee the state, or I will remand you for the entirety of the trial. Do you understand me, young lady?"

"Yes, Your Honor," I said, appreciating that he called me young lady. "Thank you."

"As for you, Mr. Lewis, you will keep any personal and political biases about transgender people out of my courtroom. Do you hear me?"

"Yes, Your Honor."

The judge then set a trial date for the week before Thanksgiving. Leaving the courtroom, I was a whirlwind of emotions though steadied by Roz's comforting presence.

"How are you doing?" Roz put her arm around me.

"I'd really like to beat the ever-loving shit out of that guy Lewis," I whispered quietly enough so that no one but Roz and Kirsten could hear me.

"I would strongly caution against that," Kirsten replied, though I could tell from her smirk that she understood I was kidding. "He's a prosecutor. Being an asshole and trying to throw the book at people is part of the job."

"I expect him to be an asshole, but misgendering me and then trying to lock me up when he was setting free the bitch who started it really pisses me off."

"Just don't get yourself into other trouble. Try avoiding the mobs of transphobic bigots if you can help it."

"Trust me, the way my body feels, I can assure you I will. Not always possible, though. And what to do I tell these fucking journalists?"

"I'll have my office prepare a statement. Send me the names and numbers of any media who contacts you. I'll get the message out."

"Well, I gotta get to work. I already blew off one client this morning." I hugged Kirsten. "Thanks so much for your help."

"You're welcome."

"You ready?" I asked Roz.

"Whenever you are."

"Just drop me off at the studio. I'll catch an Uber back home after I'm done with work." I held her in a prolonged embrace. "It really helped to have you here."

"What? I didn't do anything."

"It's not what you did in there. It's what you do every day." I gazed into those honey-gold eyes of hers. "You're always there for me. And that means a lot."

She kissed me. "You're always there for me too. We make a good pair."

CHAPTER 13
RESURFACED

"OH, kiddo, I'm so sorry. If you'd told me, I would have been there for you this morning," Bobby said after I arrived at Seoul Fire Tattoo and filled him in on recent events.

"I'm glad you weren't, Appa. It was humiliating. The prosecutor misgendered me, and it went downhill from there, dredging up all the shit from my past."

Bobby's eyes held compassion, not pity. Even so, I couldn't shake the memory of being that street rat he'd caught breaking into his tattoo studio in downtown Phoenix six years ago. Despite Kirsten's portrayal of me in court as an upstanding citizen, the truth was more complicated. I didn't always follow the rule of law. I lived by the rules of the street —survival by any means, protecting those I loved, fighting for the innocent—and if it meant breaking the law or even killing, so be it.

"I'm confident Kirsten will get those charges against you dismissed," Bobby said.

"I hope so."

"Now, call back the client whose appointment you missed. Focus your mind on your work for now."

I dreaded picking up the phone. Ever since the arraignment, I'd been getting more phone calls from the media, asking for interviews. I'd silenced all of them except those from people in my contact list, but a few of the callers had left voicemails. I had no intention of returning them.

I called my client, apologized, and rescheduled him for the following week. I then resolved to spend the rest of the day immersed in my art. No matter the chaos in my life, I could usually find solace in turning clients' bare skin into canvases of color and design.

Tattoos were more than just ink on skin to me. They were meant to reflect the wearer's true nature. I certainly had my artistic style, which *Inked Magazine* had described as "HR Giger meets Tim Burton." But I did my best to convey my clients' personalities through my personal lens of visceral imagery with whimsical undertones and dark, dreamlike fantasy.

When Maya Harris arrived, she gasped. "Oh, Avery, what happened to your face? Are you all right? Should we reschedule?"

"No, I'm fine. I just… I was attacked last night."

This was our second session together, working on a thigh piece. When we first met, she hadn't seemed like my usual clientele. She was a businesswoman in her midforties—all power suits, subtle makeup, and a three-hundred-dollar haircut. Not the kind of woman I expected would request a Gigeresque biomechanical tattoo down her left thigh. But people were often more than they seemed.

I got her prepped, with her skirt hiked up to expose her leg, and immersed myself in my work, not even bothering with small talk.

"Can we take a break?" Maya eventually asked. "I really gotta pee."

I looked at the clock and realized I'd been working for two hours straight. No wonder she'd fidgeted the last twenty minutes.

"Yeah, sure."

"Is something wrong?" she asked.

"No, why?"

"You seem... angry. Are you... is someone abusing you?" Her concern seemed genuine.

"No. Nothing like that. Like I said, I was attacked last night but not by someone I knew." I debated how much to share with her. "I got jumped by some assholes who didn't like the fact that I'm transgender."

"I'm so sorry. A jerk at my wife's office has been harassing her for weeks. HR refuses to do anything about it. We're considering filing a lawsuit."

I was surprised. She hadn't set off my gaydar. But then some queer women didn't.

"I'm sorry that's happening to her," I said. "You should definitely sue their ass."

"This guy, he's always repeating those homophobic, right-wing talking points he hears from that talk show host Sergeant Rivers. 'Queers are destroying America.' 'Lesbians are destroying the institution of marriage by luring women away from godly men.' And my favorite, 'Queers are causing a population decline in the country because they can't have kids.' Our own kids got a chuckle out of that one."

"I hate that guy," I replied.

Sergeant Rivers, a right-wing militia type, hosted the nationally syndicated talk show *The River of Truth* on satellite radio, with video segments available on his YouTube channel. I'd only ever seen clips of his shows, but they were nothing but a shit pile of misinformation, logical fallacies, blatant prejudice, and absurd conspiracy theories. And of course, advertisements encouraging his fans to buy cryptocurrency, precious metals, and guns for "when the end times come."

Whenever Rivers said anything particularly controversial, it got picked up by all the mainstream media as clickbait to drive advertising. And then all the other right-wing talking heads would echo Rivers's nonsense word for word as if it were gospel. They reminded me of a plague of grackles squawking in a palm tree.

"That asshole at my wife's work is always quoting him. He complains about people's lifestyles being shoved down his throat and how woke values are turning our country into a bunch of pussies. Last week, she overheard him telling a coworker that queer people were grooming kids."

"I know the type."

"Well, I'd better run to the ladies' room, and then we can continue."

As Maya rushed to take care of business, I discarded my gloves, feeling a mix of relief and apprehension. My phone had been buzzing with unread messages—several from unknown numbers and one from Detective Rutherford. With a deep breath to steady my nerves, I played her message.

"Ms. Byrne, this is Detective Rutherford from the Phoenix Police Department. I located your friend. Call me when you get a chance."

My heart pounded as I hit Redial, the phone feeling heavy in my hand.

"Phoenix Police, Detective Rutherford speaking."

"It's Avery Byrne. You found Danielle? Is she okay?" The words tumbled out in a rush, laced with hope and fear.

"Good afternoon, Ms. Byrne." Her voice came through tinged with a hesitance that sent a chill down my spine. "We found Danny Kirkpatrick at his home in Tempe. He appears to be… safe."

A cocktail of anger and disbelief surged within me. "Her name is Danielle! And she's a *she*."

"Please understand, Ms. Byrne. I'm not trying to misgender your friend. But she, or rather he, has detransitioned. I don't know all the details, but I can confirm they are alive and safe."

"That's bullshit!"

"I understand that's not what you wanted to hear, but I looked into it for you."

"You must have the wrong person. Danielle wouldn't detransition."

But even as I said it, a knot formed in my stomach as the memory of the letter about the canceled scholarship flashed in my mind, raising a tumult of doubts. I'd never known anyone who had detransitioned. Maybe such a devastating blow had led her to a misguided attempt to cling to her old life as a man.

"I assure you, Ms. Byrne, we have the right person."

I mulled over her words. They had the undeniable ring of truth to them. "What about my friend Sophia and her boyfriend?"

"We are still investigating. We've confirmed that the 911 call was placed locally, although the caller used a prepaid cell phone. Our techs are trying to locate it, but it takes time."

"And the cops who shot Sophia and her boyfriend?"

"We haven't received the ballistics report, and we're evaluating the bodycam footage. Beyond that, I cannot comment at this time. I promise you that if the officers acted outside of protocol, we will hold them accountable."

I took a breath in a futile attempt to calm the storm inside me. "Thank you for telling me."

"You're welcome, Ms. Byrne. You have a good day."

I considered asking her to help get the new assault charges against me dropped, but at this point, it was in the court's hands.

Bobby was staring at me when I hung up. I wondered how much he'd heard over the buzz of his tattoo machine.

"Bad news?"

I shared the details with him.

"You know as well as I do that each trans person's path is unique," he said. "A part of the transition process is grieving the loss of the former life. There can be bouts of denial. If your friend is indeed transgender, they will eventually accept it and retransition. Until then, all you can do is love and accept where they are on their journey."

"I need to talk to her," I said, pulling my purse from the bottom drawer of my station.

He took it out of my hand and dropped it back. "No, kiddo. You have a client waiting and two more after her. If your friend wants to talk to you, they know how to reach you. For now, focus on your work."

Hating that he was right, I donned a fresh pair of gloves as Maya returned from the restroom.

"Wow, you look even more upset than before. You okay?"

"Just got some unexpected news. I'm all right. Let's get back to work."

CHAPTER 14
UNCERTAINTY

AFTER ANOTHER COUPLE OF HOURS, Maya's pain tolerance was edging toward its limit. Carefully, I cleaned off the blood and excess ink from her skin and applied antibiotic ointment before wrapping the artwork with Derm Shield. We scheduled her next session for a few weeks out, allowing ample time for her skin to heal.

After Maya settled up and left, I called Sophia.

"Hey, Avery." She sounded as exhausted as I felt.

"How are you feeling?"

"Better now that I'm home. Theo has been taking good care of me. Poor thing—I've been running him ragged. He's such a good housemate."

"I'm glad." I sighed. "Have you spoken with Detective Rutherford?"

"She told me the 911 caller was local, using a prepaid."

"Did she tell you about Danielle?"

"No, what about her?"

"Rutherford said she detransitioned."

"Wow! I knew she was having financial problems, but I did not see that coming. I suppose I should use male pronouns for him now. I hope he finds peace, but we both know gender dysphoria doesn't go away."

"No, it doesn't."

She started sobbing on the other end of the line.

"Sophia?"

"I'm sorry. I just miss Étienne so much. He was such a good man. As glad as I am to be home, I can't stop thinking of him. I still feel his presence here, like a gaping hole in my life."

"I know. I went through a lot of that when Sam was killed."

"The flashbacks and nightmares are worse than the physical pain ever was."

"Yeah. It fucking sucks."

"I'm glad you've got Roz," Sophia said, her voice brightening a little.

"You'll find someone else too. But give yourself time. I started dating Roz only a month after Sam died. It was rocky at first, though we're in a good place now."

"That gives me hope. It really does."

"Is there anything I can do for you?" I asked.

"I'd love to see you when you're available. Just to have someone to talk to who's lost a lover like this."

"You got it. I've got a couple more clients, but I can stop by around seven if that's okay."

"I'm not going anywhere."

"I'll see you then," I said.

At the end of the day, when I was closing down my station for the night, Bobby approached. Frisco and Butcher had already left, and the studio was quiet—no music playing, just the buzz of the neon lights in the window.

He sat down in the adjustable tattoo chair I used for my

work. "Hey, kiddo. Why don't you tell me what happened last night?"

I filled him in on just about everything—the incident at the library, my arrest, the arraignment, and the jaw-dropping revelation about Danielle, now Daniel apparently. I didn't mention the phone calls because I didn't want him to worry any more than he already was.

I half expected him to chastise me for confronting the mob outside the library. Instead, he put a gentle hand on my arm and looked me in the eye. "I'm so proud to have you as my daughter—someone so strong and courageous. Someone willing to protect others more vulnerable than herself."

"Thanks, Appa."

"I don't know why the world goes through these cycles. Why some people spread hate and cruelty is beyond me. I used to believe our society would evolve beyond such negativity and nonsense."

"Doesn't feel that way lately," I said.

"No, it doesn't. After Melissa died, I thought about this a lot. We have so little influence on the hate and violence in the world, even if our hearts are filled with love. Was the Buddha's quest to end the world's suffering a fool's errand? It's hard to know how to respond to such an angry, spiteful world."

"I'm surprised to hear you say that."

He let out a soft, gentle laugh. "Why? You think I'm some wise Jedi master with all the answers?"

I shrugged. "Most of the time. Even if I don't always follow your advice."

"Got news for you, kiddo. We're all just winging it. Certainty is a mind trap. The best we can do is spread love wherever and however we can. To protect the vulnerable. To speak, not just truth to power but love to cruelty. Sometimes it feels like trying to fill a swimming pool with a teaspoon.

And there aren't always straightforward answers about how to do that. We each have to make our own best decisions."

"I suppose."

"I know there are things you've done that I haven't agreed with."

Terror gripped my chest. *How much does he know?* I remained silent.

"You have made hard choices to protect those you love. And you have seen tragic consequences from some of those choices."

"Appa, I..." I fumbled for words, terrified he would see me as the horrible person I was. A vigilante. A criminal. A murderer.

"I do not judge you for the choices you've made," he continued. "Your heart is in the right place. I do not know what I would've done had I faced the situations you have. So how could I condemn you?"

"Appa..."

"But let me caution you against being too eager to mete out justice. I know the legal system has its biases. But it is better equipped to handle these situations than you are. I'd hate for you to end up in prison. Or worse, dead."

"I'm letting the police handle the swatting incident."

A smile creased his face, but there was also sadness in his eyes. "I know you are, kiddo. I just wanted to share that with you."

"Thank you, Appa. Your love and support..." My voice choked with emotion as I hugged him. "They've meant so much to me. You and Melissa were the first people I considered family after the Lost Kids."

"You're my family too. Keep your nose clean, kiddo. Eventually, this campaign against the trans community will blow over. Those power-hungry transphobes will find someone else to blame for their self-made misery."

I didn't share his optimism, but I didn't want to argue. "I promised to stop by Sophia's after work."

"Tell her I hope she feels better soon." He stood up. "Oh, before you go, I have a little something for you."

"What?"

He retrieved a wrapped present that could only be a vinyl album. "I know your birthday isn't until tomorrow, but I figured I'd give this to you early."

"Thanks, Appa." I unwrapped it to reveal that it was the Damned's *Darkadelic*. I already had the digital version, but recently, Roz and I had bought a turntable and started collecting vinyl.

I hugged him again. "You're the best."

"So are you. Now, let's blow this popsicle stand. Don't want to keep Sophia up too late. I'm sure she needs her rest, and so do you."

We walked out into the parking lot together.

CHAPTER 15
REJECTED

WHAT I COULDN'T BRING myself to tell Bobby was that taking action against bullies who hurt or killed the people I loved was, for lack of a better word, therapeutic. I wasn't a sociopath or anything—I didn't get off on hurting people. And getting my revenge didn't bring loved ones back from the dead. Sam was gone forever. As was Melissa. And the Lost Kids.

But serving justice on the predators of the world kept them from hurting others. And that was better than nothing. It was certainly better than waiting for a bigoted, broken legal system to do its fucking job.

I spent an hour commiserating with Sophia and Theo then headed home. Roz still hadn't heard anything new from the embassy. The news stories briefly mentioned negotiations even as the brutal invasion of Gaza continued, including the bombing of a hospital that was doubling as a refugee camp.

Despite her worries for her family, Roz woke me the next morning by playing Moran Magal's dark parody of "Happy Birthday."

I laughed and kissed her. "You crazy bitch. I love you."

"For breakfast, we're having a red velvet cake with black icing."

I clapped. "My favorite!"

She pulled out a gift-wrapped album and box from the closet. "And I got you these. But you don't have to open it now," she teased.

"Gimme, gimme, gimme." I snatched the gifts from her and tore open the album. "*Graveyard Groove*! I thought Kimi said the new album didn't come out until Halloween."

"Well, I know someone who knows someone who got an early pressing."

"Kimi. Of course." I unwrapped the box and discovered it was a small Bluetooth speaker.

"I know it doesn't look like much, but Kimi says this is the best-sounding speaker she's listened to. Really amazing bass levels."

"Thank you." I kissed her again. "You are the best girl-friend in the world."

"Happy birthday and Happy Friday the thirteenth, babe."

To my delight, I discovered Roz had decorated the apartment with strings of crepe paper bats, plushie black cats, and life-sized cardboard cutouts of Elvira, Jason Voorhees, and Michael Myers.

In addition to a slice of cake, Roz served up a couple of sunny-side-up eggs fried in a skull-shaped mold with the yolks as eyes, along with crossed strips of bacon. It was the best birthday breakfast ever.

"Thanks," I told her as we sat down to eat.

"Figured we both needed some cheering up."

I scoffed. "We're goth. We're supposed to be maudlin."

Roz's phone rang. "Caller ID is Washington, DC," she said and answered the phone. "Hello?"

A look of shock spread across her face. "Yes, Mr. President. This is she."

I raised an eyebrow. *Mr. President?* It couldn't be.

"Thank you," Roz said after a pause. Tears blossomed in her eyes.

A lump of concern formed in my gut, and I clasped her free hand tightly.

"I… I really appreciate that, Mr. President. Thank you. Please have someone contact me as soon as you know anything. Goodbye."

She ended the call and stared down at the table.

"Who was that?"

"President Biden."

"Seriously?"

"He's calling all the family members of Americans missing in Israel. He wanted to assure me that he and his staff are doing everything they can to get my mother, Jude, and Talia back. Secretary of State Blinken is meeting with both Netanyahu and Abbas to get the hostages released."

"Um, wow," I said, completely flabbergasted. "Sounds promising. At least you know the president has your back."

"I know. I'm sorry to be such a downer on your birthday."

"Sweetie, you've got nothing to apologize for. You and me, we're family. That means your mother and brother are my family too. Okay?"

"My oldest brother, Mitch, texted, offering to fly down from New York to be with me. I told him I'm okay. I've got you."

After a long silence, I said, "Speaking of chosen family, I've been thinking about Danielle. I need to talk to her. Or him, I guess it is now."

"Avery, maybe it's best to leave him be until he's ready to reach out."

"I just feel I let him down." It felt weird using male pronouns, but it was protocol in the trans community to use someone's declared pronouns, even if they changed.

"I should have contributed more to his GoFundMe. Maybe I still can. I still have some of that cash Sam stole from the Desert Mafia. I'm going over to his house to talk with him."

"What if he's not there? Or doesn't want to see you?"

"I don't know."

"You want me to go with you?" she asked.

"I wouldn't mind."

We pulled up to Daniel's house in separate vehicles since we both had to leave for work afterward. A Subaru Forester sat in the driveway.

"Is that his car?" Roz asked when she met me beside the Gothmobile.

"I think so." My pulse increased. I made no move to walk toward the front porch. I wasn't sure what to say to a detransitioned version of Danielle.

"You okay, sweetie?"

"I suppose." I laced my fingers with hers. "Let's do this."

A moment after I rang the bell, the door opened a crack, the security chain still in place. A familiar but frowning face peeked through the gap.

"What do you want?" the voice was cold, hard, and masculine.

"Danielle, I've been worried about you. Can we come in?"

"It's Danny. And no, you can't. You need to leave."

"What's going on? I heard you've been having financial troubles. Something about your scholarship?"

"It's none of your damned business, you perverted freak! Now, get off my porch!"

"Danielle—er, sorry, Danny—I'm your friend. I'm worried about you."

"You and those groomers at the Phoenix Gender Alliance have done enough damage. You people ruined my life, brainwashing me into thinking I was trans."

"What? That's not true, and you know it. I did your prescreening interview before you joined the Hatchlings, remember? You were with your mother and were already calling yourself Danielle and dressing femme. All we did was offer you support, love, and acceptance. No one groomed you or brainwashed you."

"No! I was confused. And my mother is just another delusional woke libtard. You people took advantage of me. Filled my head with all kinds of ridiculous notions. I lost my scholarship because of you!"

"The scholarship for women? They took it away because they found out you were trans, which is a rotten thing to do, but that's not my fault or the fault of anyone at the Alliance."

"I could have applied to other scholarships. You're a goddamn cult! You should all be locked up."

"Danny, do you even hear yourself? This isn't you. Have you been talking to your father again?" I remembered him sharing during Hatchlings meetings about how his father was some wealthy Republican fat cat who'd disowned Danny and his mother when he transitioned at sixteen. *Could they have reconnected?*

"Leave my father out of this. He's the one who really cares about me. Not like you radicalized gender extremists!"

"Danny, we only wanted to help."

"By turning me into a freak? By reinforcing my delusions when I was at my most vulnerable? You people are sick!"

"If you'd rather live as a man, I've got no problem with that. But gender dysphoria doesn't go away. You can't just pray it away. Just let us inside, and we can talk."

"I'm done talking. If you freaks aren't gone in five seconds, I'm calling the cops."

The door slammed shut, and the deadbolt clicked into place.

"Shit."

"We should go," Roz said. "We both have to get to work."

I hated to give up on Danielle or Danny or however they saw themselves. But Roz was right. There was no point in trying to talk my way in. And the last thing I needed was for the cops to bust me again.

CHAPTER 16
KIDNAPPED

AT SEOUL FIRE TATTOO, Frisco and Butcher joined Bobby in singing "Happy Birthday" to me. Even George the grackle stopped by to squawk and tap on the glass door. I took it as a sign that he was wishing me a happy birthday. For the next several hours, I forgot about my troubles and enjoyed making art on my client's skin.

Near closing time, Bobby said, "You know, I've been thinking. We've got that one empty workstation in the corner. I think it's time we add another member to our crew."

From a business perspective, it made sense. At one time, that workstation had been home to Shana Trinidad, whose Polynesian-style tattoos had earned her awards and national recognition. She'd moved to LA a couple of years ago and was reportedly tattooing Hollywood's elite.

Bobby had initially found a new artist named Mark, but he was sent packing after sexually harassing Frisco. Another had freaked when he found out I was trans. So the station had sat empty for the better part of a year and a half.

"Actually, I kinda like it with just the three of us," I said.

Tap, tap, tap.

"Oh, four of us," I corrected. "Sorry, George. Didn't mean to leave you out."

"Be that as it may, daughter dear, I'm already putting some feelers out. Don't worry. If there is an issue like the ones we've had, we will deal with it. I promise."

"I'm open to it," Frisco said. "So long as they keep their paws to themselves."

"Butcher?" Bobby asked.

Butcher shrugged.

"I'll take that as a yes. Birthday girl?"

"Yeah, okay."

We closed shop shortly after. I pulled into my spot at the Stonewall Apartments parking lot and glanced at my phone. Caller ID told me it was Marilyn Hildebrandt, Zoë's mom. I figured she had a question about the Trans March or the Pride Festival scheduled for the following morning.

"Hey Marilyn," I answered, walking to our apartment. "What's up?"

"Zoë's missing."

A knot formed in my stomach. "Missing? Since when?"

"She normally takes the Valley Metro bus home from Discovery Charter Middle School and arrives around four o'clock. But that was two hours ago. She never showed up."

"Maybe she went home with a friend," I suggested, hoping against the worst.

"I called all of her closest friends. They each confirmed Zoë didn't go home with any of them. I got a hold of one of the school administrators, who said she was pretty sure Zoë boarded her usual bus."

"All right. Don't panic. Maybe she got on the wrong bus by mistake. Did you call the police?"

"I did. They're sending someone. Did she say or do anything at the meeting that might provide clues about what might have happened to her?"

"Not that I recall."

"She had so many behavioral problems before she came out. I thought we'd put all that behind us. But she's been unusually quiet since the Hatchlings' meeting. Oh, Avery, I'm so scared for her."

"You want me to come over?"

"I'm sorry. You've probably got a fun evening planned. Zoë mentioned you had a birthday coming up. I hate to—"

"You're not interrupting anything, Marilyn. Just tell me where you live."

She gave me an address in Peoria, northwest of Phoenix.

"I'm on my way," I said just as I walked through the front door.

"Thank you."

"Roz?" I called.

She appeared in the living room, dressed in a bloodred button-down shirt and a bolo tie with a skull slider. She looked good enough to eat.

"Get changed," she said with a gleeful smile. "We're having dinner at Barrio Queen. I think we both could use some margaritas."

"I can't. I was just talking to Marilyn Hildebrandt. Her daughter Zoë, who's a member of the Hatchlings, didn't arrive home after school. Do you mind if we go over and talk with her?"

Roz looked crestfallen. "Of course not. It's your birthday. You're in charge."

～

When we arrived at Marilyn's house, her face was streaked with mascara, her eyes red and swollen from crying. "Oh dear, look at your face."

I'd almost forgotten how bruised I still was. "I'm okay. Marilyn, this is my girlfriend, Roz."

"Ms. Hildebrandt, I'm so sorry to hear about Zoë."

"Thank you. Please come in. And call me Marilyn."

She led us into the living room, where her visibly distraught husband sat with a woman I guessed was a detective.

"Avery, Roz, this is my husband, David. Avery leads the Hatchlings meetings."

He shook my hand. "I appreciate all you've done for Zoë. I saw the video of what happened to you at the library that night. That was very brave of you."

I blushed in embarrassment. I hated that my bruised face was all over the internet after getting a beatdown from the right-wing mob.

"I fear I only made things worse, but thank you."

Marilyn gestured toward the woman who'd been talking to her husband. "And this is Detective Hausman. She's with Peoria Police Department's Special Victims Unit."

Detective Hausman's ice-blue eyes studied me as she stood and extended a hand. Her black suit looked expensive. I wondered how she afforded it on a detective's salary.

"Good evening, Ms. Byrne. When did you last speak with Zoë?"

"Wednesday night at our monthly Hatchlings meeting."

"Did she seem distressed or anxious?"

"With all that's happened to the trans community lately, we're all a little freaked," I replied.

"Any indication she was considering running away again?"

"My daughter did not run away," Marilyn said firmly.

Detective Hausman put a hand on her arm. "Ms. Hildebrandt, we must consider all possibilities. She's a teenager who's run away twice in the past. She has a history of delinquent behavior, including drinking, drug use, and shoplifting. It's entirely possible she's doing those things again."

"Zoë's behavioral problems stopped once she transitioned," David said. "Her therapist explained that her acting out had been a cry for help. Since she's been living as a girl, she's been happier and more communicative, with no behavioral problems. Running away now just doesn't make any sense."

Hausman paused, considering David's words. "We can't ignore her past behavior completely. We'll do everything we can to locate her, regardless of whether she ran away or someone took her." She turned to me. "Ms. Byrne, what did Zoë talk about at the meeting?"

"We talked about a lot of things—online safety, tomorrow's Trans March, the Pride Festival, and the Halloween party later this month. We also discussed the group's chairperson getting shot by the cops."

"The swatting incident. Yes, I heard about that." Hausman nodded slowly, jotting down notes. "Did the child seem especially upset by that discussion?"

"Upset about the police shooting the innocent leader of our group and murdering her boyfriend?" I said. "Of course, she was upset. Who wouldn't be? Our community's been under attack, and the cops are part of the problem."

Roz put a hand on my arm, no doubt encouraging me to take it down a notch.

"Has she mentioned anyone wishing her harm?" Hausman asked.

"You mean aside from the entire Republican party?"

"Anyone specifically? A classmate or a neighbor?"

"She hasn't said anything in the group."

"Thank you, Ms. Byrne." Hausman turned to Marilyn and her husband. "I'll issue an AMBER Alert and check with Valley Metro and the school. I'm sure she'll turn up." She gave me her business card. I was starting to build up a collection of cards from cops lately. "If you hear from her or learn anything that might help us locate her, please contact me right away."

Marilyn thanked her, and David escorted her to the door.

"What can I do to help?" I asked, feeling utterly useless.

Marilyn shook her head, wiping tears from her face. "I don't know. I was hoping she might have shared something in the group that would point to where she might be."

I racked my brain but came up with nothing. "Nothing comes to mind, but if I remember something significant, I'll call you."

"Thank you. We've contacted all of her friends. No one has spoken with her since school let out."

"Have you received any threats?" I asked. "Is there anyone who would wish her harm? Family members? Neighbors? People at your work or David's?"

"No threats. We don't really know our neighbors other than to say hi in passing. We're estranged from my parents. They were strongly opposed to Zoë's transition, my dad especially. He's very religious and set in his ways."

"You think he could have taken her?"

"No!" She shook her head dismissively. "My father may be a lot of things, but a kidnapper isn't one of them."

"What about David's parents?"

Again, Marilyn shook her head. "His mom passed a few years ago, but his father's been very supportive. He took her to the Halloween Superstore last weekend to pick out a princess costume. She said they had a great time."

"Was she dating anyone?"

"No. She's been too focused on her transition and schoolwork to worry about dating."

"Well, I'm not sure how much I can help, but I can check with other members of the Alliance to see if they know something that might help. You could contact the local TV stations, have them spread the word."

"I'll do that. Thank you. Do you think it could be those people—the ones protesting at the library?"

I shrugged. "I don't know. How closely do you monitor

Zoë's online activity? Does she share information, like what bus she rides, on social media?"

"I don't monitor it as closely as I did when she was having problems. But we've talked about the importance of online privacy. I keep thinking it must be someone she knows, perhaps a bully from school. Or maybe Detective Hausman's right. Maybe she ran away again."

A hush fell over the room. I could hear the muffled voices of Hausman and David near the front door.

"Do you need us to stay with you until she's found? For moral support, I mean?" I asked.

She shook her head. "No, but thank you both for coming out. I'm sorry for interrupting your birthday."

"Nothing to be sorry for," I assured her. "Zoë's safety takes precedence over everything else."

We headed out, and Roz and I drove in silence for a long while.

"I can see the wheels turning, babe. What're you thinking?" she finally asked.

"My gut's telling me there's a connection—Zoë's disappearance, Sophia's swatting incident, the protest at the library, even Danielle's—or rather, Daniel's—sudden detransition. I know anti-trans rhetoric and violence have been increasing, but this feels like a well-planned and organized effort. "

"How so?"

"Remember when state after state passed laws banning gender-affirming care for trans kids? The language in the bills was identical. The same with the laws restricting abortion. Turns out Arizona's own fascist organization, Patriots of Liberty, was behind it all. This uptick in attacks on the local trans community feels the same."

"Well, babe, there's not much we can do about it tonight."

"I suppose not." I stared blankly out at the passing lights

of the city and remembered something. "Can we stop at Office Oasis? I have to pick up the signs and banner for tomorrow's Trans March."

"Sure." Roz checked her watch. "We missed our dinner reservation. Probably a long wait on a Friday night. Alternative plans to celebrate your birthday?"

I considered our options. "After we get the signs, let's grab a quick bite somewhere then head over to L Street for drinks."

When she'd stopped for a red light, she leaned over and kissed me. "Anything you like, babe."

CHAPTER 17
TARGETED

AS ROZ DROVE, I typed Detective Hausman's number into my contacts list. *But what if she contacts me on a different number? What if missing her call means not being able to track down Zoë?*

The calls from the media had subsided. The reporters must have tired of being forced to talk to no one but my outgoing message. So I turned the ringer back on.

When the phone rang five minutes later, I answered without checking the caller ID, hoping it was Marilyn calling back to tell me Hausman had found Zoë.

"Fucking groomer bitch." The voice sounded male with a thick Texas accent. "I'm gonna track you down and rape you till there's nothing left."

"Who the hell is this?" I yelled.

"You'll find out soon enough, faggot!"

I hung up, fuming.

"Who was that?" Roz asked.

"Someone wishing me a happy birthday."

"Didn't sound like it."

"Or some bigot threatening to rape me."

"What?"

I realized it was time to tell her. "Ever since the arraignment, I've gotten a shit ton of calls. At first, they were from the news media, wanting my side about what happened at the Hatchlings meeting. Now the assholes must have found my phone number."

"How?"

I sighed. "Seoul Fire website, most likely."

We hadn't driven another block when my phone rang again. Before I could answer it, Roz snatched the phone out of my hand.

"Roz, you're driving."

She ignored me. "Hello?" she growled.

I hoped it wasn't a client or a member of the Alliance. From the expression on her face, I knew it was another harassing call. She hung up and handed it back to me.

"What'd they say?"

"You don't want to know."

"Someone threatening to rape me again?"

"Worse. Someone threatening to kill you. Rather graphically."

"Happy birthday to me."

We arrived at Office Oasis's printing counter twenty minutes later. When I swiped my debit card to pay for the order, the digital screen read *Transaction Not Authorized*.

"Shit!"

"What's wrong?" Roz asked.

"Card declined. I don't understand. I've got thousands in my account."

"Try it again," the woman behind the counter suggested. "Sometimes these machines glitch."

I did, and the screen displayed the same message. "Fuck."

Roz pulled out her card. "Here, let me try."

I waved her off. "No, I'll use my business bank card."

"Should you be using it for Alliance expenses?"

I shrugged. "Only in an emergency, which this is. My accountant will sort it out."

I swiped my business bank card. Again, the screen read, *Transaction Not Authorized.*

"Fucking hell! This machine must be broken." I pushed back against a rising panic in my chest.

"Here, let me try mine so we can go have a drink at L Street." Roz sounded irritated.

Not that I blamed her. It was turning into a fucking nightmare of a birthday at the end of a fucking nightmarish week.

She swiped her card and punched her PIN into the keypad. The screen read *Transaction Authorized.*

"Yay!" the woman behind the counter said cheerily.

I sighed with a mixture of relief, guilt, and anger. I hated depending on someone else, but if I had to, I was glad it was Roz.

After we put the signs and the banner into the back of her SUV, I opened the bank app on my phone and checked my accounts while Roz drove. Both were overdrawn. I scrolled through the list of transactions and found hundreds of unfamiliar charges, ranging from a few dollars to a few hundred dollars—all different vendors. Someone had been on a spending spree with my money.

"Fucking hell!"

"What is it?" she asked.

"Someone hacked both my bank accounts."

"Oy vey!"

I called the number on the back of my bank card and spent fifteen minutes navigating the automated system with increasing frustration, trying to get a hold of a live person. Eventually, a cheerful recorded voice informed me that no customer service representatives were available and asked that I leave a message. They would call back on Monday morning starting at eight o'clock Eastern time.

I stared out at the city as Roz drove. When my phone rang again, I answered it, irrationally thinking it could be the bank calling me back. Instead, some asshole unleashed a string of transphobic profanities, told me in anatomical terms where he'd like to stick a barbed-wire-wrapped baseball bat, and hung up.

"Motherfucker," I grumbled.

"Another harassing call?"

"Yeah."

"Putz!"

I muted my phone so that only people on my contacts list would ring through. If those asswipes had anything meaningful to say, they could leave a voicemail message. Then I'd have evidence to give to the police, assuming the cops actually gave a shit.

"Babe, you think it's safe to go home?" she asked with a tremor in her voice.

"Honestly? I don't know. To be frank, I'm freaking out a bit." I considered the situation. "As I see it, we have three options."

"Oh? And what are they, birthday girl?"

"Option one—we spend the night at a police station, filing a report that they'll never follow up on. Remember last month when the Gothmobile got broken into at Seoul Fire? They stole my first aid kit, a box of motor oil, my leatherbound sketchbook, and a tool kit. So I did the thing, filed the report, and… nada. They never even called me back. So fuck that."

"Okay, so…"

"Option two—we crash at Bobby's or rent a motel room, but for how long? We can't hide forever. And there's no telling when or if this would blow over."

"Which leaves…"

"Option three—we fight back."

"Babe, the police are far better equipped to deal with this than we are," she said.

"The police? You mean the ones who shot Sophia and murdered her boyfriend? The ones who arrested me for trying to protect the Hatchlings? They won't help. You know this. And whoever is behind these attacks is not going to stop. Not till someone makes them stop."

"Uh-oh. You've got that look."

"I'm not letting these douchebags run me out of my own home. If they want a fight, I'll give them a fucking fight."

"No offense, babe, but have you seen yourself in the mirror lately? I think you lost that fight."

"I lost a fight. And yes, it was stupid. I should've listened to Easton."

"Why, what did Easton say?"

"How should I know? I wasn't listening. My point is, I will find who's behind all this bullshit. After the parade tomorrow, Avery the avenger is coming out to play."

She entwined her fingers with mine. "Well, count on me to be there beside you."

"Thanks, sweetie. You're the best. Now, let's go to L Street. I need a fucking drink."

CHAPTER 18
TRANS MARCH

ALL NIGHT, I tossed and turned, replaying the past week's events in my mind—Sophia's swatting, the riot at the library, Zoë going missing, the harassing calls, and the fraudulent bank charges. Even if I couldn't figure out who was behind it all, rescuing Zoë was my priority. Detective Hausman had seemed competent for a cop. But the more people looking for Zoë, the better. I texted Marilyn Hildebrandt to see if she'd been found, but there was no immediate reply.

Roz called the embassy again in the morning, only to be told negotiations were ongoing. Unfortunately, so was the war, with the death toll steadily rising. I comforted her as best I could, but it didn't seem like it was enough. I hoped the Trans March and the Pride Festival would lift her spirits a little.

I drove us downtown and parked the Gothmobile in a lot near Thomas Road and Third Street that served as the staging area for the march. The air was refreshingly cool, although it was still expected to reach the midnineties by late afternoon. I wore a black shirt with the words We Will Not Be Erased in the colors of the transgender pride flag. Roz's shirt read, I Love My Trans Wife.

Despite all the recent craziness, my mood rose when I saw other members of Phoenix Gender Alliance. These people were my family. Around them, I found strength, safety, and a sense of empowerment.

Seven years before, Bobby had nudged me to join the group. I'd been reluctant and told him I wasn't a joiner. But the truth was, I feared being judged for having been homeless and transitioning on black market estrogen. I didn't need a bunch of rich suburban trans kids looking down their noses at me. Still, Bobby pressured me to at least consider it.

So on a chilly December day, Bobby and I met then cochair Jinx Ballou at a Village Inn for a screening interview, no doubt to make sure I was a trans kid and not some radicalized, bigoted bully.

Jinx was pretty even without makeup. She had dark hair like mine but tan skin, whereas mine was luminescent and pale. What really struck me was her confidence, and I immediately caught a cop vibe off of her. I worried this whole thing had been a setup. My fears eased when I learned she'd left the force after being outed as trans. She now worked as a bounty hunter, chasing down fugitives and bail jumpers.

My first Hatchlings meeting reminded me of when I was squatting with the Lost Kids in a house downtown. We each had our own journey. We were all considered freaks and outcasts by the outside world. But we had each other.

For the first time in years, I felt hopeful about my future. I might live to see twenty. And I wouldn't have to hide or be embarrassed about being trans.

Of course, since then, the world had taken a hard right turn. And the past week had opened old wounds and awoken Avery the avenger.

Theo and Easton soon joined Roz and me in the Trans March staging area.

"How's Sophia?" I asked Theo.

"Physically, she's recovering. Emotionally? Well, that may take a while."

"I understand. Unfortunately, Zoë's Hildebrandt's missing," I said, glancing at Easton.

Their eyes widened in horror. "Missing? As in kidnapped?"

"She didn't arrive home after school yesterday. Police are looking for her."

"Shit," Easton said. "I got a voicemail from her mom but haven't had a chance to call her back. Any leads?"

"The detective assigned to the case believes that she ran away due to the problems she had before coming out. But I'm not convinced. There's too much shit happening to our people lately. Sophia and her boyfriend. Then Zoë. Also, someone drained both of my bank accounts with fraudulent charges."

"Seriously? Damn!"

"Don't forget the harassing phone calls," Roz added. "Death and rape threats."

"That sucks!" Theo hugged me. "Have you reported this to the police?"

"Not yet. I'm not so confident they'd even give a damn."

"Has anyone heard from Danielle?"

Roz and I exchanged a glance. "We did," I said. "They detransitioned. I went by *his* house the other day to talk. He acted as if we brainwashed him."

"That's a load of crap," Easton said. "She, or rather he, came to us after already socially transitioning. All we did was provide love and support. Someone must've really got into his head with all that groomer nonsense."

"All we can do is leave him be," I said. "And hope he finds peace somehow."

"What if he changes his mind again and decides to retransition?" Theo asked. "Do we let them back into the group?"

I didn't have an answer. People who detransitioned were so rare—we'd never had a member do that before. The group had no protocol for such a situation.

"We'll figure it out if that happens."

More members of the Alliance showed up, including Jinx Ballou, Kirsten Pasternak, Shaun and his father, Tequan, and some others I hadn't seen since the last Pride Festival. I could only guess the number was in the hundreds. Still, Sophia and even Danielle—now Daniel—were a noticeable absence.

As the starting time for the parade drew near, Theo and I stretched out the banner from Office Oasis, its pastel pink, white, and blue stripes extending thirty feet from end to end. At the center was the Phoenix Gender Alliance logo I'd designed a while back, loosely inspired by the City of Phoenix logo depicting a firebird rising from the ashes. Bobby had once told me it reminded him of the Rebel Alliance logo from *Star Wars*. I thought that fitting. We were, after all, fighting against an evil empire of bigotry.

Roz and a few others passed out the signs we'd picked up that read Keep Your Laws Off My Body; Trans and Proud; and My Gender, My Body, My Life. I spotted one that bore the phrase Gender-Affirming Care Saves Lives. At the top of the hour, we exited the parking lot and began marching north on Third Street. Roz walked beside me, holding a sign that read Trans People Don't Molest Children —Preachers and Priests Do.

The sidewalks were bustling with a vibrant crowd adorned in a kaleidoscope of rainbow colors and energetically waving Pride flags of all kinds. They cheered as we marched past, and my heart swelled with joy. A rarity these days. Somewhere, an Against Me! tune was playing from speakers. At the Osborn Road intersection, Bobby and his girlfriend, Dana, stood cheering us on, with Frisco and

Butcher waving beside them. My face flushed when Frisco raised her arm in solidarity with us.

By the time we reached Steele Indian School Park, where the Pride Festival awaited, my face ached from smiling so much. My spirit was soaring. The past week's troubles seemed a distant memory.

But then I spotted the cluster of haters who gathered every year at the gates of the festival with signs that read things like God Hates Fags and Stop Mutilating Kids. There seemed to be twice as many as the year before. Some of them were in combat gear and balaclavas. My joy darkened into anger.

"Just ignore them," Roz shouted above the din. "They're just trying to intimidate us."

She was right. They were pathetic little haters with nothing better to do than rain on someone else's parade. But a chill ran down my spine when I recognized a face in the crowd that I hadn't seen in a decade. Despite the balaclava he was wearing, I knew those eyes and that pert nose. Wylie. My baby brother. He'd morphed from a skinny ten-year-old kid into a buff young man.

Wylie's eyes locked with mine, blazing with a hatred that left a sick feeling in my stomach. I'd seen that same look in our father's eyes more times than I cared to remember. *Is this my fault for leaving him behind with an abusive, alcoholic father and a milquetoast, codependent mother?*

My regret turned to terror when Wylie drew a pistol from a holster at his hip. Two of his buddies raised assault rifles at those of us marching.

"Gun!" I shouted.

They opened fire.

CHAPTER 19
BABY BROTHER

THE CHEERS abruptly transformed into screams of panic, drowned out by the deafening thunder of gunfire.

I let go of the banner and charged at my brother. He was only twenty feet away, but as the chaos unleashed around me, time slowed to a crawl. My eyes remained fixed on the boy who'd always tagged along even when I wanted to be alone or with my friends.

My mind replayed the time he'd brought me an over-nuked Hot Pocket as I recovered from one of our father's violent rages. It was burned and tough as shoe leather, but I'd appreciated the gesture.

I remembered kicking the ass of a bully who'd stolen Wylie's bicycle. These and a thousand other memories flashed through my mind in a heartbeat as I rushed toward him.

The barrel of the pistol in his hand flashed. Thunder shook the heavens. Something struck me with the force of a sledgehammer, but I kept going, driven by inertia, adrenaline, and fury.

We collided, and I grappled for the gun. My left arm didn't want to work. My body felt like it was on fire.

"Pervert faggot," Wylie growled into my ear, barely audible over the pounding of my heart.

I felt another hit with a sledgehammer, this time in my leg. With the last of my strength, I grabbed the gun barrel and twisted it away from me. Thunder erupted again, but I didn't feel it.

The world tumbled around me. Then I found myself staring up into the crystalline blue expanse of the heavens. It would have been nice except for the excruciating pain coursing through my veins. I caught a wisp of cloud in the sky and wished I could be there, away from all the screaming and gunshots and pain. My eyelids struggled to stay open.

"Stay with me, Ave."

Roz. She was staring down at me, blocking my view of the pretty cloud. I wanted to tell her to move, to let me see the cloud, but I was too tired. It was hard to breathe.

Finally, my eyelids shut. I felt cold. But it was okay. I was ready to let go.

CHAPTER 20
HOSPITAL

"AVERY, can you hear me? You need to open your eyes, sweetie." The voice was unfamiliar but gentle.

Who are you? And who the hell is Avery?

My head swam. Thoughts and emotions and body sensations overwhelmed me like the overload of a crowded Las Vegas casino. *Too much, too much.*

"Avery, open your eyes for me, honey."

Then I remembered. Avery was me. I struggled to remember how to open my eyes.

A woman was leaning over me. Kind face. *Do I know you?*

"Where?" My voice rattled like shattered glass in a garbage disposal.

"You're in St. Michael's Hospital in Phoenix. Do you remember what happened?"

"No." Pain, both dull and sharp, penetrated my mental fog.

"You were shot."

I let that filter through my brain. Vague flashes of memory. Blue sky. Rainbow flags. The Alliance banner. Crowds. Parade. Bobby. It was the Trans March. Someone shot me.

"Why." I was trying to say, "Wylie," but couldn't get out the second syllable. I remembered my brother's eyes filled with rage, like a wounded animal.

"I don't know why, sweetie. But you're safe now. No one's going to hurt you here. Okay?"

"'Kay."

She left, and I stared up at the ceiling. The room was dimly lit. I could make out the shape of the overhead light, even though it was off. The lens had a texture reminiscent of the seeds on a sunflower's head.

Breathing hurt. But I didn't mind so much. The swimming sensation in my brain, the difficulty focusing on a single thought, was more annoying.

"Ave?"

A different face. Familiar. Roz. Streaked mascara down her face.

"Hey," I croaked.

"Oh my goth! I was so worried."

Another face beside hers. Bobby. His eyes were full of tears.

"Appa."

"Hey, kiddo." He squeezed my hand. "You gave us quite a scare."

"Do you remember what happened?" Roz asked.

"Shot."

She nodded and wiped a tear, further smearing her makeup. "Yeah, but the doctor says you're going to be okay."

I must have drifted back asleep. Next thing I knew, someone else was staring down at me. Short black hair. Narrow face. Olive skin. Dark, beady eyes. Familiar.

"Fuck. Valentine."

A year and a half ago, Detective Valentine and his partner, Detective Hardin, had chased me all the way to New Mexico, suspecting I'd murdered my girlfriend, Sam. Detective Hardin had eventually earned my trust. Valentine was still just a dick with a badge, all swagger and no clue.

"Good to see you again, Ms. Byrne."

"Why. You. Here?"

"I'm investigating the Pride Festival shooting. Apparently, you were at ground zero. Imagine my lack of surprise."

"Where Hardin?"

"Retired six months ago. I'm investigating this case, so why don't you tell me what happened?"

"Not talking. To you."

"You're not a suspect, Ms. Byrne. We already have one of the shooters in custody. But we need to know what happened and if you can identify the other two shooters."

"Lawyer," I stated more firmly even though it hurt my throat.

"Ms. Byrne... Avery... help me put those responsible for this horrific massacre behind bars. Please."

"Lawyer."

Valentine sighed. "Your choice, but I would have thought that you of all people would want to help me track down the people who killed seven of your friends and severely wounded dozens more, including three children. I thought you cared about justice."

"You. Don't. Know. Justice."

Valentine disappeared, and I drifted off again.

When I woke next, I heard a woman ask, "How's your pain level on a scale of one to ten?"

I considered the question, my brain feeling like someone had filled it with molasses. "Six."

"Okay," she said. "I'll be back in a moment with something to help with that."

Before she returned, Kirsten Pasternak walked in and sat on the corner of the bed. "Hey, hero. I understand we have you to thank for stopping the attack. Well done, you."

My recall of the parade was a jumbled mess. Nothing fit together. Shouting. Gunshots. Pain. Wylie.

"Me?"

"Valentine said you shot one of the gunmen. With his own weapon, I might add. That's some badass shit."

"Don't. Trust. Him."

"Who? Valentine?" She chuckled. "Can't say as I blame you, but he arrested the one you disarmed. Who, it appears, is your brother, Wylie. Are you up to talking with me about that?"

I nodded, and it sent the room spinning.

The nurse returned and injected something into my IV port. "That should help for a bit. Let us know if you need anything else."

"So, your brother," Kirsten continued. "Have you been in contact with him recently?"

"Not for years."

"How did he know you would be there?"

"Dunno."

"Was there some conflict between the two of you?"

"No." I wanted to explain I hadn't seen him since my father kicked me out, but I didn't have the energy.

"What about other family? I know you were homeless in your late teens. Have you been in contact with any of your family since then?"

I caught myself drifting off and had to ask her to repeat the question.

"No," I answered. "No contact."

"Detective Valentine's outside, champing at the bit. But I don't think you're up for an interview right now. I'll postpone until tomorrow, when you're feeling better. I'll also insist they drop those ridiculous assault charges against you before you tell them anything."

"Tomorrow."

"You get some sleep, girl."

A question bubbled up from the depths of my consciousness, even as I felt a wave of drowsiness sweep over me. "Where Roz?"

"She and Bobby J. are just outside. You want me to bring them in?"

"Please."

"Okay, girlie. You rest up. We'll talk tomorrow."

I felt myself drift off again, only rousing when I heard Roz's frantic voice.

"Oh my goth, Avery!" I felt her shower kisses on my face, which was still tender from the fight a few days before.

"Hey, kiddo," Bobby said from somewhere in the room. "We're here for you."

"Hey." That was all I could manage.

"I was so worried we lost you!" Roz cried.

"You hurt?"

"No, I'm fine. I'm just worried about you. After all that's happened lately, I was so scared."

"Where shot?"

"The doctor says a bullet penetrated your inner left thigh. Just missed your femoral artery. Another grazed your left arm," she said. "But you're expected to make a full recovery."

"Others, sadly, weren't so lucky," Bobby said.

A knot formed in my stomach. "Who else shot?"

Roz sighed and pressed a warm hand on mine. "I don't think you want to discuss this now."

"Who?"

Roz's eyes misted up. "Shaun and his dad were both killed. Easton was hit, but their injury appears to be minor. They're home recovering."

"Who else?"

"I don't know the names of the others. Dozens more wounded. Some of them might not make it."

I was growing more lightheaded from the pain meds. "Why?"

"I don't know, babe," she said. "It's awful. But it would have been so much worse if it hadn't been for you going after the shooters. I dropped to the ground as soon as I heard the first shot. But you ran right at them. You're a goth-damn hero!" She kissed me again, and we cried together even as the pain meds pulled me deeper toward sleep.

"Tired."

"Okay, babe. You rest. You sure as fuck earned it."

My mind filled with fog despite the rising tide of anger and grief. My eyelids grew heavy, and I slipped under the waves of sleep.

The rest of the day, I drifted in and out while Roz and Bobby sat vigil in my room, occasionally giving me sips of water when I requested it. I vaguely remembered conversing with Kimi and Chupa, but the haze of pain medication made it difficult to discern if it was a genuine memory or a mere dream.

I hated relying on the drugs, but dealing with the pain was too much for me. I only hoped I didn't end up one of those people who got addicted.

CHAPTER 21
OUT OF BED

SUNLIGHT WAS STREAMING through the room when I woke again. Bobby lay snoring in a chair in the corner. No sign of Roz.

My groin burned like wildfire. My right hand found the bulky remote and clumsily tried to press the nurse call button. The television turned on instead. *Fuck.* Gentle instrumental music played as the weather report appeared on the screen. Sunny for the next five days. Highs in the upper eighties.

Headlines scrolled along the bottom, but I was too bleary-eyed to read the small text. I pressed another button, and the music got louder.

Bobby woke with a start. "Not the droids. What? Huh?"

He sat up and wiped drool from the corner of his mouth. "Avery. Good morning. Guess I drifted off. How are you feeling?"

"Hurts."

"Okay, let me get a nurse. Be right back."

He hustled off and returned a moment later, not with a nurse in tow but with Roz.

"Nurse will be here soon," he said.

"Hey, babe. How you feeling?" Roz asked in a voice so worried it broke my heart. She kissed me gently.

"She's dealing with some pain, but the nurse should give her something to help."

"I can answer for myself, Appa," I said sleepily.

"Sorry, kiddo. Guess I'm acting a bit like a Jewish mother." Then he glanced at Roz. "Oh, um, sorry. I guess that came out sounding antisemitic."

Roz managed a sad smile. "My Jewish mother is very much the stereotypical worrier. And that's why I love her. No offense taken."

"I'm going to go find coffee now and let you kids catch up."

"Is Dana here?" I asked. Over the past year, Bobby's girlfriend, Dana Kim, and I had become close despite our rather different backgrounds.

"Sorry, kiddo, but she's out of town on business. She'll be home tomorrow. She sends her best, though."

When he left in search of coffee, I asked Roz, "Any word about your family being released?"

She shook her head. "Not yet. I keep leaving messages. How are you doing?"

"I've had better days. But I'm alive, which is more than I can say for some."

Roz nodded solemnly. "Kimi and Chupa stopped by yesterday, but you were pretty out of it. They're in LA for their *Graveyard Groove* album launch, but they'll be back in a day or so. She got worried because your voice mailbox was full."

"Shit. I forgot about that. Also, my bank account is still fucked-up. What day is it?"

"Sunday."

"Shit. So I'm missing Pride."

"Pride was canceled after the shooting."

"Fuck!"

"It's all your fault," she teased. "What were you thinking, getting yourself shot like that?"

The twinkle in her eye brought my pain level down a notch. "Beats the hell outta me. Have they found Zoë Hildebrandt?"

She shook her head. "Not that I've heard. The news is still reporting her missing."

"I gotta get outta here and go look for her." When I tried to sit up, lightning bolts of pain shot through my hip and arm, taking my breath away. "Fuck!"

"Ave, don't. You'll reopen your wounds."

"But Zoë…"

"The police are looking for her. You're in no shape to do anything but rest and let your body heal."

I lay back on the bed, pissed that she was right. The nurse came by and gave me some horse pills to choke down and promised breakfast was on its way.

An hour later, I pushed aside the remains of my tepid scrambled eggs, the undercooked bacon I suspected was turkey, and the driest toast in the history of the world. No salt. Welcome to Blandsville. Population me. At least Bobby had brought me a real coffee to replace the cup of decaf sadness that came with my breakfast.

I scrolled through the list of voicemail messages from people on my contacts list. A few were from clients worried about me, having heard about the shooting on the news. McCobb, Torch, and Scott Murray from Damaged Souls left wishes for a speedy recovery, as did Frisco, who broke down in the middle of her message.

A man in a lab coat walked in. "Good morning, Ms. Byrne. I'm Dr. Martin, the surgeon who treated your gunshot wounds."

"Thanks for saving me, Doc. Now, when can I get the hell out of here? No offense, but the food here sucks."

"Avery," Bobby scolded, though he knew I was right.

"Let's give it a day or so, just to make sure there's no infection or other complications. The bullets that struck you were standard rounds. The entrance and exit wounds were relatively small. Had they been hollow points or high-velocity rounds from an assault rifle, your injuries would have been exponentially worse. Also, neither bullet hit bone or a major blood vessel. I'd say you were very fortunate compared to many other victims."

"Lucky me," I muttered.

"Now, before we can release you, you're going to need to walk."

I recalled my earlier attempt to get out of bed. "Ugh. Not sure I can stand, much less walk."

"You can do it, babe," Roz assured me.

Bobby also chimed in. "You got this, kiddo. Just breathe in strength, breathe out pain."

"I realize they shot you in a rather inconvenient place," Doc Martin explained.

"Is there a convenient place to get shot?" I retorted.

He chuckled. "Perhaps not. But getting hit in the inner thigh can make walking uncomfortable this early in the recovery process."

Uncomfortable, I thought. *That's an understatement.*

"However, walking helps you avoid pneumonia and speeds your body's healing process. Let's start with sitting up. Shall we?"

With help from both Roz and the doctor, and with a constant stream of profanity, I slid my legs off the side of the bed and sat up. The pain lancing through my body had me seeing stars. The room spun and danced, sending waves of nausea to my stomach. I stared at the floor, willing myself not to puke.

"That wasn't so bad, was it?" Doc Martin asked.

If I'd had full use of my left arm, I would have strangled the motherfucker. I thought about punching him in the throat with my good arm, but considering that he saved my life, I settled for glaring at him. "Fucking peachy."

"Okay, now let's have you stand." He stood on my injured side, Roz on the other.

"Seriously?" I grumbled. "Sitting on the edge of the bed wasn't enough for now?"

"You want to get out of here, don't you?"

Roz kissed my cheek. "They have empanadas in the cafe downstairs. If you stand, I'll fetch you one."

This was what it had come down to—my girlfriend bribing me with food to get me out of bed.

"Just one empanada?"

"Okay, two."

"Breathe in strength, kiddo." Bobby took an exaggerated inhalation.

"All right." I took a deep breath, gritted my teeth, and pushed my body to stand on the exhalation. "Gyah! Fuck!"

My inner left thigh felt like someone was jabbing it with a red-hot poker. My knees almost buckled until I put my weight on my right leg.

"You did it!" Bobby clapped like I was a toddler learning to walk. "Good for you!"

Roz kissed me on the lips this time.

"You're doing very well, Avery," the doctor said. "Now, take a step."

I wanted to tell him to fuck off—that I'd performed my miracle for the day.

"You can do it, babe!" Roz added. "I believe in you. You're a badass. Dos empanadas, remember?"

With Roz and Bobby cheering me on to walk, I suddenly felt the need to prove them right despite the pain. I considered asking for a crutch or a cane, but I wasn't sure how much it would help. I took in a deep breath and blew it out as I moved my left leg forward and put a little weight on it.

"Gyah motherfucker goddammit fuck!" I yelled as Doc

Martin and Roz kept me from collapsing. I quickly stepped again to lean on my right leg. "Fuck, that hurts."

I glanced over at Bobby, half-pissed that he was encouraging this. But the heartbreak and compassion in his eyes kept me from saying anything mean.

"One more step," the doc insisted.

My hands balled into fists. It took all my will not to knock the fucker's teeth out. Roz's silence spoke volumes. I wanted to refuse and just hop on one leg back to bed, but driven by the desire to show Roz my true badass self, I reluctantly complied. I had to prove that I was stronger than this goth-awful pain.

I took another hobbling couple of steps and plopped my ass in a chair. That hurt too. "Fuuuckkkk!" My breath came in heaving gulps, despite Bobby encouraging me to slow it down. "You fucking happy now?" I asked, glaring at the doctor.

He nodded. "That was a good start. I'll check in on you tomorrow morning. In the meantime, try walking around the nurses' station."

As he turned toward the door, I said, "Hey, Doc."

He turned. "Yes?"

"Thanks again for saving my life."

"You're welcome."

Roz pulled a chair next to mine and kissed me so deeply I almost forgot Bobby was still in the room. "That was amazing, babe. I'm sorry it hurts you so much, but you really are a badass."

"Thanks, I guess. I'm just glad you weren't hit."

"I'm really proud of you, kiddo," Bobby added.

"Now I can take care of you. Like a Jewish mother." She winked at Bobby, and a rush of endorphins helped put out the fire of pain. I kissed her, savoring the softness of her lips against mine. My groin throbbed with an intense pressure unrelated to my gunshot wound.

"I'll go see about those empanadas Roz was talking about," Bobby said with nervous embarrassment.

I was losing myself in Roz's sweet embrace, feeling her arms wrapped around me tightly, when a reedy voice suddenly interrupted our moment of bliss.

"Morning, Ms. Byrne," Valentine said.

CHAPTER 22
VALENTINE

I GLARED AT DETECTIVE VALENTINE, who stood in the doorway.

"What the hell do you want?"

"I need to get your official statement. You were a bit out of it yesterday. Feeling better today?"

"Sure as hell don't feel like talking to you. Especially without my lawyer present."

"I spoke with Ms. Pasternak yesterday. The county attorney's office has agreed to drop all charges against you stemming from the incident at the library if you cooperate with me on the Pride Festival shooting. But if you'd rather have her present, I can wait."

The smart move would have been to have her there to field any attempt by Valentine to pin something else on me, especially since my brother Wylie was one of the shooters. But between Kirsten representing me for the arrest at the library and now this stay at the Co-Pay Hotel, I would have nothing left of the cash Sam had stolen from the Desert Mafia. Besides, if it meant getting clear of the bogus assault charges, I was willing to take the chance.

"Let's just get this over with," I replied through gritted teeth. "What do you want to know?"

He turned to Roz. "Do you mind giving us a little privacy?"

"Yeah, I do mind," Roz said defiantly. "We were both there."

"Yes, but I already have your statement."

I looked at her. She hadn't mentioned talking to Valentine. "You did?"

"I told him those soldier-wannabe assholes started shooting at us just as we got to the park. And rather than duck for cover, you ran to stop them. That you were a hero."

I turned back to Valentine. "That's it. I have no more to add."

"Well, I have more questions. The person who shot you is named Wylie Byrne. Any relation?"

The mention of Wylie's name brought a flood of memory flashes. The wound in my thigh burned.

"Is this really necessary right this minute?" Bobby appeared in the door with a box of what I hoped were empanadas. "Can't you see she's still in a lot of pain?"

"Wylie's my brother," I said.

"Why would your brother shoot you?"

"Ask him."

"Have you had an argument recently?"

"I haven't seen him in years."

"Why not?"

I rolled my eyes. "My folks kicked me out when I was thirteen."

"Because you're transsexual?"

"Transgender," I corrected. "Haven't seen him since. Not till the morning of the parade."

"What happened at the parade?"

More flashes of memories assaulted me like a swarm of

Africanized bees. The thunder of gunfire and screams of terror echoed through my mind, causing my pulse to race. The air in the room became stale and suffocatingly thin. I gasped, struggling to get enough oxygen. A sharp, stabbing pain radiated from my chest. *Am I having a heart attack?* I needed to get out of there, but I couldn't move. Couldn't run. Blood, so much blood. My father screaming at me. Not my father. Wylie. It was Wylie screaming at me. Then pain, so much pain.

Roz gripped my trembling right hand, stemming the panic and adrenaline coursing through my system. "Breathe, baby. Just breathe. You're safe."

I forced air into my lungs. "I saw him point. Wylie. He pointed a gun at us. I ran to stop him."

"And you had no idea he would be there?" Valentine pressed.

"No idea." Deep breath, like Bobby and Melissa taught me. Good air in, bad air out. Calm air in, fear out.

"What happened then?"

"I... I grabbed for the gun. He shot me. Still, I reached for it. More shots. That's all I remember."

"Was this connected to the incident at the library last week?"

I considered his question before answering. *Maybe I should call Kirsten after all.*

"How the hell should I know? I tried to protect the kids. The ones in our youth group. And your jackbooted cops arrested me for it. You gonna arrest me, too, for trying to protect my people?"

"Easy there, sport." He held his hands up in a defensive gesture. "From what I saw on the video footage, my jackbooted cops, as you call them, saved you. You're not a suspect in the Pride Festival shooting. I'm just trying to understand the timeline so I can put the shooters away."

"Why should I trust you? You and Hardin chased me all the way to New Mexico to arrest me for killing my ex-girlfriend. But shocker! Your boss was the one involved in her murder, not me."

Valentine's chagrined expression told me my point had hit home. "I understand your anger and distrust. There were some bad calls made in that situation."

"Not long after that, when someone murdered my friends in the Sonoran Crows Hot Rodders' group, you chalked it up to them driving under the influence."

"Well, technically, they were driving under the influence."

"Because some asshole put fentanyl in their food. They were trying to get to the hospital. But you were in too much of a rush to close the case to do any actual detective work. I found the real killers."

"That's why I'm talking to you, Ms. Byrne. You're a smart woman. And you were at ground zero for this shooting. Help me nail these guys, Avery. Your brother's already in custody. But witnesses say there were two other shooters who escaped. Did you recognize them as well?"

"They were wearing masks. Balaclavas." I recalled vague glimpses in all the chaos.

"And no idea how Wylie knew you would be there?"

Something occurred to me. "I started getting death threats the day before. Maybe he was one of the people making them."

That got a reaction from Valentine. "Death threats? From whom?"

"We've started getting them on the studio's main phone line," Bobby admitted.

"What?" I was aghast. "Why didn't you tell me?"

"You had enough to worry about. Just a bunch of punks mouthing off."

"Do you know who the callers are?" Valentine asked.

"They didn't exactly leave their names." I turned to Roz. "Where's my phone?"

She unplugged it from a charging cord on the counter and handed it to me.

I booted it up. The phone app showed I had fifty voicemails and an alert that my mailbox was full. Most of the numbers on the call log were either unidentified or simply had a city name. A few were from friends or clients.

I started playing the messages from the unidentified numbers. The callers didn't mince words. Each voicemail was a cocktail of venom, profanity, and murder or rape threats.

One message, dripping with vitriol, had a 602 area code and vaguely resembled my brother's voice. Given that we hadn't spoken in a decade, I couldn't be certain. The caller spoke of betrayal, abandonment, and a promise that he would put my "faggot ass in the ground."

The horror on Bobby's face was more disturbing than the calls themselves. I hadn't wanted him to hear them. But he must have heard some at the studio.

Valentine looked concerned. "Have you contacted the police about these?"

"Yeah. Just now. With you."

"Anyone else?"

"They started showing up in my voicemail last Friday after the media started running stories about what happened at the library."

"I can have our team investigate, but you'd have to give me your phone."

He reached for it, but I held onto it. *What else could he find on my phone—clues leading him to my activities as Avery the avenger? And what about my clients? How would they reach me if Valentine took my phone?*

"Let me think about it. Right now, my attention is solely on healing from the gunshot wounds."

He shrugged. "Suit yourself, but if these calls continue, you might wish you'd turned over the information sooner.

Some callers may try to make good on their threats once they learn you're still alive. Despite our complicated history, I would hate for something worse to happen to you."

"Who else was killed at the festival?" The question had been in the back of my mind all day.

Valentine flipped through his notebook. "So far, I can confirm the deceased include Shaun Martell, Tequan Martell, Harper Knox, Janelle Dailey, Todd Bennett, Hilary Reese, and Soledad Melendez. There may be others. Some survivors are still in critical condition. I'm sorry."

It was as if a claw hammer had violently torn my heart apart, leaving me shattered and empty. So many innocent lives destroyed.

"I think I need some rest."

Valentine closed his notebook. "If I have further questions, I know where to find you."

That almost sounded like a threat, and I resisted the urge to respond.

"You get to feeling better, okay?"

"Yeah."

After he left, Roz stood and offered her hand. "Do you need help getting back in bed? Or did you want me to call for assistance?"

I shook my head. "Let me try it on my own."

With her on my left and Bobby on my right, I mustered the strength to stand. Lightning bolts of pain lanced through my thigh, but I refused to succumb to it. Instead, I gritted my teeth, spewed a string of expletives, and hobbled back to the bed. I plopped down harder than I intended.

"Goddamn motherfucking shit!"

"You okay?"

"Peachy." I took a deep, cleansing breath and let it out slowly. "I recall someone mentioning empanadas?"

Bobby brought over the box. The aroma of fresh-baked goodness filled the air. I grabbed one, bit into the sweet pastry, and discovered it was filled with pumpkin purée and the warm flavors of cinnamon, nutmeg, ginger, and cloves— like a pumpkin pie only better. It evoked a memory of riding with Melissa and Bobby to look at the autumn leaves in Oak Creek Canyon and Flagstaff.

"Goth, that's good. Thank you, Appa."

"You're most welcome, kiddo."

Roz's expression suddenly grew more pained.

"Something wrong with your empanada, sweetie?" I asked.

"No, I have something you should see."

"Please tell me it's not a video of the shooting. I don't think I can watch that yet. It's just… too soon."

"It's not that. Something else." She took out her phone, tapped the screen and handed it to me. A video started playing.

"Fuck me."

CHAPTER 23
THE INTERVIEW

"HELLO, patriots, and welcome to *The River of Truth*. As always, I'm your host, Sergeant Troy Rivers. Retired Special Forces. Veteran of both Iraq and Afghanistan. Recipient of the Purple Heart and two Silver Stars and the Congressional Medal of Honor. And having proudly served my country and fought for our freedoms, I'm here now fighting for truth, even as our country is overrun by the woke mafia who want to take away your rights to life, liberty, and the pursuit of happiness."

I recognized Rivers from his YouTube channel. He was an aging, heavyset man with a penchant for spreading right-wing conspiracy theories and spewing hate and lies about minorities, especially African Americans, immigrants, Muslims, and his latest passion, transgender people. His show's logo flashed in the corner of the screen.

Sitting opposite Rivers was none other than Danny Kirk-patrick, formerly Danielle. A military-style buzz cut had replaced his flowing locks. While his cheeks and chin retained a feminine softness, his eyes were flinty and cold. The chyron at the bottom of the screen referred to him as a "Reformed Trans Radical Activist."

"Our guest today is Danny Kirkpatrick, former member of the Phoenix Transsexual Alliance, a cult that encourages people, including innocent, vulnerable children, to poison themselves with experimental drugs, mutilate their bodies, and live as the opposite sex. Danny is here today to share some shocking truths about this organization. Welcome, Danny."

"Thank you, Sergeant," he answered somewhat nervously. His eyes darted back and forth.

"Now, tell me, Danny, how did you fall in with this cult of deviants?" Rivers asked.

"I was sixteen and struggling with insecurity and depression, like a lot of boys that age do. My parents were divorced, and I lived with my mother, who did her best but coddled me too much. Boys need a father figure. Unfortunately, because of the liberal biases of the courts, he was denied all visitation."

"I'm really sorry to hear that, young man."

I sat dumbfounded. *Is this really how he feels, or has he been coached?*

"I didn't really know where I fit into the world. Every time I saw pictures of beautiful women in magazines, I was attracted to them, as normal adolescent boys are. But in my confused, depressed state, I thought I wanted to be like them, to be them. Because they looked so glamorous, so happy, so successful. Everything I wasn't. I was just some skinny young kid whose only parental figure was a woman."

"Did you seek professional help?"

"I went to a therapist named Dr. Edward Ballou. But instead of helping me with my insecurities and depression, he brainwashed me into thinking that I was transsexual."

"Wow. Why would he do that?"

"He had a kid who was transgender, a son who thought he was a girl. He claimed that transitioning helped make him happier. I was so lost and distraught that I believed him. I was willing to go along with just about anything to feel better. If he had told me that dressing up in a chicken suit would cure my depression, I would've done it. That's how vulnerable I was."

Fury flared inside me. Dr. Ballou was Jinx's father and had also been my therapist. Despite my reluctance to open up about my feelings, his patience and kindness won me over. His knowledge of trans issues also helped me feel safe with him. And over a period of a couple of years, he helped me work through a lot of the trauma I'd endured during my teens.

While I couldn't know exactly what was said during Daniel's sessions with Dr. Ballou, I was sure it hadn't involved any sort of brainwashing. Dr. Ballou knew his shit and was good people. Unlike this asshole Rivers.

Sergeant Rivers nodded gravely. "It is unbelievable that quacks like this so-called Dr. Ballou are allowed to prey on vulnerable children. What did he tell you to do?"

"He told me to give in to this insane delusion that I was a girl. He told my mother to encourage this. And he suggested I join this radical transsexual group, the Phoenix Gender Alliance."

"These are the people who are running a child trafficking ring," Rivers added. "Grooming them into thinking they're transsexual, sexualizing them, and pressuring them to mutilate their bodies with experimental drugs and surgeries."

"What the fuck?" I growled. I was tempted to turn it off and hand the phone back to Roz, but I kept watching.

"The people were nice and welcoming at first. They didn't judge me, but they took advantage of my susceptible state. They kept filling my mind with ideas. I started taking estrogen and spironolactone to rid my body of the testosterone it needed. I underwent a painful laser treatment to get rid of my facial hair. I still have scars from it."

The camera focused in on Danny's face, revealing pitted skin on his cheeks.

"That's bullshit!" I told Roz. "Those scars aren't from laser treatment. Those are acne scars. He used to talk about it in the Hatchlings group. He's a fucking liar."

"Why would he turn on the Alliance like this, claiming you coerced him into transitioning?" Roz asked.

"Beats the fuck out of me. We did nothing of the kind."

Yet his tone was so sincere that I wondered if somehow we actually had pressured him.

"Did you have the sex change surgery?" Sergeant Rivers asked.

Danny shook his head. "Almost. I came to my senses before my scheduled surgery date. I'd even put down a ten-thousand-dollar nonrefundable deposit."

"And what brought you to your senses?"

"I'd just started Arizona State University on a women's scholarship. But somehow, they found out I wasn't really a woman and revoked it. They demanded I pay back the tuition money they'd already paid. They were threatening to file a fraud lawsuit against me. That was my wake-up call, when I realized that this transsexual nonsense was ruining my life."

"And what did you do after you found out about the scholarship?"

Danny let out an enormous sigh, his shoulders slumping in defeat. "I reached out to my father, the man who loved me but who knew I had been led astray by these radical activists. He agreed to help me restore my life. It was like waking up from a nightmare. I got rid of all of my women's clothing. All the makeup and hormones. And true to his word, he welcomed me back into his life with loving arms. He helped me find a godly counselor who wasn't pushing a transsexual agenda. I am now learning to be the man God wants me to be."

I stopped the video and handed the phone back to Roz. "Listening to that shit makes me sick. They're brainwashing her or him with that Jesus bullshit, and she's buying it all because she lost her scholarship."

"You think he's really trans?"

"All I know is you can't pray gender dysphoria away any more than you can pray the gay away. Believe me, I tried when I was a kid. Sounds like she got involved in some conversion therapy."

"I thought conversion therapy was outlawed in Arizona," Bobby said.

"Only for licensed therapists," Roz said. "The law doesn't apply to nonlicensed Christian clergy who weaponize their religious beliefs to brainwash queer people into thinking they're straight and cis."

"That's a hell of a loophole," Bobby said

"I knew someone who was sent to a conversion therapy camp when she was fifteen," Roz continued. "They tortured her for days. Wouldn't let her eat or sleep. Just forced her to listen to audio recordings of sermons and bible verses until she started towing the party line. She committed suicide two weeks after getting out."

I recalled my attempts to be the dutiful son while struggling with my gender dysphoria and the dreaded morning my world collapsed.

CHAPTER 24
KICKED OUT

TEN YEARS BEFORE, I'd been on my way to a track meet at my middle school. It was a fallback sport after my father decided gymnastics was, in his words, "turning me into a faggot."

He would have preferred I tried out for the school basketball team, but I was small for my age, and the thought of getting elbowed by guys twice my size terrified me.

I discovered I was an excellent sprinter. Growing up with an abusive father, I'd found the ability to move swiftly crucial for survival. As it was, my body was often a canvas of bruises hidden beneath my clothes—scattered across my torso, upper arms, and back.

He worked construction, his bulging muscles a stark contrast to my slender frame. Where I was sensitive and quiet, he was a sadistic monster, taking great pleasure in inflicting pain on my mother and me.

The morning of the track meet, my father confronted me in the kitchen. Despite it only being seven in the morning, I could already smell the booze on his breath. "Where the fuck you think you're going, freak?"

"I've got a track meet. Dean's dad is picking me up in ten minutes."

He shook his head. His eyes had a feral expression I was all too familiar with—the look of a bully who knew he had the upper hand. He smiled, but there was nothing kind about it.

"You ain't going nowhere, you sissy faggot." He tossed a gym bag at my feet. I recognized it as the one where I kept my secret stash of girl clothes—panties, a couple of bras, some frilly tops, and a dress.

My heart raced as adrenaline surged through my veins, leaving my mind clouded with panic. Frantically, my eyes darted around, desperately seeking an exit, but there was no escape—only the looming threat of another brutal beating.

"Open it," he growled.

"Dad, I'm gonna be late for my meet "

"Open it, goddamn it!" He pounded his fist so hard on the countertop that the blender fell over.

My face grew hot. Nervously, I knelt down and unzipped the gym bag. On top was the flowery dress and a pair of panties.

"Th-They're my girlfr-friend's," I lied, trembling in anticipation of the unprecedented beatdown I was about to receive.

"Bullshit. You ain't got no girlfriend."

"N-No, really! They're Kimi's. We were, uh, we were making out, and she left them."

"Kimi? That half-chink, half-wetback mongrel little bitch?"

My terror turned to anger. *Say what you like about me, you asshole. But not my friends.*

"Don't call her that. She's my friend."

"Don't you talk back to me. She ain't shit. And neither are you, you little fag."

I glared at him, ready to dodge the inevitable blows.

"I'm not gay."

"The fuck you're not."

"I like girls, not boys. I dated Dawn Tressler last year. You know that."

"Fucking bullshit. If you ain't gay, why the fuck you got these?"

"I told you, they're—"

He punched me so hard in the jaw that the back of my head hit the stove. Stars blurred my vision. "Don't you lie to me. Tell me the truth."

I took a deep breath and let it out. It was a long shot, but I might as well try the truth. "Because I'm a girl. I know it sounds strange, but—"

He burst out laughing, but it did nothing to lessen the tension in the room. "You're a fucking, cock-sucking, sissy commie faggot. But you ain't no girl."

He reached into the fridge, and just for a second, I thought I could slip past him. But he closed it, a fresh beer in his hand, before I got one step.

"Don't even think about it, fag boy." He popped the cap and tossed it toward the trash can, missing it by a foot. "Motherfucker."

"Dad, I can't explain why, but I've always felt like a girl."

"Shut the fuck up! I'm talking." He glared at me. "Can't say I'm all that surprised. Never shoulda let you join gymnastics. But your mother always did coddle you. Said the exercise would be good for you. But here we are."

My chest felt like a gorilla was sitting on it. I struggled to get enough air. "I-I can explain," I stammered.

But I couldn't. I didn't understand it. I'd tried so hard to be a normal boy, yet this drive, this compulsion, this primal need to be a girl was unstoppable and irresistible. Over the past few years, I'd binged and purged my stash of girl clothes several times. I'd tried praying. I joined the church youth group. But nothing had helped. It was like swimming against a riptide. Eventually, I grew exhausted and let the tide sweep me over to where I was told I shouldn't be.

"Nothing to explain. You're a goddamn fag. And I don't allow that shit in my house. The only girl here is your mom."

"Fine. I'll do better. I promise." A car horn sounded from outside. "That's Dean and his dad. I gotta go."

"I want you gone."

"Well, if you step aside, I'll leave. Should be back around lunchtime."

"Gone, as in, out of this house forever."

"You're kicking me out? Over a bunch of old clothes?"

"I'm kicking you out because you're a goddamn abomination. You have five minutes. If you're still here, I'm gonna beat you to death and hide your body where ain't no one will ever find it."

From anyone else, I would have thought that was an idle threat. But I knew my father meant it. The car outside honked again. I was tempted to just run out to it. But then I wouldn't have anything.

He glanced at his watch. "Time's a-ticking, faggot."

I grabbed the gym bag and raced to my room, where I filled a knapsack and one other gym bag with essentials—clothes, my laptop, some granola bars, a rainbow bracelet that Kimi had given me, and a photo of our dysfunctional family from the camping trip we'd taken to Lake Mary last year.

The front doorbell rang. I was still gathering shit together and prayed they wouldn't leave yet. I grabbed my charging cords, a roll of toilet paper, my toothbrush, a hairbrush. *What else? What else?* I asked myself, glancing frantically around my room.

"Fifteen seconds."

"Shit."

A hollow thunk sounded repeatedly somewhere in the house. I knew that sound—my brother's baseball bat. I'd felt its blows on my back and arms more times than I cared to count. I pulled on the straps of my knapsack, grabbed a duffel bag in each hand, and ran into the hallway. He stood at the other end, bat at the ready.

"You win. I'm leaving," I said defiantly.

"You ain't going nowhere till I see what's in those bags."

My heart sank. *What now?* "Why?"

"Gotta make sure you ain't stealing nothing. Show me what's in those bags."

With no other options, I opened the gym bag he found, the one with the girl's clothes in it.

He snorted derisively and poked around. There wasn't much else in there except for some toiletries.

"Now the other one."

I opened the second gym bag. It held some T-shirts, jeans, sneakers, gym socks, the rainbow bracelet, the family photos, and the collar and tags I'd kept after our dog Shadow passed away. I'd also packed two aluminum insulated water bottles, both filled from the tap.

He pulled out the water bottles and, one by one, emptied them onto the open bag, soaking my clothes and the photos. He then stuffed the empty bottles back into the gym bag and zipped it closed, a smug look of satisfaction on his face.

"Now the backpack."

"Just let me leave. You won't ever have to see me again."

"Don't back talk me, faggot. Open the backpack."

I slid it off my back and handed it to him. He immediately pulled out my laptop.

"You ain't going nowhere with this."

"But it's mine."

"The fuck it is. I paid fifteen hundred bucks for this. Besides, girls don't need computers. You just need makeup and dresses to look pretty for the other fags."

He threw the laptop onto the hard floor and smashed it

repeatedly with the bat. The screen cracked and crunched with each blow.

My humiliation gave way to a fiery rage. This wasn't about who paid for what. He just wanted to hurt me and show he had absolute power over me.

From the pack's front pocket of the pack, he pulled out my iPhone. "I also paid for this."

He tossed it on the floor next to the remains of my laptop and pounded it into shards with the bat. He sorted through the rest of my things in the pack, including a spiral-bound notebook, some pens, and photos. He left them, handing me back the knapsack.

"Now, get the fuck out or else." He whacked the bat on the floor a few more times to make his point.

I raced out the door, but Dean and his father were long gone.

What now? Where can I go? There was only one possibility.

I ran down the street and knocked on Kimi's door. She was the only person who I'd told about being trans. And to my relief, she never judged me.

Unfortunately, her parents refused to allow me to stay. When they offered to call the cops and report my father for abuse, I told them not to bother. It wouldn't have helped. The cops had been to our door many times. Nothing ever changed.

Eventually, Kimi had handed me a wad of bills—her entire life savings, which amounted to fifty-three bucks, a lot of money for a thirteen-year-old. I'd hopped a bus to downtown Phoenix.

And here I was a decade later, wounded by none other than my own brother. It was a chilling realization, seeing him transform into a mirror image of our abusive father.

My lunch arrived shortly after watching Daniel's dreadful interview on *The River of Truth*. Roz occupied herself with her phone. She had her earbuds in, and I guessed she was watching more videos. Judging from her expression, I was pretty sure I didn't want to know what they were.

Bobby had left to work on some of my clients at the tattoo shop, since I clearly wouldn't be in on Monday. He'd been hovering like a mother hen, and both Roz and I had encouraged him to go. Eventually, I pushed aside the remains of my overcooked hamburger with the soggy bun. A stupid game show played on the TV mounted on the opposite wall.

"You didn't eat much," Roz said. "You want something from the cafeteria?"

"I could use something with some flavor."

"I'll head down and see what I can find." She leaned over and kissed me. "So glad to see you're on the mend."

"So glad I've got you taking care of me."

We were embarrassingly precious, like a couple of lovesick teenagers, but I didn't care. I had someone who loved me and treated me with respect. Someone who knew all of my darkest secrets and didn't judge me.

When she left, I grabbed my phone and checked the recent calls. The number of unrecognized callers had decreased in the past day but was still several an hour. The voice mailbox was full. Scrolling down the list of calls, I realized I'd missed a few from friends. But I didn't have the mental or physical energy to call them back.

I opened the web browser and started doomscrolling the news feed. I found a few stories about the Pride shooting. One identified my brother, Wylie, as one of the shooters. It also mentioned that an unidentified woman in the Trans March had heroically disarmed him.

I snorted. *Yeah, me, the big bad hero.* I was just glad I didn't have reporters trying to talk to me again. I'd gotten enough publicity lately—all of it rotten.

I remembered the fury in Wylie's eyes as we wrestled for

the gun. I gripped my chest as panic once again sent my heart racing. *Boom!* A sharp sting in my arm—a graze, the doctor had called it.

Boom! The second shot. A white-hot lance of fire in my inner thigh. Still, I fought Wylie even as my strength waned.

Boom! A third shot. He'd cried out this time, not just in anger but in pain. Despite my injuries, I'd somehow turned the gun on him, hitting him in the chest or abdomen. The last thing I remembered was the fear in his eyes and then the blue sky.

Valentine had said he'd arrested Wylie. But with a gunshot wound, my brother had to be in a hospital somewhere. Working on a long shot, I pulled up the hospital website and found a search page to look up patient room numbers. For privacy's sake, a patient's last name and ID number were required to log in and run a search.

I checked my wrist and found my patient number on my ID bracelet. I used it to log in and pulled up my room number, 515. Now that I was logged in, the search page also let me search for other names. I typed *Wylie Byrne* into the search bar and crossed my fingers.

It must have been my lucky morning because his name and room number appeared. My heart fluttered in my chest. He was in room 520. Same floor. Maybe the same unit.

It had been ten years since we'd spoken. I'd never had the chance to say goodbye. Now he'd tried to kill me and my friends. I needed answers.

CHAPTER 25
WYLIE

WITH GREAT EFFORT and clinched teeth, I swung my legs back over the side of the bed. I was still hooked up to the IV, but it was on a mobile stand I could use for support. *Will I be able to make it to Wylie's room? And what will happen if I do? What will I say to him?*

I took a deep breath, and as I blew it out, I stood, trying not to scream at the pain. The room spun for about fifteen seconds while I clung to the IV pole for balance. After a few more breaths, my mind cleared. I took a hobbling step, drawing on my anger for strength. My hospital gown flapped open behind me, but I didn't give a shit. I had to talk to my brother. I needed to know why he and his buddies had murdered my friends.

I emerged into the main part of the unit. The rooms encircled the nurses' station, with mine opposite the corridor leading to what I guessed was the center of the hospital.

As I studied the room numbers, looking for 520, a male voice said, "Oh, let me help you."

In an instant, a CNA named Mark was at my side. He cinched up my hospital gown in back and draped another over my shoulders so I wasn't showing my ass to the world.

"Good to see you up and around, Ms. Byrne," Mark said in a cheerful voice.

"Thanks."

I spotted room 520 at the edge of the unit closest to the corridor. A uniformed cop sat outside the door, staring down at his phone. Naturally, Wylie would be under guard as he recovered.

Still, I was determined to get inside that room, no matter what. Step by painful step, I hobbled around the nurses' station. When I was within ten feet of Wylie's room, the cop looked up at me, putting away his phone and standing. He must have sensed my intended destination.

"Can I help you, miss?" His name tag read Rivera.

"That's my brother's room. I need to speak with him."

"And your name?" Rivera asked.

"Avery Byrne."

"You're a patient here?"

"No, I just like walking around hospitals, dressed in flimsy gowns, with an IV needle stuck in my arm." I held out my wristband.

He studied it then shook his head. "Sorry, Ms. Byrne, but even if you are his sister, no one gets in without proper authorization."

"Detective Valentine said that I could speak with him since I'm family." It was a lie, but how would he know?

The mention of Valentine's name caused Officer Rivera to raise an eyebrow. "You spoke with the detective?"

Something about this guy set off my gaydar, and I figured I'd use that.

"Yes, he interviewed me earlier this morning. I was shot during the Pride Festival massacre while attempting to disarm the shooters."

"That was you?" he asked.

"Watch the videos. They're all over the web."

"I thought you said this guy was your brother."

"He is. He's also one of the shooters, the one I disarmed even after I was shot."

He seemed to consider that but then said, "I'm sorry, but I'd get in big trouble if I let you in."

Another idea occurred to me. "Valentine wanted me to talk to Wylie, see if I could get him to give up the identity of the other two shooters. He won't even need his lawyer here since I'm not a cop. I'm family."

"That may be, but I'll need confirmation from Valentine or his lieutenant." He pulled his phone back out. "Just a minute. Let me see if I can get him on the line."

I felt deflated. Valentine would never let me inside the room.

"Look, Officer Rivera, I'm recovering from two gunshot wounds. I'm in a lot of pain and don't have the strength to stand here while you play phone tag with Valentine. Just let me inside so I can talk to my brother and convince him to rat out his buddies before they kill someone else."

Rivera ignored me. "Yes, this is Officer Gabriel Rivera. I'm guarding the suspect Wylie Byrne's room at St. Michael's Hospital. I've got a woman named Avery Byrne, who claims to be the suspect's sister. She also states you authorized her to speak with the suspect to identify the other two shooters."

"Fuck," I muttered. My pain level ratcheted up, sapping my strength. My knees grew wobbly. I hobbled over to a wheelchair parked against the wall before my legs gave out. *Well, I tried. I guess I'll just have to find another way.*

Rivera hung up and approached me with a serious expression on his face. "Valentine says he never asked you to talk to your brother."

I stared down at the linoleum.

"However, Valentine told me you could go in anyway. But only for a few minutes. And I'll be at the door, listening."

I looked back up at Rivera, shocked at my sudden turn in

luck. A surge of energy flowed back into me. I was in. *Holy fuck.* Against all odds, my plan had worked.

With Rivera's help, I got back to my feet. He opened the door for me.

"Yo, asshole!" Rivera said. "Someone here to see you."

I hobbled into the room and took the chair next to Wylie's bed. He looked so different from when we were kids. He still had our mother's red hair and our dad's nose. But his face was hard, and his eyes burned with that same malevolent glare that I'd seen so many times with my father. He also had a lightning SS tattoo on his neck. My brother was a fucking neo-Nazi. Hardly surprising since he'd grown up with our racist dad.

The bedsheet covered most of his body, so I couldn't see where he'd been shot—where I'd shot him. Guilt nagged me about that. I'd shot my baby brother, even if it was in self-defense.

"Hey, Wylie," I muttered, not knowing what else to say.

He didn't reply at first, just glared at me. After a few minutes, he said, "What the fuck you want, freak?"

All the questions that I'd wanted to ask him evaporated from my mind. His voice sounded identical to our father's— the same slurs, the same hate. My body stiffened as traumatic childhood memories played on a loop in my mind.

Finally, I steeled myself and asked, "Why?"

He winced, but I didn't know if it was from my question or the pain. "Someone has to protect the kids."

"Protect kids from what?"

"You groomers."

"We're not groomers. All we do is offer support for people who already identify as trans."

"Bullshit! Everyone knows you're brainwashing kids into thinking they're transsexual. Sergeant Rivers has proof. I've seen it on his YouTube channel."

"Dude, can we get past the right-wing propaganda? No

one groomed me. No one brainwashed me. I've known I was a girl since I was five. I don't know why I'm this way. Just how my brain was wired."

He scoffed.

"You think Sergeant Rivers knows who I am better than I do? The man is a known liar and conspiracy theorist. A few years ago, he was convicted of slander for claiming the Avondale school shooting was a false flag and that the victims were paid actors."

"Witch hunt."

"Come on, Wylie. You were always a smart kid in school. Can't you see past Rivers's bullshit?"

Wylie didn't respond right away. He just glared at me. But I could see him doing the calculations in his mind.

"When you ran away, Dad started beating me. Every fucking day."

His words were a punch to my gut. I'd always feared that would happen—not that I had a choice about leaving. All those times that our dad went into one of his alcoholic rages, I'd protected Wylie. Without me there, he'd been defenseless.

"I didn't run away, Wylie. Dad threw me out. I didn't have a choice."

"Bullshit. Dad said you thought you were too good for us and went off to live your perverted transsexual lifestyle."

"Dad told you that? News flash, kid! Dad is a drunk and a bully and a liar. I protected you from his abuse for as long as I could. But he was bigger than the two of us combined. I'm really sorry if he hurt you, but I didn't have any choice about leaving."

"He wasn't the only one."

I tilted my head. "Who? Mom?"

"No. Father Sebastian."

That was another name I hadn't heard in a very long

time. Father Sebastian had led the youth group at Saint Katharine Drexel Catholic Church.

"How did Father Sebastian hurt you?" But I knew the answer. Something about Father Sebastian had always bothered me. My friends at the church and I had steered clear of him, calling him Father Sebastard.

"What do you care?" he asked.

"Why do you think? You're my little brother, Wylie. What did he do to you?"

His face turned red, and his eyes closed. "I'd rather not talk about it."

"Did he molest you?"

Wylie looked like I'd punched him in the gut. "Yes."

"Multiple times?"

"Yeah."

I didn't need to know the details. And I didn't want to cause him further pain by sharing them with me.

"You tell Mom or Dad?"

"Fuck no."

"I'm sorry that happened to you. Is he still at St. Kat's?"

"Died a few years back. Heart attack."

"I hope he suffered," I replied. "And if there really is a hell, I hope he's there now, screaming in agony."

Wylie opened his eyes again, and we looked at each other for a long while without speaking.

"Wylie, who were the other two shooters at the Pride festival?"

A smirk crept eerily across his face. "You didn't recognize them?"

"They were wearing masks."

"One of them said they remembered you."

"Remembered me from where?"

For a moment, I thought he would tell me. "Doesn't matter. I ain't sayin'."

"Why not? You can cut a deal, reduce your sentence."

"You working for the cops?"

"No. I hate cops."

"Right. Then how come they let you in here?" he asked.

"Doesn't matter. Your buddies murdered my friends, Wylie. Who the fuck were they?"

"Better for you if they remain anonymous."

"What the fuck's that supposed to mean?"

"One of them's got dirt on you. Serious dirt. He saw you kill someone."

I wanted to laugh off his statement as posturing, but there was steel in his words. A chill ran down my spine. *Who are these people? And how would they know I killed someone? I always cover my tracks any time I let Avery the avenger out to play. Unless I missed something.*

"Tell me, Wylie," I said more forcefully. "Who were the other two shooters?"

"I ain't no snitch. I'm a loyal patriot. Unlike you fairy-ass perverts." His eyes had turned flinty again.

Back to this bullshit. "Look, I understand you wanting to protect your friends. But they're murderers. Patriots don't murder innocent people."

"You perverts are not innocent. Just a bunch of men in dresses who molest children."

"The Phoenix Gender Alliance doesn't molest children. The only men in dresses who molest children are people like Father fucking Sebastard."

"Sebastian was a fag, just like the rest of you."

Anger rocketed me to my feet. I ignored the pain jetting through my leg. "Goddammit, Wylie, tell me who murdered my friends!"

The door opened. Rivera appeared. "Times up, ma'am. You need to leave."

I ignored Rivera. "Tell me, Wylie! Don't be like Dad. Grow some balls and have some fucking integrity."

Rivera grabbed my arm. "Come on, ma'am. This isn't helping anyone."

"I know who took that missing girl," Wylie said with a sneer. "I'm guessing she was part of your group."

The shock of his words nearly caused my knees to buckle. I shrugged off Rivera's hand. "What'd you say? Who took Zoë? Where is she?"

"Fuck you, faggot! I'll never tell."

I reached for him, determined to force him to tell me, but Rivera was stronger and pulled me away.

"Come on, Ms. Byrne. I'd hate to arrest you too."

I desperately wanted Wylie to tell me where Zoë was, but it was futile. Riviera was already leading me to the door. I hobbled out of the room in defeat.

When the door shut behind me, I said to Rivera. "Contact Detective Hausman at Peoria PD. She's investigating the kidnapping of Zoë Hildebrandt, a trans girl who went missing last week. Wylie just admitted he knows where she is. Maybe Hausman can get it out of him."

"I'll pass along the message to Peoria PD. In the meantime, I think it best you return to your own room."

"Hey!" Roz emerged from my room, carrying a couple of closed Styrofoam containers. "There you are. I was afraid something had happened."

"Thanks for letting me talk to my brother," I told Rivera.

He nodded and went back to his phone.

"You want a wheelchair?" Roz asked as I limped painfully back to the room.

"No. I need to walk so they'll let me out of here."

CHAPTER 26
MOM

ROZ HELPED me settle back into the bed and opened the containers she'd brought from the cafeteria downstairs. Inside each was a small pizza. Hers was veggie all the way. Mine was topped with pepperoni, bell pepper, and mushroom. Everything a healing body needed.

I inhaled the wondrous aroma. "Goth, that smells fantastic. You are a lifesaver."

"Need anything else?" she asked.

I shook my head, biting into a slice with great fervor. "It's good," I said through a mouthful of cheese and pepperoni.

I caught her up on my family reunion with my brother.

"Wow," she replied. "I'm so sorry that happened to him. But it doesn't excuse what he did at the Trans March. Not by a long shot."

"No. It doesn't."

"Look, I know you don't want to give Detective Valentine your phone. But something has to be done about these harassing phone calls, especially the rape and death threats. Bobby called me when I was getting lunch because he couldn't get a hold of you."

"Shit. I left my phone in the room."

"He's getting threats at the studio. The police have shown up twice over bomb threats."

I nearly choked as a wave of fury washed over me. It was one thing to come after me. But going after the people I loved was where I drew a hard line.

Guilt tempered my anger. Neither of us would be getting these calls if I hadn't thrown down with that bitch at the library. If anything happened to Bobby, Frisco, or Butcher, I couldn't live with myself.

"I agree that something has to be done. I just hate giving him my phone. Who knows what he and his techs could dig up on me. You know?"

"I think I found a solution that will work for both of you. There's an app on my laptop that will allow me to download your messages, including all the metadata. We can put it all onto a flash drive and give that to Valentine."

"You think he'll go for that?"

Roz shrugged. "Doesn't hurt to try. I'll run by the apartment and get my laptop. You need anything from home?"

"Clothes would be nice. Something loose, like sweatpants and T-shirts."

"Got it. Anything else?"

I nodded. "My makeup kit. I feel the need to goth out. I can't shower yet, but a little black eyeliner and lipstick would help improve my mood."

"You got it, babe." She gave me a kiss, and I felt my body respond.

"I'm sorry to be such a bother." And I meant it.

She shot me a confused expression. "How are you a bother?"

I gestured with my arms spread. "All of this. Asking you to get me meals, dealing with my phone issues, helping me walk, all this shit."

She gazed soulfully into my eyes. "Babe, you've got nothing to apologize for. You're the goddamn hero. Remember? You risked your life to take down a shooter and scare off the other two. Who knows how many more people would've died if not for you?"

"I don't feel so brave."

"Brave people rarely do. You did what you needed to do, despite the danger, despite the fear. That's what makes you a hero."

I scoffed, not sure what to make of that. I was a lot of things—a tattoo artist, a vigilante, a murderer. But a hero? That label just didn't fit.

She kissed me again, more deeply this time. "I'll see you in a few, babe."

When she left, I called Bobby back and told him what Roz had planned.

"Well, I hope it works. I know you did what you felt you had to at the library, but…"

"I know, Appa. I'm truly sorry."

"No need to be sorry. You're not the one making these calls. Hopefully, Roz can provide the police with the information they need to track down these bullies. How are you feeling otherwise?"

I filled him in on my conversation with my brother.

"Doesn't sound like he's ready for a family reunion," Bobby replied. "At least, not a healthy one. But perhaps one day."

"Yeah, when he's serving twenty to life."

"Trust the process."

That was one of Dr. Ballou's favorite catchphrases. I was never sure what this process was supposed to be or why I was supposed to trust it, though he assured me I would figure it out eventually.

"Thank you for taking care of some of my clients."

"It's all fine, kiddo. We've got a new artist starting tomorrow, and they'll be able to help as well. You just get some rest. I'll be by a little later."

After I hung up, I scrolled back through the endless call log and returned calls to friends and clients who'd left messages before the mailbox was full. I thanked them but rebuffed their questions about the shooting. The wounds, both physical and emotional, were still too fresh.

I was just hanging up with my third client when my room door opened. A familiar figure stood in the doorway. She was fiftyish and still rail thin. Her mousy-brown hair, now streaked with gray, hung limply around her face. She wore a tan cardigan, a matching knee-length skirt, and sensible loafers.

"Andy? It's Mom."

A hornets' nest of emotions buzzed inside of me— sadness, confusion, and anger.

"My name is Avery," I said sharply.

She shuffled in tentatively, avoiding my direct gaze. "You'll always be my little Andy, my precious firstborn son."

More anger now. "Don't call me that. I'm not a boy, and my name isn't Andy. It's Avery."

I'd been an idiot to talk to Wylie. Now I had to deal with my mom and all the horrible baggage she brought with her. I didn't need this shit. I was supposed to be recovering.

"Get out," I demanded.

"Please. I'm hoping we can at least talk. It's been so long."

"Fine. But you call me Andy again, and I'll have you escorted out of here."

"I will do my best. I was just talking to your brother. He's in a lot of pain. They had to take out a section of his intestine from where you shot him."

"Who cares? Wylie shot me first, Mom. Twice. He and his neo-Nazi militia buddies murdered several of my friends and wounded dozens more, and you're worried about him?"

"I talked with our lawyer," she continued as if I had said nothing. "He thinks he can get the charges reduced to a misdemeanor if you're willing to help and testify on Wylie's behalf."

Now the hornets' nest was in full swarm. I could taste bile in my throat. "Why the fuck would I help him? Aren't you listening to me?"

She placed a gentle hand on my injured arm. I considered jerking it away, but doing so would cause me more pain than it would cause her.

"Because we're a family, Andy—uh, Avery. Sorry." Her eyes grew tearful. "I always knew you were troubled. Always the sensitive one. Every day since you ran away, I wondered what happened to you."

"Ran away? Is that what he told you?"

She looked taken aback. "Well, of course. That's what happened."

"I didn't run away, Mom. Dad threw me out. He threatened to murder me if I didn't leave."

"I'm sure it was just a misunderstanding. You know how he said silly things when he got upset. We just needed to talk it out like a family."

"Talk it out like a family? When the fuck did we ever talk anything out like a normal family?"

"Please don't use that kind of language with me."

"Dad was a bully. He beat you. He beat me. And he beat Wylie. There was no talking to him, no reasoning with him. He was a fucking monster. And there was no misunderstanding. He would've killed me. He killed my dog, Mom. When I didn't do what he said, he took Shadow to the pound and had her put down. All I had left was her collar. He was a motherfucking monster."

"Your father was... complicated. He had trouble expressing his feelings."

I scoffed. "Bullshit. How many times did you and I end up in the emergency room after he'd expressed his feelings?

Remember that time when he fractured your eye socket because you put too much salt on his dinner?"

She stared down at the floor. "As I said, he was complicated."

"And where is he now?" I was genuinely curious. *In light of this glorious family reunion with Wylie and her, where the fuck is dear old Dad?*

My mother stared at the floor. "He's down in Florence."

"Prison?" I was pretty sure he hadn't traveled to Italy.

"Seems he lost his temper one too many times. And that jury just didn't appreciate all the pressure he'd been under. They found him guilty of aggravated assault and attempted murder."

"When was this?"

"In April."

"And who did he try to murder? You? Wylie?" I asked.

"He'd had a disagreement with our neighbor, Mr. Sanders, about a tree and the leaves that were falling into our yard. It was messing up the cool deck for a pool. A total disgrace."

I felt a smile creep across my face. Bill Byrne finally got his comeuppance. About fucking time. "He's in prison now, and you're still making excuses for him. Tell me you're not still married to him."

"Of course I am. I'm his wife."

"You weren't his wife. You were his punching bag. Why didn't you just divorce him?"

"Because we're a good Catholic family."

I let loose with a belly laugh. "A good Catholic family?"

"I'm not saying we were perfect."

"We were a fucking after-school special."

She didn't reply.

"Did you know Wylie was sexually abused by Father Sebastian?"

A mix of surprise and shame washed over her face. "Father Sebastian? Don't be ridiculous. He never would have done such a thing. You shouldn't speak that way about him."

"Wow. I can't tell if you truly believe that, or if you're just so used to towing the patriarchal line that you just can't stop yourself. You care more about predators than you do their innocent victims, even your own kids. You really are a shit mother."

Tears ran freely down her face. "How can you say that? I gave birth to you. I raised you and your brother under very difficult circumstances. Maybe I wasn't Mother of the Year…"

"Gee, ya think?"

"I did the best I could. If I'd left your father, if I'd tried to divorce him, what do you think would've happened? What do you think he would've done to the three of us?"

I didn't answer right away. I had never considered that. I'd simply blamed her for playing along, for refusing to protect Wylie and me, and for refusing to get out. But it was easy for me to judge. I hadn't had to make that choice. And my dad's best friend was a cop who intervened any time we showed up at the hospital with suspicious injuries or the neighbors complained about the screaming.

My mom was the one who'd held everything together with her little side hustles—dog walking, selling candles, tutoring the neighbors' kids in English—to bring in income when my father got himself fired or there was just no work.

"I don't know what would've happened if we'd left," I said. "Maybe he would've come after us. Possibly killed us. But he's locked up now. He can't hurt you. So stop making excuses for him. Stop downplaying his abusive behavior."

She sighed and appeared to consider my words. "For twenty-five years, I had to convince myself that the only way to survive was to play along—to give him no reason to hit me or you kids. Some habits are hard to break."

"Dad didn't need a reason to hit us. He just hit us and made up a reason later."

"I brought you and Roz cappuccinos." Bobby walked in with a tray of coffees and set one down on my bedside table. "Oh, hello," he said cheerily and extended his free hand to my mother. "I'm Bobby Jeong, Avery's father."

Well, this is a little bit awkward. But I smiled, glad to have an ally in the room.

My mother appeared taken aback. "His father? Andy's father is in prison. Who the heck are you?"

A confused look crossed Bobby's face. "Who's Andy?"

"Appa, this is my biological mother, Jacqueline Byrne." I looked her in the eye. "Bobby and his wife Melissa took me in after that bastard you married kicked me out."

Realization dawned on Bobby's face. "A pleasure to meet you, Ms. Byrne."

"I should probably go," she replied.

"She was just here to ask me to drop the charges against my murderer brother. Because that's the kind of useless mother she is."

"Avery, don't talk that way to your mother," Bobby replied.

"Melissa was more of a mother than that woman ever was. My bio mom let my father beat me and my brother time and time again. She should be in prison along with him for child endangerment. At least I got out when I did. We see how my brother turned out."

I saw the sting of my words hit their mark and felt more than a little satisfaction as my mother once again started crying.

"I am really sorry I wasn't a better mother."

"Did you even look for me after I disappeared? Did you file a missing person report?"

I could see Bobby growing uncomfortable with the situation. I was sorry he had to be pulled into the middle of this.

"Your father wouldn't let me. He said you ran away and that we had to respect your choice."

"My choice? I didn't have any choice in the matter."

"Yes, I realize that now." She turned to Bobby. "Thank you for caring for Andy when I could not."

"My name is Avery!" I spat.

"Please, kiddo, give her some time to adjust," Bobby said.

"Thank you, Bobby," my mother said. After an awkward pause, she spoke again. "Well, I suppose I should head back to Wylie's room. I just wanted to say hello after all these years. I'm glad you're still alive, Avery. I'm sorry for what your father and your brother did to you. And thank you, Bobby, for taking care of her when I could not."

"She has been an unexpected blessing in my life," Bobby assured her.

"I hope... I hope we can stay in contact, Avery."

Do I want a relationship with this woman? I wasn't sure, but we exchanged phone numbers anyway.

"I don't claim to understand why you made the choices you did. Perhaps it's because, when I was pregnant with you, I hoped you would be a girl. And if that's the case, I'm sorry."

I shook my head. "I don't think that has anything to do with it. It's just how I turned out. It's nobody's fault. I did what I had to do. And hard as it is to admit, you did what you had to do. Or at least what you thought you had to do."

"Maybe it would've been better if the three of us had run off to a shelter. But I was just so afraid. Your father had powerful friends—people who could find those who didn't want to be found. I was afraid if we ran away, it would only get worse. That he might kill you or Wylie."

Something from my conversation with my brother popped into my head. "If you want Wylie to avoid a lengthy prison sentence, get him to tell the cops where Zoë Hilde-brandt is."

"Who is she?"

"A trans girl who was kidnapped. Wylie knows where she's being held. He also needs to give up the names of the other two shooters. Otherwise, he and Dad can rot in prison together."

Again, my mother nodded. "I'll talk to him. It was good to see you again." With that, she walked out the door, wiping the tears from her eyes.

I turned to Bobby. "Well, that was uncomfortable."

"She seems like a troubled woman."

I scoffed. "Troubled? Pathetic's more like it."

"What you endured growing up, no one should go through. But she must've had it rough, too, being married to such a monster. Perhaps now the two of you can start fresh. It sounds like she could use a positive influence like you in her life. Especially with your brother being in trouble."

He was probably right. But there was a lot of blood under the bridge, and it wasn't easily swept away with rationalizations, good intentions, and platitudes.

Roz walked in with her laptop bag and a small suitcase. "Who was that woman I saw walking into your brother's room?"

"My bio mom."

"Ooh," Roz said. "Guess I missed the fireworks again."

CHAPTER 27
RELEASED

ROZ DOWNLOADED the voicemail messages onto her laptop, deleted the ones from people I knew, and then transferred them to a flash drive. I called Valentine, who picked it up an hour later. That evening, Bobby stopped by, as did Frisco and Butcher, each carrying a bouquet, which we put with the other flowers and gift baskets that arrived. Roz and Bobby had a tough time finding room for them. Still, it felt good to be loved rather than reviled.

The next morning, I was halfway through an omelet that Roz had brought me when Dr. Martin, stepped into the room. Bobby was at the tattoo studio, taking care of another one of my clients.

"Morning, Ms. Byrne," the doctor said. "How are you feeling?"

"Better, I suppose."

"Where is your pain level right now?"

"Most of the time, it's about a three. When I walk around, it can jump up to about a six."

"Do you mind if I check your wound?"

"Sure." I pushed aside the bedside tray, taking one last

bite of my breakfast. I removed the bedsheet covering my legs and grunted as I pulled down my sweatpants.

The doctor peeled away the bandage. "It's looking much improved. No signs of infection, and the wound appears to be healing. I do good work. I think you can go home today."

It was the best news I'd heard in more than a week. "That'd be great. Hard to get a decent night's sleep with nurses checking on me every couple of hours."

Martin chuckled. "I understand. I'll write you a prescription for the pain that should take you through a week. After that, over-the-counter medication should suffice. No bathing for at least five days. Showers are okay. Just no soaking in a tub. If you see any signs of infection, contact your primary doctor."

"Will do." I extended my hand, and he shook it. "Thanks for your help, Doc."

"You're welcome."

After he left, Roz turned to me, her face glowing. "Freedom! Yay!"

"I hate to see what this little hospital stay is going to cost me. At least now I can sleep with you next to me."

She kissed me. "I missed having you home. The bed's been awful empty without you there."

While we waited for the paperwork, I finished breakfast and called my bank. After ten minutes of navigating the bank's automated call system, I finally reached a live human being named Jai. I explained that both my personal and business accounts had been hacked and drained of funds via fraudulent transactions. With Jai's help, I identified the last legitimate transactions on each of the accounts.

"Everything after that is bogus," I explained. "I need my money back."

"That won't be a problem," Jai assured me. "I'll flag those transactions for further investigation and restore the funds to your accounts. I also suggest, as a precaution, that we cancel your debit cards, and issue you replacements with a new card number. Is that okay with you, Ms. Byrne?"

"When will I get the new cards?"

"You should receive them within five to ten business days."

"Two weeks?"

"I'm afraid so, ma'am. I am sorry. I can request they put in a rush order on it. Would you like me to do that?"

"Well, yeah, I need access to my money."

"Happy to do so. Is there anything else I can assist you with today?"

"No, thanks." I ended the call before he could continue anymore canned customer-service speak. I then called Bobby.

"Hey, kiddo. I'm on my way to the airport to pick up Dana. You need me to bring you anything while I'm out?"

"No, Appa. They're releasing me. Just waiting on the paperwork."

"Wonderful news, kiddo. We can stop by your place a little later if you think you'll be up for visitors."

"For you and Dana, I'm always up for visitors."

An hour later, Rob from Transport showed up with my release papers and a wheelchair. Roz put all my belongings into the suitcase she'd brought the day before. I sat in the wheelchair, holding a partially eaten gift basket of gourmet foods.

As Rob rolled me out of the room, I noticed there was no longer a uniformed police officer sitting outside Wylie's room. *Has he been released by the hospital and taken to jail?*

"Hey!" I pointed toward my brother's room. "Can we go that way around the nurses' station?"

"Sure. I suppose. Why?" Rob asked.

"My brother's in room 520. I want to say goodbye." I really wanted to press him again to see if I could learn where Zoë was. Maybe my mother had gotten through to him.

"I've got two other patients waiting for transport. I don't have time for you to stop and visit."

"I promise I'll be quick." I caught Roz giving me a wary glance. At Wylie's door, I handed her the gift basket. "Be right back."

"Good luck."

I opened the door and slipped inside. My brother was awake and typing away on his phone. He looked up at me and glared. "What the fuck you want?"

"I see the cop's gone."

"Made bail."

"While still in the hospital?" I asked.

"What do you care?"

"Did Mom speak to you about talking to the cops?"

"I don't rat on my friends."

"You might reconsider that when they throw you in prison. Tell them where Zoë Hildebrandt is."

"Who?" he asked.

"The girl who was kidnapped. You said you knew who had her."

"Did I? I don't recall."

"Her parents are worried sick. She's been missing for nearly a week."

He smirked. "He ain't no girl. And the sooner he realizes it, the better off he'll be."

"What the fuck does that mean? Where is she?"

"That's for me to know and you not to find out."

"She's going to be found eventually, Wylie. As are your two buddies who murdered my friends. The only question is how long you'll spend in prison for it. And how many times you'll get fucked in the ass as someone's prison bitch."

It was a cheap shot, but considering his arrogance and history with Father Sebastard, maybe he would see reason and talk.

"Fuck you, you perverted freak."

There was a knock on the door. I ignored it and grabbed a butter knife off the tray on his bedside table. "If she's been hurt, getting raped in prison will be the least of your worries. I'll fucking end you."

He burst out laughing. "Yeah, bitch, I'd like to see you try."

The door opened. "Ms. Byrne, we gotta get going," Rob said.

"One thing Dad taught me was how to be ruthless." I tossed the butter knife onto the floor. "You won't see me coming." I limped out the door and settled back into the wheelchair.

"That did not sound like a happy family goodbye," Rob said as he wheeled me down the corridor.

I was too pissed to speak.

"They're a complicated family," Roz replied.

CHAPTER 28
HOME

FORTY-FIVE MINUTES LATER, Roz pulled into our apartment complex after dropping off my prescriptions at the pharmacy. She promised to pick them up after I got settled in the apartment.

The grueling walk from the parking lot to our front door seemed a thousand miles long. The aluminum crutch from the hospital helped, but only a little. My pain rose steadily with each step.

"Keep going. You've got this," Roz said when I started losing steam thirty feet from our door. I put my good arm over her shoulder, and she helped me through the last stretch and into the apartment. "Where to? Living room or bedroom?"

"Living room," I said between heaving breaths. "Closer."

"You gonna be okay while I pick up your prescriptions?" She eased me into my recliner.

I gave her a reassuring smile. "I think I'll survive."

I shouldn't have been so smug. Even sitting in my chair, the burning in my groin was uncomfortable. To distract myself from the pain, I started scrolling my news feed, but every other post was about the shooting.

My name now appeared in many of the stories as the woman who disarmed one of the shooters. That explained the surge in anonymous callers. Fortunately, my phone still only rang for callers on my contact list.

One article reported that Wylie and I were siblings and speculated whether the shooting was a hate crime or a domestic dispute. Worse, loudmouthed blowhards like Sergeant Rivers dominated the feed with their transphobic rants. And rather than refute the obvious lies, the mainstream media used the quotes as clickbait headlines to generate more ad revenue. But the bottom line was that cops still hadn't identified the other two shooters, and Zoë was still missing.

I called Marilyn, hoping for good news.

"Avery?" Her voice was weak and lifeless. "How are you feeling?"

"I'm fine. Thanks for the flowers. Any word on Zoë?"

"Detective Hausman has talked to her teachers, friends, and classmates as well as David and my parents. No one has seen or heard from her."

"Has there been a ransom?"

"No, not really. Detective Hausman followed up on a few online posts claiming to have her, but they turned out to be false." Her voice grew shakier. "I don't know what I'm going to do, Avery, if… if… I… I just can't imagine not seeing her again. This is my worst nightmare."

Hearing her sob hurt more than the pain in my thigh. "If the police can't find her, I will. Somehow."

"Oh, Avery, I appreciate your assurances, but there's nothing you could do that the police aren't already doing. Especially in your condition."

"I can't just lie around while she's still missing. We will find her. I promise you."

"You just focus on getting better, Avery. Easton, from the Phoenix Gender Alliance, stopped by. They told me what you did at the Trans March—how you disarmed that shooter. You're a hero to the community."

"I'll feel more like a hero once Zoë is home safe with you and those other shooters are rotting in jail."

"Avery, you've done enough. You need to rest and recover."

I hated to admit she was right, but I wasn't in any condition to track down a missing girl. *Doesn't matter*, I told myself. *I'll walk through hell before I give up on Zoë. I just needed a plan.*

"I'll talk to you soon, Marilyn." I hung up and tried to think.

Wylie was the closest thing to a lead I had. Although he was still in the hospital and determined not to talk to me, his claim to know who had taken Zoë rang true. The kidnappers had to be whatever right-wing militia group he was a part of. But who were they? The news stories didn't say.

My pain level was creeping up to a six, making it hard to think. I popped two extra-strength Tylenol and washed them down with a beer from the fridge. An ice pack on my groin helped a little but only lasted twenty minutes.

By the time Roz arrived home with my meds—an hour after she'd left—my pain was at an eight, and I was spewing an unbroken stream of profanity.

"Sorry," she said. "There was a long line. One pharmacy tech was handling both the walk-up customers and the drive-thru."

Rather than reply, I tore into the white paper bag she held out to me and swallowed two horse pills and a bitter-tasting antibiotic with the last of my beer.

"You okay?" Roz asked, watching my desperate performance.

"I will be."

"Not sure you should mix alcohol with the pain meds."

"It's one goddamn beer!" I snapped, immediately regretting my tone. "Sorry. Pain's got me grumpy."

She smiled. "I understand. No offense taken. Why don't I get you to bed? You look like you could use some rest."

"Yeah, okay."

She helped me shuffle to the bedroom. "I heard from Mr. Goldstein at the embassy."

"Yeah?"

"A few hostages were released as part of a prisoner exchange, but my family wasn't among them. The IDF's killing of Palestinian civilians and rearresting previously released prisoners is complicating matters. Mr. Goldstein insists he's doing what he can to get all Americans released, but it's tricky when dealing with a conflict that goes back so many centuries."

"Shit. I'm so sorry, sweetie."

"Nothing we can do but wait," she said with a sigh. "Get some sleep."

Before long, the meds took effect, and I fell into a deep, dreamless sleep.

When I woke, the light streaming through the bedroom window told me it was late afternoon. Voices drifted in from elsewhere in the apartment. I struggled to my feet. The room rocked gently thanks to the meds still coursing through my system. My pain was at a dull ache.

My hair looked like a raven's nest, and my makeup was smeared. The once-vibrant Damaged Souls T-shirt I wore was faded and frayed at the seams. My sweatpants weren't in much better shape. But both were comfortable, so I didn't care.

I shambled like a zombie into the living room and found Kimi, Chupa, and Torch crammed together on our love seat. Roz occupied a chair from the kitchen while Dana sat in Roz's recliner, with Bobby perched on the arm.

The short walk from the bedroom was enough to set my

heart racing. I'd have to get myself back in shape if I was to rescue Zoë and track down the other two shooters.

"Hey, everyone."

"There she is," Chupa said. "The belle of the ball."

"More Beast than Belle," I replied.

"Come, sit." Roz got up and kissed me then led me to my recliner.

"Good to see you home, kiddo," Bobby said when I eased into the chair and raised the feet.

Dana reached over and gripped my hand. "I'm sorry I wasn't able to visit you in the hospital. I was so worried about you."

Our gazes met as I squeezed her hand. "Not your fault. I missed you, but Bobby and Roz took good care of me."

She wasn't Melissa, my foster mom, but she had become a good friend once I got over my hang-ups over her relationship with Bobby. When they'd first started dating a year and a half before, I thought she was an uptight, pushy know-it-all. Not a good fit for Bobby. But eventually, I got to know her once I admitted that my antipathy toward her stemmed from grieving Melissa's death. It was such a corny cliché, but it didn't make it any less true.

Dana didn't have any problem with me being trans. She admired my abilities as a tattoo artist and respected my choices in fashion and music. We'd even gone shopping together a few times.

"Me and the boys dropped by the hospital the first day you were there," Kimi said. "Not sure if you remember. You seemed pretty out of it."

"I vaguely remember." The memory was little more than flashes.

"McCobb would've come tonight, but he had a prior commitment. I'm glad you're home, though. It's no fun being in the hospital."

I glanced over at Roz. "Yes, I much prefer Roz's bedside manner to any of the nurses or the doc."

"Yeah, she's a keeper," Kimi said, exchanging a glance with Roz. "It's been a horrible week for a lot of us."

Torch, who would normally be cracking jokes with Chupa and McCobb, stared down at the floor, shoulders hunched.

"Any word about your family?" I asked.

Torch sniffled. "Not yet."

"Whole fucking world's gone crazy."

"Seems those that want to make war are winning," Kimi said.

"That's why we must stick together," Bobby said. "And keep a check on her own anger."

"I think we have a right to be angry," I replied. "All these innocent people getting murdered here and overseas."

"You do have that right, kiddo. But anger leads to hate. Hate leads to—"

"Appa, don't," I said.

"Sorry. Old habit."

"Well, we have a refrigerator full of food, thanks to all your generosity," Roz said. "So who's hungry?"

As we ate, Bobby told me that a new artist named Dakota Ellis had started work at Seoul Fire that morning. "You'll like them. They're nonbinary and recently moved from Los Angeles. I've talked with a few of your clients, and they agreed to let Dakota pick up where you left off."

"You're giving away my clients?"

"No, Dakota is just filling in until you're back on your feet."

After dinner, I started drifting off again. I'd taken another pain pill before we ate, and it was kicking in at full force. Sleep was enveloping me like a heavy blanket. I rallied to stay awake, but it was a losing battle.

"You want me to help you to bed?" Roz whispered, startling me awake again.

"No, I'm fine. Just a little tired."

"I think we should head on out," Kimi said to Chupa. "Avery needs to rest, and we've got a long drive to our gig in Albuquerque tomorrow."

"Come on, babe. You need sleep." Roz helped me to my feet.

"Thank you all for coming," I said. "It's great to have family like you."

Everyone came around for a group hug.

"Group grope," Chupa joked with his signature goofy laugh.

CHAPTER 29
REPLACED

I SPENT all of Tuesday trying to take it easy—watching horror movies on Shudder with Roz, listening to the new albums I got for my birthday, walking from one end of the apartment to the other to build up my stamina, and sleeping off and on. But in the back of my mind, I still worried about Roz's family and Zoë.

The next morning over breakfast, I told Roz, "I want to meet the new artist at Seoul Fire."

"Babe, you've only been home a couple of days. Give your body a chance to heal."

"I can heal just as easily at the studio as I can here. Besides, this Dakota's filling in for me while I'm recovering. I deserve to meet them. Make sure they're up to snuff."

"I doubt Bobby would've hired them on if they weren't up to snuff."

I gave her a look.

"All right," she said with a shrug. "I'll be your chauffeur."

"I can drive myself," I insisted. "You should go back to work at Spy Gal. I'm sure Polly could use a break."

She folded her arms and stared at me. "You're not driving yourself while you're on those pain pills."

"Fine. You can drive. But please don't coddle me. I'm not disabled."

"I wouldn't coddle you even if you were disabled. But you are recovering from a serious gunshot wound. Two gunshot wounds, in fact. I'm here to help."

"I hate sitting on my ass with nothing to do."

"Just breathe in peace, exhale frustration," she replied in her best imitation of Bobby.

"Funny."

"I'll drive you to the studio, and we'll see how it goes, okay?"

When I walked in, Bobby, Frisco, and Butcher all came over to hug me. It was a little overwhelming, but they were family.

"Missed you, kid," Butcher said. That was volumes, coming from him.

"Glad you're back, girlie," Frisco added.

Bobby led me over to the formerly vacant workstation. "Kiddo, I want you to meet Dakota Ellis. Dakota, this is my daughter, Avery Byrne."

A tapestry of black ink tattoos covered the medium-brown skin of both Dakota's arms. I had to admit I liked their style, which blended African and Mesoamerican patterns with three-dimensional shading that really made it pop. My client, Magnus Petersen, reclined in the chair while Dakota added the color and shading to the dragon design I'd outlined on his biceps.

Dakota stopped and extended an elbow in greeting to avoid replacing their gloves. "The legendary Avery Byrne," they said with a grin.

I bumped elbows with them. "Legendary?"

"I saw your spread in *Inked Magazine* last year. Nice

work. Also heard what you did at the parade. I'm glad you're okay."

"Thanks. I should be back working soon."

"No rush," Magnus reassured me. "Dakota here's doing a great job."

I felt a pang of jealousy, watching Dakota work on one of my clients. *Am I that easily replaced?*

Over the years, I'd bailed on more than a few client appointments when Avery the avenger was busy taking revenge on those who'd hurt my chosen family. Bobby always warned me that my clients would find another artist if I wasn't dependable. He was right. Here Dakota was, stealing my clients, and I had no one to blame but myself.

A tapping at the front door caught my attention. George the grackle stood outside, long black tail feathers gleaming in the sun.

"Hey look," Dakota remarked. "Tapper's back."

"Tapper?" I asked. "His name is George."

"We renamed him Tapper," Frisco replied. "Kinda fits, don't ya think?"

The pangs of jealousy intensified. Not only was Dakota taking my clients, but they'd also renamed my grackle. Well, he was not my grackle per se. Even so, Dakota had no right to rename him.

I reached for the tattoo machine in their hand. "I think I can handle it from here."

Dakota raised an eyebrow. "Excuse me?"

"Ave," Bobby interjected. "Could you and Roz give me a hand with something in the back?" The look on his face told me I was in for one of our father-daughter lectures.

Roz and I followed him to the back storage room. The short walk was enough to leave me winded.

"What are you doing, kiddo?"

"Just getting back to work," I replied innocently.

Bobby shook his head. "While I'm happy to see you up and about, you still need time to recover. You just got out of the hospital. We don't need you coming in here, causing chaos."

"I'm not causing chaos."

Roz shot me a look. "Babe, I hate to say it, but Bobby J.'s right. You don't need to be here. Dakota is taking care of your clients, so you can recover. You're out of breath just walking in here."

"Am not," I said impatiently.

"Are too," Roz replied with a playful smirk.

I sighed. "Okay, fine. Maybe I'm a little out of breath."

They both stared blankly at me.

"And maybe I'm a bit jealous of Dakota working on my client, filling in a design that I created and outlined."

Roz said, "No one's replacing you. Dakota's just helping out. Your clients will still be your clients. Besides, jealousy is not a good look on you."

"Okay, fine," I conceded. "But did they really have to rename my grackle?"

"It's a bird, kiddo," Bobby said. "It's not yours or anyone else's. It's its own bird. Whether we call him George or Tapper, it doesn't matter. It's just a bird."

I hated that they'd ganged up on me like this, but what really got me was that they were right. "Whatever. I'll go home and let you people work."

Bobby and Roz both hugged me. In the back of my mind, I could hear Chupa saying, "Group grope." I was getting a lot of these kinds of hugs lately.

For most of the ride home, we didn't speak. About a mile from the apartment complex, Roz asked, "You okay?"

"Yeah."

"You're awful quiet."

"I'm always quiet."

"With strangers, yes, but not with family. You still mad at Dakota?"

"No. Just thinking about all the other shit going on."

"It's a lot," she said solemnly.

"I can't sit around and do nothing, Roz. I'll go fucking bananas."

"I understand." At a red light, she gave me a knowing look. "I feel helpless not being able to help my family. But sometimes the best thing we can do is take care of ourselves. Avery the avenger needs time to recover."

"I think Bobby's starting to rub off on you."

Despite all the casseroles and other dishes in our fridge, Roz stopped to buy a couple of pints of ice cream for lunch on the way home. We settled into our respective recliners and started streaming the new Mike Flanagan series, *The Fall of the House of Usher*. I'd always been a fan of Edgar Allan Poe, and after enjoying Flanagan's previous miniseries, including *The Haunting of Hill House* and *The Midnight Club*, I hoped this would be just as entertaining. I wasn't disappointed.

In the middle of the second episode, Roz got a call. "Hello? Hey, Polly. What's up? Yeah, okay. I'm on my way." She hung up. "Will you be okay for a while on your own?"

"Sure. What's going on?"

"I got to go to Spy Gal. Polly's babysitter called her and said her daughter is running a fever. She's hoping it's not COVID. You need anything before I go?"

"No, I'm good. There's plenty to eat and drink. I've got something to keep my mind occupied for a while."

"No alcohol," she said with a wink. "Not while you're on those pain meds. And no wild parties."

"Aw, come on! Just one teensy-weensy wild party?" I stuck out my bottom lip. "Tell Polly I hope her daughter feels better."

"Will do." She kissed me, and I already missed her. "Later, babe."

During the opening credits of the third episode, I spied the dish on the kitchen counter where I kept the keys to the Gothmobile. I really did need to give my body time to heal. But Zoë was in danger. And there had to be something I could do about it.

CHAPTER 30
POSSIBILITIES

I PULLED Detective Hausman's business card out of my wallet. Maybe I didn't need to go traipsing across the Valley looking for Zoë if Hausman was close to finding her.

The line rang three times before a familiar voice answered. "Peoria Police, Special Victims Unit. Detective Hausman speaking. How can I help you?"

"Detective, this is Avery Byrne. I met you at the Hildebrandts' the night Zoë went missing. Have you found her yet?"

"We're still following up on leads."

"I've got a lead for you," I said.

"Oh?"

"My brother, Wylie Byrne, knows where she is. He was arrested as one of the shooters in the Pride Festival massacre."

"Phoenix PD already contacted me about this. I looked into it. It's not a viable lead."

"He knows where Zoë is."

"I haven't found any evidence to suggest your brother is involved with Zoë's disappearance. Everything points to her running away from home. We're checking with friends as well as all the shelters, bus stations, and the other usual places a kid like her would go."

"Her parents supported her transition. They love her."

"She's a fourteen-year-old kid, Ms. Byrne, with a history of delinquent behavior, including running away."

"That was before. I know Zoë. She's shared with our youth group that she's much happier at home than she used to be. There's no reason for her to run away."

"I'm sorry, but I can't discuss our investigation with you. But I assure you, my team is doing everything we can to return the child home."

"Bullshit." I hung up, pissed at her ignorance, arrogance, and incompetence. Well, if she refused to consider Zoë a kidnap victim, then I would find her myself. And if she was still alive, I would bring her home.

In the year that Zoë had been a member of the Hatchlings, I'd watched her blossom, not just physically but emotionally and mentally as well. When she first joined, she was withdrawn and still carrying the weight, shame, and trauma of having hidden her gender dysphoria. But over time, she opened up, knowing that within the group, she was safe. She wasn't alone in her experiences and would not be judged.

She shared her joy at being able to live as her true self and learning to trust her parents and their unconditional support. I had to admit, I was a little jealous while also happy for her. Which was not to say her life was perfect. She envied her female classmates, whose bodies were further along in maturing to womanhood. She feared her voice was too deep from waiting so long to start testosterone blockers. And of course, there were the schoolyard bullies and the teachers who turned a blind eye.

But there was no talk of running away—no desire to act out in the ways she had before. No substance abuse or cigarettes, having been warned by her doctors of the greater health risks now that she was on HRT.

So where is she? Who has her? And how will I find her?

For an hour, I sat and pondered my next step. Some of the protesters at the library had been dressed in combat gear the same as my brother had. Little tin soldiers who got off on harassing and murdering trans people. *Who the hell are they, where is their base of operations, and who is calling the shots?*

I scanned every news story on the Pride Festival massacre I could find, but none mentioned the name of the group responsible. I wondered if running a background check on my brother would yield some clues.

When Roz and I were first dating, she'd used an app called SkipTrakkr to help me figure out who had murdered some friends of mine. The app provided background checks, criminal records, bank transactions, phone logs, and more. The kicker was, it was only for licensed private investigators, which neither Roz nor I was. But she was able to use her late father's private eye license to set up an account.

Unfortunately, Roz had her laptop with her at work. And she probably wouldn't want me tracking down my brother while I was still recovering. I'd have to wait until she got home. Unless Wylie had been lying. Maybe Hausman had followed up and found it really wasn't a lead after all.

Yet there was something there. My brain was just too muddled from the pain meds to sort it all out. And I couldn't think of any way to locate my brother—not without Roz running a background check on SkipTrakkr.

I pulled out my phone and called her.

"Hey, babe," she said. "What's up? You need something?"

"I do. I want you to run a background check on my brother."

"Ave, you're sleuthing again."

"Am not."

"Are too."

"I'm just trying to reach out to my brother. Reestablish family ties."

"Reestablish ties with your neo-Nazi brother who hates you? You need to be resting."

"I need to find Zoë Hildebrandt and bring her home. My brother knows where she is."

"Call Detective Hausman and let her know," she said.

"I did, but she doesn't believe me. She said she already checked it out and doesn't think it's a lead."

"Well, at least she checked it out. I'm sure she's doing everything that can be done to find Zoë."

"I just..."

"You just need to rest and let Hausman do her job. I love you, babe. I'm not trying to coddle you. But you can't go looking for your terrorist brother. You're not up to the task. And it hurts to say that. Sometimes you've just got to let things go, at least for a while. I would love nothing more than to fly over to Israel and rescue my family, but it's not an option."

"You won't even run the background check?" I asked.

"Get your Poe fix on and go back to watching *The Fall of the House of Usher*. I love you. I'll see you tonight." She hung up.

I sat and stewed. I knew she was right. But a girl was in trouble. I had to find her.

Perhaps another approach would yield results. Marilyn had said Zoë was last seen getting on a Valley Metro bus at her school. Even if she'd boarded the wrong bus, she would have turned up by now. Someone could have intercepted her on the ride home.

If a stranger had forced her off the bus before her stop, surely she would have put up a fuss. The bus driver would have intervened. At least, I would hope they would have.

Unless someone had drugged her, making her more

compliant. *Would a fourteen-year-old know not to eat or drink something from a stranger?* I'd been pretty naive when I hit the streets at thirteen. Then again, I hadn't had parents who gave a shit until I found Bobby and Melissa.

Another possibility was that she ran into someone she knew and trusted, someone who pretended to be her friend but lured her somewhere. *A classmate pretending to be romantically interested in her? Her estranged grandparents? A neighbor?*

Marilyn had said Zoë wasn't dating anyone, but a memory from a few months back surfaced. Zoë had shared that she had a crush on a boy at school. *What if this boy found out about her crush and used it to hurt her?*

There was one more possibility that I didn't want to consider but couldn't ignore. While her parents had allowed her to transition, there could still be trouble at home. I didn't know David Hildebrandt as well as I knew Marilyn. *Could he have been molesting her or abusing her?* I had no reason to believe that, but that kind of situation was not always obvious. After all, Kimi had been surprised when I'd told her about my dad.

Of course, all of this was pure speculation. I needed to talk with someone who knew her better than I did— someone she saw every day and trusted with secrets she might not tell her parents. When I was living with Bobby and Melissa, there'd been things I didn't tell them, even though I'd known they loved me. Such was the nature of teenagers—always full of secrets. And sometimes we shared them only with people our own age.

Zoë might have trusted the members of the Hatchlings, but it was a big group that met only once a month. There was not always time for deep personal confessions. Her close friends might know something she hadn't shared either at group or with her folks. It was a long shot, but it was all I had.

I called Marilyn. "Hey, it's Avery. Could you give me the contact info of Zoë's closest friends?"

"Her friends? Why?" She sounded even worse than the last time we'd spoken.

"Because Hausman is looking for Zoë at shelters and bus stations. You and I both know she wouldn't run away." I hesitated to continue. "Maybe her friends know something that could point me in the right direction."

"Avery, you've been such a great friend and mentor to Zoë. But you just got out of the hospital. You need to recover. Detective Hausman has already spoken to her friends. Besides, I wouldn't feel right giving out their private information to someone they don't know."

"Not even to save Zoë's life? Hausman's had nearly a week, and what has she turned up? Zilch. If there's a chance I can track her down, don't you think that trumps her friends' privacy? It's a long shot, I know, but maybe it will help me find her."

For a long minute, she said nothing. I figured this was another dead end. She only knew me as the Hatchlings youth group leader. She didn't know about Avery the avenger.

"She's got two friends, Liana Romano and Benji Clarke. I can't imagine Zoë would tell them anything that she wouldn't tell David and me, but I'll give you their phone numbers." She rattled them off, and I wrote them down.

"Thank you, Marilyn," I said. "I'll find her and bring her home."

"I hope you do. I've barely slept since she disappeared. Thank you, Avery. Be careful."

I called the number for Liana Romano, but she didn't answer. No surprise, considering it was in the middle of the school day. I left a message explaining that I was Zoë's mentor and that her mother had given me her number to help find Zoë.

I expected to leave a voicemail for Benji Clarke, but to my surprise, he answered. "Who is this?"

"My name is Avery Byrne. I'm a friend of Zoë Hilde-brandt. I lead the trans support group she's a part of."

"Yeah, Zoë's told me about you. What do you want?"

"I'm hoping you can help me locate her."

"Aren't the police looking for her?"

"They say they are. But it's been almost a week, and she's still missing. I think the more people looking for her, the better. Don't you?"

There was a pause before he answered. "Yes, I suppose so. What do you want to know?"

"Was Zoë having any problems at home?"

"Not since she came out. She's been really happy now that she can live as a girl. Her parents have been the best. I'm a little jealous. My father freaked when I came out as gay. My mother cried. They're coming around, but they're not nearly as supportive as Zoë's parents have been."

"What about school? Was she having any problems there?" I asked.

"Who doesn't have problems at school? Especially when you're queer like us."

"Has someone physically harmed her?"

"No. Mostly, it's just comments in the hall between classes. Soon after she transitioned, some asshole taped a photo of her from before and wrote the word *fag* on it. Nothing recent, though. You think someone here at school attacked her?"

"I don't know. I'm looking into all possibilities. So no one was threatening her?"

"Not that she told me. I figured someone must've grabbed her after she got off the bus."

Of course. Why didn't I think of that? The pain meds really had me off my game. *Why force Zoë off a bus with so many witnesses when you could kidnap her on the walk home? She attends a charter school, so there were probably fewer kids getting off at the stop.*

"How far is her house from the bus stop?" I asked.

"About a half a mile, I guess."

"Has she had any problems with neighbors?"

"No, I don't think so."

I tried to think of other questions to ask but came up empty. "Thanks for your help, Benji. I'm gonna find her."

I was about to hang up when he said, "You know, there is one thing. Probably nothing, though."

My heart leapt. "Yeah, what?"

"Her grandpa. Zoë told me she's been in touch with him recently."

"Which grandpa?"

"Her mother's father."

"I thought they were estranged," I said.

"They were, but she kinda missed him. I don't know if he reached out to her or the other way around. But she was happy to hear from him. And she was afraid to tell her folks."

And there it was.

"Do you know his full name and his phone number or address?" I asked.

"Only that she calls him Grandpa Joe, like from *Charlie and the Chocolate Factory*. You really think her grandfather would take her and not tell her folks?"

"At this point, anything is possible. But maybe if she's with him, she's safe."

"I hope so."

I gave him my phone number. "If you can think of anything else, call me, okay?"

"Will do."

I hung up and sent Marilyn a text, letting her know that her father might be involved and asking for his contact information.

CHAPTER 31
SEARCHING

TEN MINUTES LATER, I received Marilyn's reply.

> MARILYN:
>
> My father's been talking to Zoë?

ME:

That's what Benji sed. What's ur father's
name & where's he live?

> MARILYN:
>
> Joseph Patterson. In Sun City West.
> Hausman already spoke with my parents,
> doesn't think they're involved.

ME:

Hausman's convinced Zoë ran away. I don't
buy it. Give me ur father's address. I'll talk
to him. Maybe he knows something.

She didn't reply immediately. I wondered if I'd pushed too
hard.

MARILYN:

> I spoke with David. He's agreed to talk with
> my father. You focus on recovering. But
> thank you for your diligence.

I wanted to press her, but as Zoë's mother, it was her call.
Perhaps David would have better luck than I would.

ME:

> Okay. Let me know what he finds out.

MARILYN:

> Will do.

I sat there, growing increasingly restless. Nothing interested
me, not even *The Fall of the House of Usher*. I tried reading
Desert Queen, a lesbian vampire romance from Kayla Cara.
But try as I might, I kept losing my place in the story,
worrying about Zoë. The walls felt like they were closing in.

Finally, I decided that while David Hildebrandt was
following up with Grandpa Joe Patterson, I would again
look at my brother. Roz was unlikely to have changed her
mind about running a background check on Wylie. She'd
probably be pissed I'd been contacting Zoë's friends. Wylie
still probably wouldn't tell me anything. And maybe he'd
just been yanking my chain about knowing where Zoë was.

But then why would he bring it up in the first place? He had
to know something. One thing I'd learned was that angry
people sometimes let things slip. *In furia veritas.* Maybe I
could provoke Wylie enough that he revealed clues to Zoë's
whereabouts. I might learn which neo-Nazi militia group he
was a part of.

Is he still at St. Thomas, or did he get released? I pulled up the hospital patient directory on my laptop once again, only to remember that it required a patient number to access.

Shit. I'd tossed my hospital ID bracelet the moment I got home. *Has Roz taken out the trash?* I dug through the bathroom wastebasket and found nothing but tissues, discarded bandages, and one of Roz's used tampons. *Ick.*

The kitchen trash can was nearly full. Good news—Roz hadn't emptied it since I'd gotten home from the hospital. I spent thirty minutes digging through food scraps, dirty paper towels, and empty cartons and soup cans before I found my ID bracelet.

I rinsed it off under the sink, returned to my laptop, and punched in the number. But when I searched for my brother, the results page showed zero hits. He must have been discharged. *Shit.*

His bail had been posted, so he wasn't in jail. He had to be at home. *So where the fuck does he live?* Since Roz wouldn't run a background check, I was left with only one option—I would have to talk to my mother.

"Andy, it's so nice to hear from you. I'm sorry, I meant Avery," she sputtered. "I'm still getting used to the new name. How are you feeling?"

"Where's Wylie?" I demanded.

"Wylie? At home. Why do you need to know?"

"Where's he live? I need to speak with him."

"Honey, I don't think he's ready to talk with you yet. He's still working through some stuff."

"A girl has been kidnapped, Mom. He knows where she is, and he won't tell the police."

"I don't know anything about that."

"Who bailed him out? Did you did you put up the house as collateral?"

She sighed. "I sold the house years ago to pay your

father's legal bills. I don't have anything that I could've put up for collateral."

"Then who posted Wylie's bail?"

"Some of his friends, I suppose. He doesn't talk much about them to me. He has his own life now."

"He's a member of one of those neo-Nazi right-wing militias. Which one is it? The Proud Boys? Oath Keepers? White Nation?"

"Like I said, he doesn't confide in me anymore."

"What's his phone number?" I asked.

"I don't think he would want me to give that out."

"He's a murderer and a kidnapper, Mom. He tried to kill me, and you're worried about what he wants? You're protecting him just like you protected Dad when he was abusing us. Has Wylie threatened you?"

"Don't be silly. Wylie would never do anything like that. And I'm not siding with him. I love you both equally. I wouldn't give him your phone number either."

"Where does he work?" I asked.

"I don't know exactly. One of those indoor gun ranges, I think. But I don't know which one."

Well, that tracks. Where else to meet like-minded ammosexuals than at a shooting range?

"Where does he live?"

"Again, I don't think I should give you that information."

"He's a murderer, Mom, I'm trying to save a girl's life. And you won't help because you're worried about his privacy? Where the fuck are your priorities?"

"Please don't use that kind of language with me. I'm still your mother."

"No, you're just the woman who gave birth to me and turned a blind eye when Dad was abusing me and Father Sebastian was molesting Wylie."

"The police have Wylie's information," she replied more sternly. "If you think he's involved with this missing girl, tell them. You shouldn't be running around after him. Best just to leave him alone. I would hate for something else to happen to either of you."

"You still haven't changed. Still protecting abusers and predators no matter what they've done. Why am I not surprised?" I hung up before she could answer. I was going to have to find Wylie another way. Plan C or D or whatever it was—I would search social media.

Since the incident at the library, my own social media accounts had blown up with thousands of hate-filled messages. But I wasn't logging on to interact with followers and trolls. I was tracking down Wylie in hopes he'd lead me to Zoë.

I was surprised to discover there were a lot more Wylie Byrnes than I'd expected. Even when I filtered for people in Arizona, there were multiple hits. If I've been using Skip-Trakkr, I could have used his middle name and birthdate to narrow down the list. But those weren't filter options on social media.

After fifteen minutes of scrolling results, I found what I suspected was his Facebook account. There was no profile picture, just an image of red crosshairs over a white background. But this Wylie Byrne posted a lot of conspiracy theories, religious blather, and bigoted memes. His employer was listed as the Red Mountain Gun Club in Mesa.

I was frankly surprised he hadn't closed his account or at least privatized it, considering his arrest. Sadly, a lot of the comments were supportive of his vile posts. Still, it was a lead that got me one step closer to Zoë.

According to their website, the Red Mountain Gun Club was on Thomas Road, near Higley and the Loop 202. They sold a wide range of firearms, offered a members-only indoor firing range, and held classes on gun safety, marksmanship, self-defense, and tactical training.

Their blog touted their latest sales, reviews of firearms,

and posts about how the liberals were trying to take away their Second Amendment rights.

I didn't know how bad Wylie's injuries were. He probably wasn't back at work yet. But I could try to sweet-talk his coworkers into giving me his address. *Only one way to find out.*

After a quick shower and a fresh set of clothes, I felt almost human again. Still, the simple tasks of getting dressed and putting on makeup left me winded, as if I'd run a marathon. *Am I really up to tracking down and confronting my brother?* Maybe not, but I couldn't sit on my ass with Zoë still in peril.

It had been three hours since my last pain pill, so I grabbed my purse and keys then walked gingerly out to the parking lot, where I slid behind the wheel of the Gothmobile. I took a deep, cleansing breath, inhaling the car's scent of leather and desert dust from sitting for days. I felt a surge of my old strength coming back. *Breathe in energy, exhale fatigue. Breathe in strength, exhale weakness.*

I turned the key in the ignition. *Ruh-ruh-ruuhhh...* The engine turned but didn't catch.

I tried again. Closer, but still not quite there. I pumped the gas a couple of times, tried once more, and the Gothmobile roared to life.

I was going to find Zoë. No matter what.

CHAPTER 32
MISFIRE

I WAS grateful that the Gothmobile was automatic and not a straight shift. The pressure from the seat belt digging into my hip every time I braked was painful enough. If I'd had to push in a clutch with my left leg, the drive out to Mesa would have been unbearable.

I was reaching the limits of my pain tolerance when I pulled into the parking lot that the Red Mountain Gun Club shared with a bar called Iron Eagle. Guns and alcohol—a rather lethal combination. I repeated the breathing exercises, hoping to channel more positive energy, strength, and anything else that would help me save the girl's life.

"You can do this," I told myself as I stepped out of the car.

The gun club was a rustic wooden building with a wrap-around porch. Climbing the three steps from the parking lot felt like having a knife twist in my groin. Refusing to let it stop me, I stepped through the glass door.

A few customers milled about the place, carrying bags I assumed contained guns and ammunition. Glass display cases offered a wide selection of guns—pistols, revolvers, hunting rifles, shotguns, and assault rifles. Ammunition lined the shelves along the back wall.

The astringent smell of spent gunpowder hung in the air. The irregular staccato thumps of gunfire drifted from the back of the building. My breath caught when a vivid flashback of the Trans March shooting played in Dolby Vision in my mind. The stench of blood filled my nose. Screams of pain and fear. Panic rising.

I took a deep, steadying breath. *You're here. You're safe. It's just a firing range. Breathe in peace. Release fear.*

I focused my attention on a sign by the front door: "Customers must keep all firearms unloaded and secured in carrying cases."

The guns-guts-and-glory crowd always cried foul about any limits on carrying in public, but here in their holy of holies, they had to keep their toys unloaded and locked away. I approached a woman who stood behind the counter, wearing a Red Mountain Gun Club T-shirt. Mounted behind her was a sign listing the prices for membership and use of the gun range.

"How can I help you today?" she asked.

"I'm looking for Wylie Byrne."

Her pleasant expression hardened into a scowl. "I'm not talking to reporters. And you don't look like you're law enforcement. This is a private gun club. I'm going to have to ask you to leave."

"I'm not a reporter or a cop. Wylie's my brother." I volunteered my driver's license as proof. "I need to talk with him."

She glanced at my ID and studied my face. "Yes, I can see the resemblance. He never mentioned he had a sister. Why is that?"

"We've been estranged for a while, but we reconnected in the hospital. I'm hoping we can become a normal family again."

One of the other employees across the room shouted. "Hey, I know you! You're that chick with a dick. The one that shot Wylie."

Something about this guy looked familiar, but I couldn't place him. His name tag read Cam.

The woman behind the counter glared at me. "You said you were his sister."

"I am."

"Wylie ain't got no sister," the guy said. "You're his faggot brother, the one that shot him at the parade while he was exercising his constitutional right to protest."

Suddenly, all eyes in the room were on me. Being a transgender woman in Arizona could be dangerous at the best of times. But walking into a gun store run by Wylie's bigoted buddies had probably been a bad idea.

"Look, he shot me. His buddies killed several of my friends. But I'm willing to let bygones be bygones if he'll just talk to me. I care about him."

Cam stalked toward me. "I think you best leave before you end up in a body bag."

Clearly, my opportunity for getting information about Wylie would not end well if I pressed the issue here.

"Fine. I'll go." I pulled out my business card and laid it on the counter. "Have Wylie call me. I can help get some of the charges against him dropped."

I hobbled back to the Gothmobile, the pain in my hip skyrocketing with each step. Maybe Roz and Marilyn Hildebrandt were right and I should have been home recovering, no matter how maddening it might feel. My phone pinged just as I reached the car and slid behind the wheel. I expected a text from Roz, wondering where I was or maybe a follow-up from Marilyn Hildebrandt, letting me know what her husband had found out at Joseph Patterson's house.

But to my surprise, the text was from Danny. I glimpsed the first line.

DANNY:

Srry, Avery. Im an idiot.

CHAPTER 33
ALPHANINJA45

APPARENTLY, Danny's phone service had been restored.

ME:

Where RU? We shld talk.

DANNY:

Home. Srry 4 what I did. I dont deserve 2 live. Worlds better w/o me.

My pulse raced. I didn't like the sound of his words despite all the horrible things he'd said on *The River of Truth*. He sounded suicidal.

ME:

Dont do anything rash, Danny. Ur my friend. Lets talk.

DANNY:

Thanx 4 being a friend. I hurt you & Sophia & evryone in PGA. Pls forgive me.

ME:

On my way thr. We can talk this out.

DANNY:

Dont bother. Its 2 late.

Pushing through the throbbing ache in my hip, I tore out of the gravel parking lot and onto the bustling Loop 202. Danny's house was only twenty minutes away. I desperately hoped I'd reach him in time.

I screeched to a halt in front of his duplex, rapidly limped up the driveway, and pounded on the door after I confirmed it was locked. "Danny, let me in. It's Avery."

When he didn't answer right away, I pounded again. "Danny, please open the door. I'm worried about you."

When he still didn't respond, I pulled the lockpicks out of my purse. It took forever to get the tumblers aligned. Once the cylinder turned, I rushed in and began searching the house. I found him lying unconscious on the bathroom floor, an empty pill bottle clutched in his hand. Surprisingly, he was wearing makeup and a dress.

I shook him. "Danny? Can you hear me?"

When he didn't respond, I checked his neck and found a weak pulse. He was alive, but for how long? I pulled out my phone and called 911.

"I need an ambulance now. A friend of mine overdosed. His... or her pulse is weak." I wasn't sure what pronouns to use at this point.

"What's your location?" the operator asked.

"Maple Street. No, Avenue. Maple Avenue." My brain was in a fog of panic. I couldn't remember the house number. I pulled up my contacts and rattled off the full address.

"An ambulance is on the way. Are you or your friend in any physical danger?"

"No, just get here now."

"What's your friend's name?"

"Dan... Danielle Kirkpatrick."

"What medication did Danielle take?"

I examined the amber pill bottle. "Hydrocodone acetaminophen."

"What's the dosage?"

"It says five milligrams slash five hundred milligrams."

"How many pills did she take?"

"I don't know. The bottle's empty. It originally had twenty, but it looks like it was filled a year ago."

"Okay, stay on the line. The ambulance is on its way."

As I waited, I kept checking her pulse. "Hang in there, girl. Help's on its way."

A piece of paper on the floor caught my eye. She'd written a suicide note. I read it and felt sick to my stomach. I crumpled it and stuffed it in my purse.

A few minutes later, a male voice called from the front door. "Tempe Fire and Medical. You called for assistance?"

"We're in here. In the bathroom."

Two paramedics, one carrying a large case, appeared in the doorway. I stepped out of the bathroom to let them work, hoping they could save her.

A female cop met me in the living room. "You called it in?"

"Yeah."

She introduced herself as Officer Zepeda and asked me for a rundown of what had happened. I told her about getting a text from Danielle and finding her in the bathroom unconsciousness.

"Has she been depressed lately?"

"Her scholarship got revoked. And she's been dealing with gender dysphoria. So yeah, I'd say she was depressed."

"Gender dysphoria? What's that?"

"She's transgender."

Zepeda nodded. "Where did she get the pills?"

"No idea. Her name was on the label, so I assume from her doctor."

"Where were you when she texted you?"

"In Mesa," I replied, being deliberately vague.

"You live in Mesa?"

"No. I live in Phoenix."

"What were you doing in Mesa?"

"Visiting my brother. He lives there."

That seemed to satisfy her. She asked how long I'd known Danielle and a series of other inconsequential questions. I wasn't sure if she was trying to pass the time, get more information out of me, or test the veracity of what I was saying.

"You mind if I call my girlfriend? I want to let her know what's happened."

"Sure, go ahead," she said. "But stay close. I may have more questions."

I wandered into the kitchen for some privacy and punched Roz's number.

"Hey babe," she said. "You climbing the walls yet?"

"I'm at Danny's. Or Danielle's. She texted me. She attempted suicide."

"Holy shit. She okay?"

"Paramedics are working on her. She overdosed on Vicodin."

"I thought they were going by Danny now."

"I found her in makeup and a dress. So your guess is as good as mine."

"Well, I'm glad you were there for her, but you need to rest, babe. You should have just called 911."

"I didn't know exactly what was going on. Besides, I was kinda in the area." I couldn't keep any secrets from her.

"What were you doing in Tempe? You're not out looking for Zoë, are you?"

"Maybe."

There was silence on the line for a moment before Roz said, "You need me to come over?"

"No, you've got the shop to run. How's Polly's kid, anyway?"

"Running a low fever and coughing. But otherwise okay."

I considered my next statement before I spoke. "Roz, there's something else." I dropped my voice to a whisper so Officer Zepeda wouldn't hear me in the other room. "She's AlphaNinja45."

"I don't know what that means. What's AlphaNinja45?"

"She's the gamer who swatted Sophia and Étienne."

"Fuck me. Are you sure?"

"It was in the suicide note she wrote. She apologized for it. I think that's why she attempted suicide. She felt guilty for what she'd done."

"Has she been arrested?"

"You're the first person I told. I haven't shown the suicide note to anyone. I don't know what to do about it."

"You should hand it over to the cops, babe. That's evidence. She's responsible for Sophia getting shot and her boyfriend killed."

"The SWAT team shot her and her boyfriend." But I knew that was only half the truth. "Sweetie, you don't know how scary and confusing and depressing it is to be trans sometimes. She screwed up. She was scared. That scholarship fund was coming after her for last year's tuition money. They were threatening to sue her for fraud."

"You're right—I don't know what it's like to be trans. But Danny or Danielle broke the law. Her actions were reckless and led to Etienne's death. You know what it's like to lose people to violence. Shouldn't your loyalty be to Sophia, who is an innocent victim?"

Her words struck home. *Why the fuck am I protecting Danielle when she betrayed our community in such an unforgivable way?* I had become just like my mother, protecting a perpetrator rather than the victim. *Shit.*

"You're right. I don't know what I was thinking."

"You saw a friend dying, and you didn't want to make things worse for her. I get it. No one wants to choose between two friends. But she hurt Sophia."

"You're right. I'll turn over the letter."

"I love you, babe."

"Love you too, sweetie. I'll talk to you later."

I returned to the living room to find it empty. No sooner did I step into the hallway than the paramedics were coming my way with Danielle on a stretcher. I stepped out of the way, relieved that she was still alive.

"Where are they taking her?" I called out to Officer Zepeda.

"Scottsdale Osborn."

When the ambulance took off, I followed in the Gothmobile. My pain level was creeping up again. In the hospital parking lot, I took another couple of pain pills. It was reckless to be driving while taking them, but I couldn't stand the agony any longer.

I gave my name to the ER receptionist and waited for the better part of forty-five minutes before a woman in scrubs asked for the family of Danielle Kirkpatrick.

I stood and hobbled over. "That's me."

"She's stable. Do you want to come see her?"

"Yes, please." I followed her through the corridors of the emergency ward. She pulled back a curtain, and I saw Danielle lying on a bed, eyes closed, lips smeared with what looked like black lipstick.

Her eyes opened, and tears formed in her eyes. "Why'd you save me?"

I struggled for what to say. "Because you're my friend. Despite what you've done."

She avoided my gaze. "Shoulda let me die."

"Why did you do it? Why'd you swat Sophia? And why'd you say those awful things about the Alliance?"

She sobbed and shook her head. "Everything was going great until they took away the scholarship."

"Because you're trans. That was a shitty thing for them to do to you. So why'd you swat Sophia? Her boyfriend's dead because of you. What'd she ever do to you?"

"Nothing," she sobbed. "There's no excuse."

"Then why? Why turn your back on your own community—the people who loved and supported you when your own father treated you like shit?"

I watched her cycle through a range of emotions and settle on anger.

"Where were you all when the Quinn Fund canceled my scholarship? When they threatened to sue me for fraud? All I got from Sophia and the rest of you was prayers and positive vibes."

"I contributed two grand to your GoFundMe."

"Wasn't enough. The Quinn Fund was demanding the seventy-five grand they gave me last year. Plus interest."

"Well, I'm sorry, but I didn't have a spare seventy-five grand lying around. Not many people do."

"My father did," she said bitterly. "But he would only give it to me if I detransitioned."

"I get it. You were between a rock and a hard place. Sometimes we have impossible decisions to make. But why turn on us?" I pulled her crumpled note out of my purse. "Why would you swat Sophia? And why go on Sergeant Rivers's bullshit show, spewing things you knew weren't true?"

She was back to sobbing again. "My dad said he'd only help me if I went to counseling."

"What's that got to do with what you did?"

Her body trembled at my question. "He sent me to a conversion therapy camp."

"Son of a bitch. What did they do to you?"

She squeezed her eyes shut and grew even more visibly disturbed. "You don't wanna know, but after two weeks, I was willing to say or do anything they told me."

I didn't want to think of what they'd done to her. I'd heard my share of horror stories.

"I was angry, Avery. Angry at God for making me this way. Angry at my mom for allowing me to transition. Angry at the Quinn Fund for taking away my scholarship. Angry at Sophia and the Alliance for not helping me out more. Angry at myself that I couldn't make these feelings go away. Just so fucking angry at everyone."

"But Danielle…"

"I know it wasn't rational. I know you all were being as supportive as you could. But I was pissed at the unfairness of the world, and I lashed out. And now someone is dead because of me."

Despite my anger at her for what she had done, I held her as her body shook. "The world can be a real dumpster fire."

My phone dinged, and I stepped back.

She wiped her face. "That's why I wanted to end it all. I'm so tired of fighting. So tired of trying to be what I'm not. It's so fucking hopeless. And now I'll probably be sent to a men's prison and get raped to death."

Neither of us spoke for a few minutes. I debated about what to do. What Danielle had done was unforgiveable. She'd destroyed Sophia's life and killed her boyfriend. She'd hurt all of us with the nasty lies she'd said on *The River of Truth*.

At the same time, she'd found herself in a no-win situation and endured goth knew what in the conversion therapy camp. *Am I now prepared to send a trans woman to a men's prison?*

"I haven't turned this over to the cops." I held up the crumpled suicide note.

"Why not? I deserve to be punished. Their blood is on my hands."

"You know about these other attacks on our community?"

She nodded. "The shooting at the Trans March. I heard."

"You have anything to do with that?"

"No."

"Also Zoë Hildebrandt has been missing for about a week now."

"I heard."

"Any idea where she is?" I asked.

Danielle shook her head. "I haven't seen her since I aged out of the Hatchlings and joined the main Alliance group a year ago."

"The people who ran this conversion therapy camp, you think maybe they grabbed her?"

"No."

I couldn't tell if she was telling the truth. "I'm sorry your scholarship got taken away. I'm sorry your dad is such an arrogant, transphobic prick. And I'm sorry for what you went through at that camp. You're still family."

"Some family," she said with a sigh.

A thought occurred to me. "Did you go after me too?"

"You?"

"Yeah. Someone hacked my bank account. Ran up a bunch of bogus charges."

The surprise on her face appeared genuine, but I wasn't sure.

"I wouldn't even know how to do that," she said.

"What about the angry mob who showed up at the Hatchlings meeting?"

"I... I may have mentioned the meeting to some people."

I could feel a flicker of rage building up inside me. Swatting Sophia was bad enough, but sending the bigot squad after trans kids? "Who did you tell? Sergeant Rivers? People at the camp?"

"Maybe. I don't remember. I'd just as soon forget it all happened."

My fist tightened around the suicide note. *How could I even have considered letting her off the hook after the harm she caused?*

"You might want to forget, but it doesn't change the facts. You put the Hatchlings in danger. You got Sophia shot and her boyfriend killed. You're a fucking traitor and a murderer. I'm done caring about what happens to you." I turned to leave.

"Avery, wait. I'm really, really sorry for everything I did."

"Are you? Turn yourself in. Maybe your rich daddy can pay for a fancy lawyer. Then you can tell the judge how sorry you are."

"Avery..."

I walked out.

CHAPTER 34
EXPIRED

I WALKED out of the hospital and checked my phone. Marilyn Hildebrandt had texted me.

MARILYN:

David talked to my mom. She hasn't heard from Zoë.

ME:

What about your father?

MARILYN:

He was @ doc appt. My mom said he hasn't seen her either. Her friend must be mistaken. I'm at my wit's end, Avery.

ME:

I will find her, Marilyn. I promise.

MARILYN:

Detective Hausman doesn't want you interfering with the investigation. Says it could put Zoë at risk.

ME:

What do you want?

MARILYN:

Please let the police handle it for now.

I couldn't believe it. *Wouldn't she want as many people as possible looking for Zoë?* But she was the mom. It was her decision.

I called Detective Rutherford, but it went to voicemail, so I left a message. "This is Avery Byrne. I know who swatted Sophia Bitsui and her boyfriend. But I want something in return. Call me."

I drove back to the apartment, trying hard not to speed excessively or give the cops a reason to pull me over. The last thing I needed was to get busted for driving while on pain meds. Roz was already home when I limped in. My pain level was again on the rise, and I was emotionally and physically drained.

"I've been worried about you." Roz hugged me at the door. "Come take a load off."

I hobbled to the kitchen. "Gotta take a pain pill first," I said through gritted teeth, debating whether to take the usual two or try to get by with one. My supply was getting low, and I needed to start weening myself. But my wound felt like someone was jabbing a knife into my crotch.

"You should've been home recovering." She filled a glass with water and handed it to me.

I settled for a single pill, hoping it would at least be enough to take the edge off the pain. I then hobbled to love seat and lay down. "I was worried about Zoë."

"Any news?"

I shook my head. "Nothing so far. Marilyn's husband checked with her folks, but they haven't heard from her either."

"And Danielle? She still alive?" There was a bitter edge to her voice.

"Yes."

"What'd you do with her confession?"

"In my purse. I plan to use it as a bargaining chip to make sure those trigger-happy bastards who shot Sophia and Étienne go to prison too. I left a message for Rutherford to call me."

"Any word on your family?"

Her eyes misted, and she shook her head. I feared the worst.

"There's been a news report that the IDF shot and killed three hostages who managed to escape. I don't know if it's them or not. I've left a message for Mr. Goldstein, but he hasn't called back."

Despite the gnawing pain in my thigh, I launched myself off the couch and hugged her. "Oh, sweetie, I'm so sorry. Why would the IDF shoot them?"

"I don't know. The story I read said IDF saw them near the building in Gaza where they'd been held and mistook them for Hamas."

"It's probably not them. Hang in there, sweetie."

Her expression darkened. "I also heard from Torch. Seventeen members of his family were killed when an IDF missile struck the hospital where they'd taken refuge. He used to visit them every summer. And now they're gone. Four generations of the Shaheen family, including a baby only a few months old."

My chest felt tight. "Poor Torch. This world's gone fucking bonkers." After a somber moment of silence, I added, "I can't do much about the shit going on overseas, but I'm determined to find Zoë and find out who's responsible for these attacks on the trans community. I know they seem random, but after talking with Danielle, I think there is some base level of coordination."

"Are you saying Danielle was following someone's orders?"

"Maybe not orders specifically. Her father agreed to help her out of her financial crisis if she detransitioned and went to conversion therapy. They turned her into a weapon against our community. Organizations like the Patriots of Liberty feed talking points to assholes like Sergeant Rivers and other right-wing talking heads, who in turn get their crazy followers to harass and murder us."

"I thought the Patriots of Liberty was defunct after their CEO went to prison for distributing child porn and soliciting minors."

"So now someone else is calling the shots. I'm going to find out who," I said.

"And do what? Even if the things they're saying are horrible lies, they're entitled to free speech."

"Free speech has limits. When what they say leads to violence against my community, I'm not going to sit on my hands. The Nazis rose to power while following the rules. Then they changed the rules, and six million Jews were slaughtered. And that's what's happening here. This isn't just free speech. This is a fucking war, Roz. I plan to go all French Resistance on their asses."

"You think you can stop these attacks?"

"I don't know. But I have to protect my community. These people have to be brought to justice. And if the police aren't gonna do it, then I will. Starting with finding Zoë and returning her home safely."

"Assuming she's still alive," Roz said.

"And if she's not, I'll kill the motherfuckers who hurt her."

"So, what's your plan?"

"My brother knows who took Zoë. I want to run a background check on him. Find out where he lives, who he's been talking to, everything."

"Don't you think the police already looked into your brother's background?" she asked.

"Hausman said it wasn't a lead."

"Maybe she's right. She's a cop, and she looked like she'd been doing this a while."

"I think she's full of shit. And I won't sit on my ass until Zoë is home. Can you please run a SkipTrakkr background check on my brother?"

"Okay. Let me get my laptop."

Moments later, the two of us sat at the kitchen table while Roz logged onto the site. Disappointment crossed her face. "Well, shit."

"What's wrong?"

"My dad's PI license expired. SkipTrakkr won't let me log in."

"Fuck. I wonder if Jinx could help. She's a bounty hunter and private investigator. And she owes me a favor for helping protect Leia Ripley from her father."

"I guess it wouldn't hurt to ask," Roz said.

"Hey, hero! How are you feeling?" Jinx asked when I called.

"Better," I replied, tired of answering this question. "But I need your help."

"Sure. What do ya need?"

"My estranged brother, Wylie, was one of the Trans March shooters, the only one the cops have identified."

"Shit. You serious? I remember hearing the last name Byrne and wondering if he was a relative."

"He's a member of some militia group. More importantly, he knows who took Zoë Hildebrandt. He told me so but wouldn't give me any more details."

"Wow, that's a twist. So, what do you need from me?"

"I need you to run a background check on him. His address, phone calls, criminal record, known associates, bank transactions, everything."

"Aren't the police looking for Zoë?"

"The detective thinks she ran away. But it's baloney. She wouldn't have. I know her. She's been so happy since she came out. She was doing better at school. There was no reason for her to run away."

There was a pause on the line. Finally, Jinx answered. "I don't normally run SkipTrakkr background checks on people that I'm not officially investigating."

"So help me investigate. Our community is under attack. I've had my bank accounts hacked and have been receiving death threats. Not to mention the mob at the Hatchlings meeting."

"Avery, nothing would give me more pleasure than to bring these fuckers to justice. But I'm dealing with a heavy caseload right at the moment. I'm pursuing four different fugitives all across the state and one who may have already gotten as far as California. I haven't got time to add a new case."

"I helped you and provided a safe place for Leia Ripley and her mom when her asshole father came after them. You owe me. I'm calling in that favor."

"Okay, how about this. I'll run a background on your brother, and we'll see where it goes."

"That's all I'm asking."

"What's his name?"

I gave her Wylie's full name and date of birth then heard her tapping on her keyboard.

A few minutes later, she said, "Okay, his rap sheet shows a couple of assaults—got probation on the first, did a year in county for the second. He's been arrested a few other times, but it doesn't look like they ever went to trial."

"Known associates?"

"Nothing listed."

"Where does he live?" I asked.

"I have three possible addresses—one in Scottsdale, one in Gilbert, and one in Mesa."

She gave them to me, and I wrote them down. Mesa seemed the most likely, considering it was closest to where he worked, but I couldn't assume anything at this point.

"Who's he been texting?" I asked.

"There's a conversation with Jacqueline Byrne. A relative, I'm guessing."

"My mom."

"Makes sense. Looks like a typical rebellious-son-nosy-mother conversation. There's a conversation with a MacKenzie Sanders. Hard to be sure, but I'm guessing a girl-friend. Her asking when he'll be home from work, that kinda shit. None of it appears to be of any substance at a cursory glance. I can send you the file. Maybe you can find something by digging deeper."

"What about his call history?"

"A lot of calls in the past month," she said. "Most of the names are also in the text log. Some don't show a contact name, only a number. Unfortunately, I don't have time to run any of the other numbers. Like I said, I'm on a time crunch right now. I'm sorry."

"And bank records?"

"I can send you his latest three bank statements and a list of transactions in the current month. Anything else?"

"Thanks, Jinx. Maybe I'll get lucky and find something that leads me to Zoë."

"Happy hunting. Wish I could do more."

Ten minutes later, I received an email with several CSV and PDF files attached. I scoured them, starting with Wylie's bank records. Most of it seemed pretty mundane—purchases at local grocery store chains, utilities, a car payment, a mort-gage payment. There were several Amazon transactions, but I had no way of knowing what they were for.

I did notice that each month on the first, the Red Canyon

Gun Club debited forty-five dollars from his account. Wylie also made other larger purchases from the gun club throughout the month. I guessed the former was a monthly membership fee and the latter were for guns or ammo. Probably par for the course for someone like him.

Wylie's text history was similarly innocuous, as Jinx had said. Our mother was inviting him over for Thanksgiving, wanting to meet his new girlfriend. Wylie appeared noncommittal on the subject. None of the conversations mentioned the militia he was a part of. No rants about the trans community or any other right-wing talking points. The call logs were all but useless. The few listings that showed who Wylie had spoken with gave me no indication of the nature of their conversations.

A lot of calls displayed only phone numbers without names. It would have required several other searches on SkipTrakkr to figure out who they were and whether they were relevant to my investigation. The bottom line: Jinx's information didn't reveal anything that would help me find Zoë, other than the three addresses that were listed. I decided to start there.

But I was too exhausted and in too much pain to do anything more that night. I called Torch and shared my condolences. He thanked me and said he was hoping things turned out better for Roz's family. I spent the rest of the night brainstorming how I would get Wylie to tell me where Zoë was. I didn't come up with answers.

CHAPTER 35
FAKE ALLIES

THE NEXT MORNING, Roz was up early. With the influx of snowbirds, she now opened the store at eight o'clock. Apparently, plenty of the Valley's part-time residents were interested in amateur spyware like nanny cams, security cameras, and less-than-lethal self-defense devices.

"So, what are you gonna do with your day?" she asked as she prepared to leave.

"Oh, you know, sit around, get drunk, pop pain pills like they're Pez, watch *The Price Is Right*."

She laughed. I was kidding of course. I'd only taken one pain pill before going to bed the night before. When I'd woken up this morning, I figured I'd try just a couple of ibuprofen instead. I'd seen what addiction had done to people I'd known when I lived on the street. I didn't need to go down that path. I had a girl to rescue and assholes to punish.

"You're not going to do anything dangerous, are you?" Roz grabbed her keys out of the bowl on the counter. "You still need to heal."

I clasped her hand. "Roz, I love you. And I appreciate

that you're concerned for my safety. But I don't need you worrying over me."

"You're not at full strength. If you get in a fight…"

"No fights. I promise. But Zoë is still missing. Sitting around, thinking about what she may be going through, is torture. I can't do it, babe."

Roz sat down next to me and hugged me, pressing her forehead to mine. "I get it. I do. If I'd been in Israel, I would have charged into Gaza and stopped at nothing to rescue my family. Zoë deserves nothing less. What are your plans?"

"I've got three possible addresses for my brother. I'm just going to check them out. Nothing crazy. I probably won't even talk to him."

"You want me to come with you?"

I shook my head. "You've got to open the shop. Polly's kid is still sick. You don't need to call her in on my account. I'll be safe. I promise."

"I worry about you," she said.

"I know. I love that about you."

She kissed me, and I felt it throughout my body. We hadn't had sex since I'd been shot, and I could have really used it—a little sexual healing, as one of those singers in the 1980s used to say.

"I'll be home around five thirty," she told me.

"I'll see you then."

After she left, Rutherford called back. "Ms. Byrne, I was surprised to hear from you. In your message, you said you knew who swatted Ms. Bitsui. Would you mind telling me who?"

"First, I want your assurance that the cops who shot her and her boyfriend will be arrested."

"I can't give that guarantee at this time. The officers who discharged their weapons are currently on unpaid leave while we investigate. These things take time. But if you give me the name of the person responsible for making the unlawful 911 call, I can assure you that we will prosecute them to the fullest extent of the law."

"So you haven't fired them yet?" I asked.

"Who? The officers? Not yet. We're still reviewing the evidence. Once we have everything, if we feel charges are warranted, we'll impanel a grand jury."

"Well, when you've arrested them for murder, call me. Otherwise, I've got nothing to say."

"Ms. Byrne, if you are withholding evidence, you could be charged with hindering a murder investigation."

"Well, that would be just like the cops to arrest the victims rather than the perpetrators."

"If you tell me who the perpetrator is, I'll arrest them instead," Rutherford said.

"You're not going to arrest me. Haven't you read the headlines? I'm the fucking hero who stopped the Pride Festival massacre."

"You can be a hero again by telling me what you know."

"When those trigger-happy cops have been arrested, call me." I hung up.

She called back, but I sent it to voicemail and started getting ready to do some investigating of my own.

I was in the middle of taking a shower when my phone rang again. I peeked out of the shower stall at my phone. The caller ID said Juniper Library.

"Hello?" I asked, turning off the water.

"Is this Avery Byrne?"

"Yeah."

"This is Mary Holmes from the Juniper Branch of the Phoenix Public Library. We've decided that the Phoenix Gender Alliance will no longer be welcome to hold meetings here."

"What? Why not? Because we're trans?" I asked.

"No, because of the risks. After the incident at your last meeting, we no longer feel it is safe for our employees and patrons to allow the meetings here. I hope you understand."

"No, I don't understand. It's not our fault those fanatics are attacking my community. Ban them, not us. We're just trying to run a support group. And you're siding with these fascists. Well, heil Hitler to you!"

"We're not siding with anyone, Ms. Byrne. And I don't appreciate your attitude. We sympathize with your plight. We consider ourselves allies of the transgender community. But our branch has received hundreds of death threats for allowing your group to meet. I have the safety of our employees and patrons to consider."

"And so you ban us? You think that will stop the threats? Next, these fascists will demand you ban queer books. And when you cave on that, they'll demand you ban queer patrons. They'll keep pushing the goalpost further and further. They won't stop. Any inch you give them, they'll just keep demanding more."

"I understand what you're saying. If it were up to me, I would still welcome you. But the decision's been made at the administrative level. I'm sorry."

"Yeah, right. Well, fuck you and your fellow fake-ally librarians." I hung up. "Fuuucck!" I shouted so loud I could feel the floor vibrate. I hadn't done shit yet, and already this day had gone to hell.

I dried myself off and got dressed, hoping my luck would change. When my damp foot got caught on the inside of my pant leg, the bullet wound burned, and I seriously reconsidered taking a pain pill or two. But I wanted to be clearheaded when I tracked down Wylie.

Once dressed, I called Sophia.

"Getting better every day," she said when I asked. "How about you?"

"Same. The library called. They've banned Phoenix Gender Alliance from meeting there."

"Shit."

"I'm sorry for getting into a fight with those protesters. I was just trying to get them to leave. I didn't mean to cause problems for the group."

"You did what you felt you needed to do. I have no qualms about it. We'll find another place. You and I just have to focus on healing." Then she asked, "Any word on Zoë? I haven't heard anything on the news."

"Not so far. The cops think she ran away, but they're wrong. She wouldn't have run away. Her parents have been nothing but supportive since she came out."

"Yeah, I've known trans kids who ran away. She didn't strike me as the type."

"A friend of Zoë's told me she'd been in contact with her mom's folks."

"The ones who are transphobic? You think they would've kidnapped her?" Sophia asked.

"I don't know. Zoë's mom, Marilyn, says her husband talked to them, and they denied hearing from her. But my gut tells me something weird is going on. I just don't know what it is yet."

"Did you tell the cops?"

"I'm sure Marilyn told the detective on the case. A female detective named Hausman. I also told Hausman that my brother knows where Zoë is, but she ignored me." I told her about talking with my brother. "I'm gonna find her, Sophia, no matter what it takes. We have to protect our own because the cops aren't going to. Not unless someone forces their hand."

"Be careful, Avery. You've been through so much already. I would hate something worse to happen to you."

I struggled to find the words to say next. "Sophia, I think you need to talk with Danielle."

"I thought she—or I guess, he—detransitioned. I saw the video of the Sergeant Rivers interview."

"Yeah, well, there's been a recent development. She tried to commit suicide. I managed to call 911 in time."

"Wow. You're a hero many times over."

Again, that word *hero* got under my skin. "Soph, you need to talk to her. Her phone is working again. I think she's got some things to tell you."

"Like what?"

"It's better if she tells you."

"Oh, okay. Be safe looking for Zoë. I'll see if I can't find us another place to meet."

"Thanks, Sophia. I'll talk to you soon."

I hung up with her and finished getting ready.

CHAPTER 36
SURVEILLANCE

SINCE ROZ OWNED the Spy Gal shop, she had some interesting toys at home. Most were legal, a few not so much. Before leaving to follow up on the addresses that Jinx had given me for Wylie, I dug through her toy box and selected a few things I might need—namely, a parabolic mic, a stun gun, a pair of binoculars, and a burner phone with a cloning app installed.

Now I just had to figure out which of the three addresses was Wylie's residence. I first drove to Scottsdale, since it was closest. The address was an apartment building south of Old Town Scottsdale that looked like it had been built in the 1970s but was well maintained. A young Black man in a U of A sweatshirt opened the door when I knocked. Something about him set off my gaydar, though I'd learned that wasn't always reliable.

"Does Wylie Byrne live here?" I asked.

"Sorry, no." He seemed wary, like at any moment, I might try to sell him solar or ask him if he wanted to join the Jehovah's Witnesses.

"How long have you lived here?"

"About two years. Why?"

"I'm looking for my brother. I think this used to be his place."

"You said Wylie Byrne? I've heard that name recently."

"Probably on the news. He was one of the Pride shooters."

"Shit," he replied, his expression growing ever more suspicious. "That dude was your brother?"

"Estranged."

"Wait, I recognize your face. You were the one that stopped the shooting."

"Not nearly in time."

"Shit. Wow. Why're you looking for him? Shouldn't he be in jail?"

"Someone bailed him out. And he has information about a missing trans girl."

"Zoë something, right?" he asked.

"Yeah, Zoë Hildebrandt. I'm trying to find her."

"Aren't the police looking for her?"

"I'm following leads they won't. I'm hoping to get my brother to tell me what he knows."

"Well, good luck," he said.

I struck out again the Mesa address, where Trump and MAGA stickers covered the back of a Dodge Ram pickup in the driveway of a small ranch house in a seedy neighborhood. A skinny bleached-blonde woman with a scabby face answered the door. For a moment, I thought I'd hit pay dirt.

"Is Wylie Byrne here?"

Her eyes narrowed. "Who wants to know?"

"I'm his sister. Our mother gave this as his address."

"You don't know where your own brother lives?"

"We sort of lost touch a few years ago. I'm trying to orchestrate a family reunion in time for Thanksgiving."

"He lived here a while back, but he moved to Gilbert."

I nodded and tapped the side of my head. "Of course.

Mom's always getting things mixed up these days. Long COVID." It seemed as a good an excuse as any.

"COVID's a myth. Everybody knows that," she declared. "Just an excuse to put the 5G in our bodies so they can control our minds."

I wanted to laugh in her face, but I had better things to do than argue medical science with someone who looked like she'd dropped out in junior high. Come to think of it, I'd dropped out in junior high. But at least I'd learned some basic critical thinking skills first.

"Well, thanks for your help."

The Gilbert address had to be the right one. As I drove south on Country Club Boulevard, I realized I needed a stealthier approach than just knocking on the door. Wylie probably wouldn't be any more inclined to talk to me now than before. But maybe I could use some of Roz's toys to do some old-school surveillance.

I picked up some snacks and a bottle of water then parked a couple of doors down from the final address Jinx had given me. A classic car like the Gothmobile didn't exactly blend in with the other cars and trucks parked on the street. I should have asked Roz to switch with me for the day. But there was nothing I could do about it now.

The house in question was a well-kept beige ranch with sage-green shutters and patches of brown grass and bare dirt for a lawn. A Reelect Trump 2024 sign in the yard was my first clue. The name Byrne had been painted in scrolling letters on the mailbox. This was the place.

So I sat, watching the house, listening to Damaged Soul's new album on my phone. A bag of Funyuns, three spicy chicken taquitos, and one large bottle of water later, I was getting a little antsy. And my bladder was getting full, which added pressure against the wound in my hip. This wasn't working.

"Fuck it." I marched up to the door and knocked.

A woman with straight hair almost to her waist answered. "Whatever you're selling, we ain't interested."

"I'm looking for my brother, Wylie."

Her eyes narrowed. "If you're one of them fake-news journalists, he ain't got nothing to say to you."

"I'm not with the press. He's my brother. My mother asked me to talk to him."

She studied me much like the woman in the gun shop had. "Yeah, I'll see if he wants to talk to you."

She shut the door, and I wondered what I was thinking, driving all the way out there.

A few minutes later, Wylie came to the door, sneering at me. "What the fuck you want, freak?"

I could see from his expression that Wylie was still in a lot of pain—which I'd caused him. A certain amount of satisfaction crept in as I considered the pain he'd inflicted on me and so many in my community.

"Where's Zoë Hildebrandt?"

"I ain't telling you shit," he sneered.

"Her parents are going out of their minds. They're worried about her. If you won't tell me where she is, at least tell those who have her to let her go somewhere safe so she can return home to her family."

"His groomer parents are the reason he's in this mess," he retorted. "He's with people who aren't trying to put a lot of crazy ideas in his head or pump him full of girl hormones."

"She wants those hormones. Being a girl makes her happy, Wylie. Who gave you the authority to decide who someone should be?"

"God did!" With that, he slammed the door shut, and I heard the deadbolt click into place.

I returned to the Gothmobile, still not knowing where Zoë was. But based on what Wylie had said, Zoë had to be alive—possibly at a conversion therapy camp like the one Danielle had been sent to. *But where?*

I'd also managed to clone Wylie's cell to the burner I'd brought along. I quickly scrolled through his text messages. I found nothing new, but I wouldn't have to contact Jinx again the next time Wylie sent a text. I should also be able to listen in on his phone calls.

By that point, I really needed to pee. I was putting the key in the ignition, when a shiny black Mercedes pulled into Wylie's driveway. A familiar-looking man in a dark suit and conservative haircut got out, carrying a briefcase. *A lawyer perhaps?*

I pulled out the binoculars and read the license plate. GETUOFF. *Definitely a lawyer.*

I aimed the parabolic mic at the front door and plugged the other end of the cord into my phone. The stiff in the suit rang the bell, and a moment later, Wylie came out.

"Hey, Mr. Harrow, glad you're here."

Harrow. I remembered where I'd seen him. He'd represented that bitch who attacked me at the library. Ethan Harrow. Fucking weasel. Of course, he'd represent my brother.

"How are you doing, kid?"

Wylie shrugged. "I'm managing."

"The organization appreciates you keeping quiet about the other two shooters."

"Anything for the cause, right? I appreciate them paying your fees and my bail."

"They haven't approached you with any plea deals, have they?"

"Not since you showed up."

The lawyer nodded. "Good. They're not supposed to make any offers without me present, but you never know with these people. They can be pretty unethical if it suits them, especially in a high-profile case like this."

"The only person I've talked to outside of the organization is my brother. The one who shot me. I told him to fuck off."

"Good boy. Shall we go inside and discuss the details of the case?"

They entered the house.

"Shit," I muttered. I was really hoping to listen in on their conversation to find out more about this mysterious organization and the other two shooters and possibly get a lead on Zoë's whereabouts.

I pointed the parabolic mic at one of the house's front windows, having read that glass could pick up vibrations. I was getting snippets of muffled conversation when someone across the street started running a leaf blower, drowning out everything else.

Fuck. Then I remembered I'd cloned his phone. One of the app's features was that I could turn on the original phone's mic and listen in on conversations. *Goth bless modern technology.*

I pulled the burner out of my purse, opened the app, and activated the microphone. Despite the din of the leaf blower, I could make out what Wylie and the lawyer were saying. "I've filed a motion to disallow most of the forensics —gunshot residue, ballistics, and fingerprints," Harrow said. "Without that, it's just he said, she said. They've got no case. I've also filed for a directed verdict. With a little luck, we can get this case thrown out, and you're home free."

"What about the Hildebrandt kid?"

"Why are you asking?" Harrow asked.

"My brother was here a while ago, asking about him."

I bristled at being misgendered.

"We're working hard to undo the brainwashing he got from his woke parents. It's not going as smoothly as we'd like, but sometimes, it just takes time. My associates are going to be helping the grandparents get legal custody and file abuse charges against the parents."

"That's cool."

"Thanks again for keeping your mouth shut. If worse comes to worst and you're convicted, we've got people on the inside who can keep you safe."

"You think we'll lose?" Wylie asked.

"It's a roll of the dice. If I can get these motions to suppress approved, it improves our chances of getting the case dismissed. But one step at a time. This is a marathon, not a sprint."

"Okay, I guess."

"I'm headed back to the club to meet with the leaders and discuss the next phase of our operation. Those freaks won't know what hit them."

"Can't wait," Wylie said.

I heard footsteps, then the front door opened. Harrow shook hands with my brother and left.

CHAPTER 37
MEMBERS ONLY

AS HARROW STROLLED BACK to his car, I snapped a photo of him and debated what to do next. I could keep watching my brother's house, hoping he'd call someone and give me another clue as to Zoë's whereabouts. Or I could follow Harrow. Maybe find Zoë. Maybe find out what this mysterious organization had planned next. Maybe put a stop to it before anyone else in my community got hurt.

And at some point, I needed to take a piss.

I opted to tail the lawyer. I ducked down in my seat when Harrow backed out of the driveway and drove past. I could only hope he didn't notice me. But considering I was driving a classic Cadillac, it would be hard for him not to. The one thing in my favor was that he didn't know I was the one driving it.

Once he reached the corner, I turned around in a driveway and followed. At the intersection with the main road, I lost sight of him. I made my best guess and turned right. A block later, I spotted a black Mercedes with the same vanity plate. I followed at a distance as Harrow drove north.

I replayed their conversation in my mind. *Headed to the*

club. Was he referring to the gun club? Is that where this organiza-
tion is based? Is that how Wylie got involved?

As we crossed over the Red Mountain Parkway, my suspicions were confirmed. He pulled into the gun club's parking lot. I parked in the far corner, facing the front door.

By the time I shut off the ignition, he was on the wrap-around porch, speaking with someone, though I couldn't see who it was. With the binoculars, I could tell she was a woman, but Harrow was blocking my view of her face.

When they shook hands and Harrow continued inside, I nearly dropped the binoculars from shock. The woman was Detective Hausman.

"Motherfucker!"

It's not what you think, I assured myself. *She must have realized that Zoë didn't run away, and she's here, following the lead I gave her.* But part of me wasn't convinced. I wondered why she was all friendly with Harrow.

I watched Hausman get into her car and drive off. *Now what?* I'd cloned Wylie's phone, but I had no way of listening in on the lawyer's conversations.

I considered calling Roz to ask for her advice. She'd probably tell me to go home. I wasn't ready to do that.

After a few minutes, with my bladder near to bursting, I climbed out of the Gothmobile and strode toward the building, hoping the people who'd recognized me before weren't working that day. I had no formal plan. But it beat sitting in the car, waiting for something to happen.

I once again caught the astringent smell of gunpowder and the steady rhythm of gunfire from the indoor gun range. I balled my fists as flashbacks from the Pride Festival massacre threatened to unsettle me. *Focus.*

Harrow was nowhere in sight. Neither were the two people I'd spoken with on my last visit. I approached the counter, where a lumberjack of a guy stood.

"Welcome to Red Mountain Gun Club. How can I help you?"

I held up my phone and showed him the photo I'd taken of Harrow. "Have you seen this guy?"

The lumberjack studied the photo for a second and shook his head. "Nope. Don't look familiar." His expression told me otherwise. "Why you looking for him?"

I considered my options. "A girl's been kidnapped. I think he knows where she is."

The guy tried to maintain an innocent face, but I caught the tell in the corners of his eyes. "Haven't seen him. Sorry."

I considered pressing the issue, but clearly, I wasn't getting any honest answers out of this guy. If Harrow wasn't in the showroom, he had to be in the firing range in back.

"How much to use the firing range?"

"Are you a member?" he asked.

"No, just looking into it."

"I'm afraid our firing range is only available to members."

"How much is it to become a member?"

"Annual membership is four hundred dollars. But first, you have to complete two of our safety courses for liability purposes." He handed me a brochure with the headline *Basic Firearm Safety 101*.

I gave it a cursory glance. "When's the next class?"

"Two weeks. Do you want me to sign you up?"

"Let me think about it."

"You can sign up on our website as well. Until then, you're welcome to look around."

"Okay, thanks."

There was nothing left for me to see, so I headed back to the car. I really needed to pee. As I was considering using the restroom at the Iron Eagle bar next door, Sophia called.

"What's up, Sophia?"

"It's Danielle. She…" Her voice choked with emotion.

A flurry of conflicting emotions swirled inside me. "What about her?"

"I can't believe it. She's been arrested. Detective Rutherford called. She said Danielle confessed to making the bogus 911 call. That she's the reason Étienne is dead."

"Wow." I tried to sound surprised. And in a way, I was surprised that Danielle turned herself in after all.

"Why would she do that?" Sophia asked. "We were nothing but nice to her."

"I don't think it's anything we've done. She's just been going through a lot of shit lately. Money problems. Issues with her phobic dad. People do stupid things."

"But we're her family."

"I know. It's fucked-up. She fucked up."

"Well, she's about to find out." There was steel in Sophia's words. "I never thought I'd say this about another trans woman, but I hope she spends the rest of her life in prison—in a men's prison."

"I hear you." I dreaded to think what Danielle would endure, but karma really could be a bitch sometimes, even without my help.

"Any news on Zoë?" Sophia asked.

"Nothing definite. Just a few leads I'm following."

"What about the police?"

I recalled Detective Hausman chatting with Harrow on the steps of the gun club. "Who knows?"

I started wondering if Zoë had been sent to the same conversion therapy camp that Danielle had. I needed to talk to Danielle. But now that she'd been arrested, I wasn't sure how.

Roz called in on call-waiting. "Hey, Soph. I gotta go. Roz is calling. But thanks for the update. Take care of yourself."

"Talk to you soon, sister."

I switched over to the other call.

"Hey, sexy," Roz said. "How's the sleuthing going?"

"Very revelatory. I cloned my brother's phone and listened in on a conversation between him and his lawyer." I filled her in on the details.

"You're not doing anything dangerous, are you?"

"Who, me? No, I'm safe. Just surveillance."

"So, what's your plan now?" she asked.

"I don't know. I drank too much water when I was watching my brother's house. My back teeth are floating."

"The joys of surveillance. That's why my dad always carried an empty bottle. Of course, it's a bit trickier when you're a woman."

"Tell me about it."

"Well, good luck, and keep me updated. And stay safe."

"Always. Love you," I said.

"Love you too."

I made a beeline for the bar. "Where's your restroom?" I asked the bartender.

He pointed to a hallway past the pool tables.

"Thanks."

As I sat in the stall, emptying my bladder, I noticed the graffiti. You could always get a sense of a place by the shit random people wrote on the wall, especially after they'd had a few. I expected the usual dirty messages, but what I read on the wall at the Iron Eagle was on a whole other level. It read more like the garbage posted by anonymous trolls on Twitter—more racist and homophobic than raunchy.

I got out of there as quickly as I could and left with a quick thank-you to the bartender. *Note to self: limit liquids when conducting surveillance.*

Once outside, I scanned the parking lot for Harrow's Mercedes. It was gone.

"Fuck!"

Now what? I could drive all the way out down to my brother's house in Gilbert, but what good would it do? After a few minutes, I started the Gothmobile and drove home.

CHAPTER 38
THE AMBUSH

I ARRIVED home at two thirty in the afternoon. The wound in my hip was burning. I considered taking a pain pill, but if I had to go out again, it would be a bad idea. I was stupid to have driven while on the pain pills before. *No use pushing my luck.*

After an hour, the pain worsened, and I relented. The ibuprofen just wasn't cutting it, so I took one pill, hoping that would suffice. Meanwhile, I kept an eye on the clone phone. So far, nothing—no phone calls, no texts. I'd managed to access Wylie's social media feeds, which were filled with right-wing propaganda but nothing indicating where Zoë might be held or the identity of this mysterious organization that was paying Wylie's legal bills.

I started compiling a list of the people Wylie followed and those following him. Most of the accounts didn't have actual names, just handles. I had no idea if any of them were local. They were just a bunch of anonymous trolls who could be anywhere in the world.

Around four o'clock, Wylie sent a text to Cameron. The name sounded vaguely familiar, but with my head swirling from the Tramadol, I couldn't place it.

WYLIE:

Harrow says cops are seriously looking for you. Suggests you lay low.

CAMERON:

Cant, dude. Gotta work. But ur sis was at the club again today.

WYLIE:

That thing aint my sister. It was my brother. Now its just garbage.

CAMERON:

Amen, bro.

WYLIE:

Cops still dont know ur nm AFAIK. Aint told them shit. Maybe take some time off.

CAMERON:

Cant. Used my PTO when I got sick last mo.

WYLIE:

Do what you gotta do, bro. But watch your back.

CAMERON:

U2.

I stared at the screen, wondering how I could use this to my advantage. I couldn't get Wylie to talk, but maybe I'd have better luck with his buddy Cameron. As the Tramadol took the edge off the pain, a plan coalesced in my mind. Avery the avenger could get Cameron to talk.

Roz got home a little after five thirty.

"How was your day?" I asked.

"Long. It was dead this afternoon. I just wanted to come home and be with you. I have to think of ways to drum up some business, especially with the holidays coming. Any new developments?"

"I think I know one of the other shooters from the Pride Festival massacre." I told her what I'd learned and what I planned to do.

"Avery, this sounds dangerous. Especially with your injuries. And these guys don't play."

"That's why we have to be smart about this. I've given it a lot of thought. I can make this guy talk."

"You sure about that?" She looked skeptical.

"I'm pretty sure."

"Pretty sure?"

"Sweetie, that poor girl's life is on the line. You've heard the horror stories about conversion therapy. It's fucking torture. But if you're not willing to risk it to save a little girl's life…"

"I didn't say I wasn't willing to risk it." Roz sat next to me on the love seat. "If you believe this guy knows where she is and you can get him to talk, I'll back your play. But you remember what happened when you followed that guy who robbed the Yushan microchip plant last year. You nearly got us both killed."

"I know."

"You should tell that detective who's looking for Zoë what you learned. They get paid to risk their lives."

"Roz, she may be in on it. I saw her talking to Wylie's lawyer. In front of the gun club no less."

"Shit."

"Yeah, shit. So if that fucking detective is dirty, what chance does Zoë have unless we do something?"

Roz didn't say anything for several minutes. I could see the worry on her face. Not that I blamed her. My plan was ridiculous and probably wouldn't work. It might just get us both killed. But it might also be the only way to save Zoë.

"Okay, I'm in. But let's try to keep this as low-risk as possible. Wait here." She disappeared into the bedroom for a minute and returned holding a large handgun, a Glock by the looks of it.

My jaw hit the floor. I'd lived with her for a year and never knew she owned one of those. "You've got a gun?"

"Bought it a few years ago. I was closing up the shop one night, and there were these two creepy white guys hanging around the parking lot."

"Did they... did they sexually assault you?"

She shook her head. "No, they were just hanging out, smoking. A couple of high school kids by the look of them. But what if...? So I bought this just in case. Took some classes, got my concealed carry permit. Whole nine yards."

"How did I not know you had one?"

"After a few months of carrying it around in my purse, I decided it was more trouble than it was worth. The legal liability seemed to outweigh the physical risks of not carrying it. If I shot at someone and missed, I could hit an innocent bystander. I could be liable for murder or, at the very least, involuntary manslaughter. I could go to prison. So I put it away and forgot about it. Does it bother you I have it?"

"No, just surprised as hell is all."

"I haven't cleaned it in over a year. At this rate, I might get off one good shot before it jams."

"Then let's clean it," I said. "May come in handy. Are you a good shot?"

"Against paper targets? Sure. Against a human target? Guess I won't know until I'm in that situation."

I nodded. "Well, let's hope you don't have to find out. If my plan works, we won't need it. Do you have another one?"

"No, just the one. I do have a Taser."

"I guess that will have to do."

I used the cloned phone to send a text to Cameron, hoping it wouldn't alert my brother.

ME:

> Dude, we need 2 talk in person. Meet me at the bldg supply warehouse past the club at 2300 hrs. Do not reply. Radio silence. Cops watching.

I wasn't sure if he would show up, but I was running out of options. Even if Zoë was still alive, I had to stop these fuckers from torturing her before she took her own life or was killed.

CHAPTER 39
CAMERON

AT ELEVEN O'CLOCK, we arrived at the Summit Building Supply, a half mile west of the Red Mountain Gun Club. The lights of Mesa gleamed to the south while the western sky held the glow from Phoenix. To the north, the flat desert of the Salt River Pima reservation stretched into inky blackness.

The building-supply parking lot was dark, with not even security lights to blot out the stars twinkling above. Roz parked her SUV next to a mud-caked dump truck.

I took out the Bluetooth speaker Roz had gifted me for my birthday. I'd listened to some of my playlists on it, and the clarity and power were unbelievable.

"You planning on listening to some tunes while we wait?" Roz asked.

I stepped out of the Gothmobile. I hadn't had a pain pill in hours, and my mind was clear. "Nope. I have another use for it." I placed the speaker by the front wheel of the car then walked around to the other side of the dump truck and connected my phone to it. "Testing, one, two, three, four." My voice came out of the speaker.

"Holy shit, babe. Sounds like you're right over there."

"That's the plan."

Roz drew her pistol and handed me the Taser. It was heavier than I'd expected, and I hoped I could use it well enough on the first shot. We hid on the far side corner of the dump truck and waited.

Right at eleven thirty, a large pickup pulled up next to the Gothmobile. Peeking around the dump truck, I recognized the driver as the man who'd called me out at the gun club. Another flashback hit me hard. Once again, my ears echoed with the memory of gunfire. My nose burned with the stink of gunpowder. Cameron was one of the shooters at the Pride Parade. Anger rose up hot inside me and raced through my veins. It was time for payback.

I spoke into my phone, dropping the register of my voice to sound more masculine. "Hey, Cameron, I'm over here. Behind the Caddy."

Cameron turned and walked toward the speaker. "Where the hell are you? And why meet here?"

"Over here," I again said through the speaker.

He picked up the speaker, his back to us. "What the hell?"

I stepped out from behind the truck and fired the Taser, hitting him square in the back. For a moment, I feared he might be wearing a Kevlar vest. You never knew with these gun nuts.

But luck was on our side. His body went rigid, and he collapsed onto his side as the current surged through him. I rushed over, grabbed his wallet and the pistol I found in his waistband, and secured him with a pair of flex-cuffs. Roz had all the best toys.

"Whud da..." He grunted.

I gave the wallet to Roz then stood in front of him, Taser in one hand and his pistol in the other. "Surprise, motherfucker!" I exclaimed, a line I'd wanted to use ever since I'd heard Sergeant Doakes say it on an episode of *Dexter*.

Cameron scowled at me. "You? Wylie's tranny brother?"

"Sister actually. And you're Wylie's buddy Cameron. One of the Pride Festival massacre shooters."

Roz stuck her Glock in her waistband and dug through his wallet. "Driver's license says he's Cameron Shrike. Lives on Cullumber Avenue in Gilbert."

"Cameron Shrike. I remember you. A fucking junkie who went by the name Cammy Shakes back when you hung out with that loser, Vinnie D."

"Till you killed him," Cameron said.

A thrill of anger lanced down my spine. My grip on his gun tightened. "He shoulda kept his hands to himself."

"I showed up at that house, looking for you. That house you and your little friends were squatting in. Except you weren't home. So I did the next best thing."

A flood of memories surfaced. Vinnie D. had been a pimp who liked beating up on his girls, including two of the Lost Kids. So one night, I crept into the dump where he lived and found him, Cammy Shakes, and another junkie passed out after shooting up with heroin. I refilled the syringe sticking out of Vinnie's arm and gave him an overdose.

Cameron must have been one of the junkies on the filthy couch nearby. He'd seemed pretty out of it, but he must have noticed me. And later, he took his revenge. I'd returned to the house after fencing some stolen goods to find the other Lost Kids slaughtered.

"You murdered the Lost Kids."

"Who?"

"The kids I was living with in the house."

A nasty smirk crossed his face. "You hurt mine. I hurt yours. And I'm gonna fuck you and your bitch girlfriend up good when I get out of this."

I zapped him again with the Taser, silencing his taunts. "Listen up, asshole. You aren't gonna do shit except answer my fucking questions. And if you don't, I'll keep lighting you up like a motherfucking Christmas tree. You got me?"

Despite the pain, he laughed. "Ain't telling you shit, bitch." Another jolt of the juice wiped the smile off his face. "Grnnngh."

"I wonder how many times I can do this before his heart gives out?" I asked Roz.

"I suppose there's only one way to find out," she replied.

"Okay, okay. Fuck."

"Question number one: What paramilitary group are you and Wylie a part of?" I asked.

All mirth was gone from his expression. His eyes blazed with murderous rage, a look I'd seen many times with my father.

"I'm waiting, Cammy."

"Sovereign Sons."

My eyes tracked to the lightning SS tattoo on his neck, identical to the one that Wylie had. *SS—Sovereign Sons. Makes sense.*

"Who's in charge?"

"Not. Telling. You," he growled between breaths. Another jolt had him screaming in pain. "Help! Please! Somebody!"

"Cammy, dude. We're in the middle of nowhere at midnight. No one's going to hear you but the coyotes and the ringtails. Who's in charge of the Sovereign Sons?"

"Fuck you!"

I kicked him in the nuts. "You want to live, you'd best start talking."

"Colonel Odin," Cameron grunted.

"That's his name? Colonel Odin?"

"That's what everybody calls him. Don't know his real name. Honest."

"Where would I find him? Where's he live?"

"Dunno."

"How about the third shooter at Pride Festival massacre?"

"That was him. Colonel Odin."

I decided to move on to what I really wanted to know. "Where is Zoë Hildebrandt?"

When he refused to answer, I shocked once more, this time for several seconds. He passed out, and I kicked him till he came to. "Where's Zoë, Cammy? I know you know."

His cries echoed across the desert with no one to hear him. "Stop," he whimpered. "Please, stop."

"Tell me what I want to know, and you and my brother can go back to playing heil Hitler."

He gasped. "Okay, okay. The kid's at our camp with a bunch of other queers."

"Where?"

"In the national forest south of Ironwood."

"Where exactly?"

"Dunno. Down some of the dirt roads up there."

"Who knows where it is exactly?"

"Colonel Odin. He's the girl's grandfather."

"Zoë's grandfather? Joseph Patterson?" I asked.

"Yeah, I guess."

"He's the leader of your little neo-Nazi group?"

Cameron nodded.

"Is Detective Hausman working with you people?"

After a moment, he said, "Yeah."

"Motherfucker! Who's in charge? You know I'll just keep shocking you until you tell me. Or until you die screaming."

"We are the Sovereign Sons," he replied mechanically. "We stand strong in our sacred duty to protect this country. To keep it pure. We are a new nobility based on blood and soil. We shall destroy all enemies of God. We are the Sovereign Sons."

I'd seen this rant before, though I wasn't sure where. *At the gun club? No. Somewhere else.*

"Who's in charge of the Sovereign Sons, Cameron? Tell me, or I swear I will kill you."

"Then do it, bitch," he grunted. "'Cause when I get free, I'm gonna rip your head off and rape you both. You're gonna feel the wrath of the—"

I pulled the trigger but not on the Taser. Cameron's gun thundered, and a hole oozed blood from his temple. A puddle of gore spread on the pavement, surrounding his head like a halo.

Roz gasped. "Shit!" she said, her voice barely audible over the ringing in my ears. She stared in shock at the body.

I quickly wiped down Cameron's gun with my shirt and tossed it beside him then yanked the Taser darts from his back. "Come on! We gotta go."

"You killed him," she said.

"Yeah, well, he had it coming. He murdered my friends—not just a week ago but a few years back, when I was homeless. So fuck him. Now, let's go!"

When she continued staring at him, I guided her into the passenger seat of the Gothmobile, hopped behind the wheel, and made for the Red Mountain Parkway.

CHAPTER 40
RULES OF WAR

WE DROVE BACK to our apartment in awkward silence. There were so many things I wanted to say, but I wasn't sure where to start. I was feeling a thousand different emotions, and I was sure Roz was too.

Cameron wasn't the first person I'd killed. And not the last, the way things were going. But I'd learned a long time ago that the legal system and justice were two very different things. More often than not, the legal system did little more than protect powerful white men from the consequences of their actions while the rest of us struggled for equality.

When we got home, Roz lay down on our love seat, staring blankly at the wall.

"You coming to bed?" I asked.

"Not yet. I've got some thinking to do."

"You mad at me for what I did?"

"I just keeping seeing you killing that man in cold blood. A man who was unarmed and handcuffed. You executed him."

"You think I should've uncuffed him and given him his gun back? Make it a fair fight? What do you think he would've done? He already slaughtered several of us at the

Trans March. He murdered the Lost Kids. The rules no longer apply when it comes to human garbage like that."

"I know, but..."

"We're at war, Roz. These people are actual Nazis. Zoë's own grandfather kidnapped her and took her to this conversion therapy camp. And Detective Hausman, who was supposed to be looking for her, is involved in her abduction. So if the cops aren't playing by the rules, why should we?"

"I hear what you're saying," she said.

"You told me your great-grandfather was a Nazi hunter. He hunted down those bastards who escaped Germany after the war. Right?"

"He did."

"You think he worried whether the fuckers he killed were unarmed? These Sovereign Sons neo-Nazis are literally rounding people up, putting them in camps, and torturing them. And half the people who undergo conversion therapy attempt suicide. It's the Holocaust all over again, only with queer people."

Rather than reply, she simply hugged me and held me for several minutes. Before I knew it, we were sobbing in each other's arms. We only released each other when her phone rang.

"Hello? Hey, Mr. Goldstein. Yes, I heard." Her face flushed, and she broke into tears. "You're sure? Absolutely sure?"

I clasped her hand for support.

She nodded. "Thank you for telling me."

When she hung up, I asked, "Well?"

She took a deep breath. "The hostages that IDF shot, they weren't my family."

"Oh, thank goth."

"But they were somebody's family. They were our age."

"It fucking sucks. Did he know anything about your family?"

"He said they're making progress on the negotiations. It's still just wait and see."

I sighed. "Roz, I understand if you don't want to be involved in helping me track down Zoë."

She cradled my face in her hands, and her eyes locked with mine. "Babe, I'm already involved. You're my family. I hate that it's come to this—that we have to kill in order to protect ourselves. But you're right. We are at war. We're fighting for our very survival. And I'll be fighting alongside you."

Emotion made me choke on my words. "Thank you."

"So, what's our next move?" she asked.

"Zoë's grandfather and Detective Hausman know where that camp is. But I don't know how to force them to tell us where it is."

She nodded. "Let's get some sleep. We'll figure it out in the morning."

CHAPTER 41
TROUBLE AT SEOUL FIRE

ALL NIGHT LONG, I debated my next move. I now knew that the Sovereign Sons were behind the Pride Festival massacre, Zoë's kidnapping, and probably other recent acts of violence against the trans community. Cameron had also confirmed that both Zoë's grandfather—Joseph Patterson—and that bitch Detective Hausman were involved. If I could track down Patterson, I might be able to get the location of the camp and rescue Zoë.

When I finally got up, I texted Marilyn.

ME:

> Zoë is at conv therapy camp. Hausman & ur dad are involved. Tell me whr he is. Ill find her.

During breakfast, I searched the internet for the Sovereign Sons. Their website was spewing typical Nazi, right-wing, fascist nonsense with a blog full of clips from Sergeant Troy Rivers's *River of Truth* YouTube channel and links to bogus news stories accusing trans people of being arrested as sexual predators or for assaulting women in restrooms.

A quick search of the actual stories revealed that in each case, the trans people were the victims, not the perpetrators. But that didn't stop Sergeant Rivers or the Sovereign Sons from twisting the facts to make us look like the villains.

I also found social media pages for the Sovereign Sons, but again, no direct way to contact them, and most of the followers used fake names and had no profile photos—typical troll behavior.

I then researched Sergeant Troy Rivers, since he was local and a key player in the spread of hateful transphobic misinformation. But aside from clickbait stories in mainstream media that highlighted Rivers's latest outrageous claims, there was nothing of substance.

Rivers had pushed his own daughter to betray her community. His rhetoric fueled the violence against us. But I wasn't sure what to do about him.

Marilyn called back as I was getting dressed. "Avery, are you sure about all this? She's at a conversion therapy camp?"

"Somewhere near Ironwood. Your father knows the exact location."

"I… I don't know what to say. How do you know this?"

"Best you don't ask."

"And Detective Hausman?" she asked.

"I saw her talking with my brother's lawyer. They looked awfully chummy. They're all part of a neo-Nazi group called Sovereign Sons."

"Oh, Avery. What am I going to do? Who can I trust?"

"You trust me, Marilyn. Just tell me where he lives. I will find him. I will make him tell me where she is. And I will bring her home."

"He lives in Gilbert." She gave me his exact address.

"Text me his photo. I'll bring her home. I promise."

When I hung up, Roz asked, "So, what's the plan?"

"I'm going to pay Colonel Odin, aka Grampa Joe Patterson, a visit."

"I'd go with you, but Polly's daughter is still sick. But I don't think you should go alone."

"They're torturing her, sweetie. Someone has to step up for her."

Roz hugged me. "Please be careful. And try not to kill anyone."

"I'll try, but no promises."

That got a smile out of her.

I found Patterson's place in a neighborhood of two-story houses. There was a Ford Explorer with a veteran license plate and a decal in the window that I recognized as a service ribbon for Operation Desert Storm. I knocked on the door, and a few minutes later, a gray-haired woman in a sweater answered. The security screen door remained between us.

"Can I help you?" she asked.

"I'm looking for Joseph Patterson."

"Well, I'm sorry, young lady, but he isn't here."

"Where is he?"

"Who are you?"

"I'm a friend of Marilyn's."

"And why are you looking for my husband?"

"I think you know why," I replied with steel in my voice. "He kidnapped Zoë. I intend to bring her home safe. So tell me where they are."

"I don't know who you are, miss, but you need to leave before I call the police."

I wasn't sure if she was bluffing. She might not dare call the cops when her husband was the one who abducted a kid. Unless she called another dirty cop like Hausman.

"Tell me where they are, lady. There are laws against kidnapping children."

Rather than reply, she closed the door. I heard muffled voices like she was calling someone. *Shit.*

I drove off, struggling to come up with another way to locate Zoë. But I was too pissed and frustrated to think straight. No matter what I tried, I seemed to run into roadblocks. I couldn't call the cops or even the feds because I didn't know who I could trust.

I trusted Detective Rutherford some. And Detective Valentine seemed honest if incompetent. But they both worked for Phoenix PD. Zoë lived in Peoria. So unless I could prove that she'd been kidnapped within the Phoenix city limits, they would have no jurisdiction.

I remembered something that Bobby had told me once: "Whenever you're feeling blocked, do something else for a while. Trying to force a solution rarely works. But while your conscious mind is focused on something else, your subconscious mind will continue picking at the problem until a solution presents itself."

He'd been talking about creative blocks. At the time, I'd been struggling with designing a tattoo in the style that my client had requested. And Bobby was right. After I'd spent a few hours doing housework, an idea popped into my head out of the blue. That design had earned me a writeup in *Inked Magazine.*

But would it work for something like rescuing Zoë? I wasn't sure. The last thing I wanted to do was put my search on hold and sit at home. I'd sooner eat glass or listen to Kenny G.

I called Bobby.

"Hey, kiddo. How's the leg?" he asked.

"Better. I'm thinking of coming back to work."

"You sure? No need to rush things. If you need help financially…"

"I'm fine. I can stand and walk. I'm off the pain pills. I'm ready."

"Well, okay, then. I look forward to seeing you. Although you might want to park behind the building."

"Why?"

"There are... well, you'll see when you get here."

I didn't like the ominous tone in his voice. "Appa, what's going on?"

"Just park in back. Everything will be fine. I'll see you soon, kiddo."

When I stepped outside, the air was noticeably cooler, a welcome relief from the blistering summer temperatures. I took it as a good omen for the day. The feeling was short-lived, however.

Around ten o'clock, I pulled into the parking lot for the shopping center that Seoul Fire Tattoo Studio shared with a hair salon and a Mexican bakery. A boisterous crowd of about forty people was gathered outside. A dozen were clearly members of the Sovereign Sons—with combat gear, balaclavas, and assault rifles slung over their backs.

Others held signs with transphobic slogans, many of them misspelled: Arrest the Groomers... HRT Is Child Abuse... Transgenerism Is a Diseese... Stop Mutalating Kids. Two mentioned me by name, sort of—Avery Burns Is a Pedaphile, and Avery the Perv.

Fury rose up in me, and I was tempted to confront them. But I kept my cool, continuing around to the back side of the building. This wasn't the time or place for a confrontation. I didn't need a reenactment of what had happened at the library. In war, strategy and tactics mattered, and when one was grossly outnumbered, open combat was foolish.

Even inside the studio, the shouts and chanting from the crowd were loud enough to rattle my nerves. Bobby was the only one working on a client. Everyone else sat at their empty stations.

"Where's everyone's clients?" I asked.

"Scared off." Frisco poked a thumb toward the mob

outside. "Got one client coming in an hour, but I'm afraid she might cancel when she sees what's going on."

"I had no idea what I was walking into when I came on board," Dakota added.

"How long has this been going on?" I asked Bobby.

He sighed. "A couple days."

"And you didn't mention it?"

"They'll soon grow tired, and things will return to normal."

"They were protesting even though I wasn't even here?"

Bobby shrugged. "They're bigots, kiddo. Don't expect them to be rational. All they know how to do is spew hate and cause trouble. They're sheep."

"We should call the cops," I said.

"We already did," Frisco said. "A couple of Glendale cops showed up but insisted they had a right to protest."

"This is private property," I said.

"I spoke with the landlord," Bobby said. "He didn't want to get involved."

"I did some research on him." Frisco sat in her chair, reading the latest issue of *Skin Deep*. "He's a Trumper, so he's going to side with them. Personally, I wouldn't give a shit, but they've been harassing our clients. I've had two people cancel just today. I wish there were a few more parking spaces in back."

"There's got to be something we can do. We'll lose business."

"It will all blow over in a few days," Bobby insisted. "If you agitate them, it will only make things worse."

So much for trying to get my mind off of finding Zoë. Those bigoted bastards just wouldn't let up. I called Joni Loloma, a longtime client who lived up in Tuba City. Eager for me to finish an elaborate back piece I'd been working on for six months, she agreed to come in later that morning.

"There's a protest going on out front," I warned her.

"Park on the far side of the lot, away from the building, then walk around and knock on the back door. I'll let you in."

While I waited for Joni to show, I looked up the city of Ironwood on Google Maps, hoping I could spot where this Sovereign Sons camp was located. But the national forest south of the city was home to several campgrounds accessed via a maze of paved and unpaved roads. Some offered cabins to rent. Others were run by church organizations. None had any obvious connection to the Sovereign Sons.

When Joni arrived, she looked spooked. "What's with the protests?"

"It's about me. A bunch of right-wing haters found out I work here."

"That's right. I forgot you were transgender."

"I wish I could forget. But these idiots won't let me."

We reached my station, and she pulled off her jacket and shirt, revealing a bikini top. The design I'd been working on was three-quarters complete and was healing up nicely.

"Have you called the cops?" she asked.

I started getting her prepped. "Bobby did. Apparently, they don't care, and neither does the landlord."

"Aren't you afraid they'll attack the shop?"

"A little. But there's not much we can do until that happens."

I got to work on the design—a stylized scene depicting the legend of Spider Grandmother helping the Hopi people emerge into the Fourth World. I felt honored that she allowed me to do it, considering I was Anglo. The design was coming along well, and she was pleased with the results so far.

Periodically, I glanced outside. Despite what Bobby had predicted, the protesters seemed to be growing in number and becoming louder. I could barely hold a conversation with Joni because of the din.

CHAPTER 42
SISTERHOOD

AN HOUR OR SO LATER, I nearly jumped out of my skin when Butcher yelled, "Son of a bitch!"

I looked up to see him with his phone in his hand. "What's wrong, Butch?"

"Another client canceled. Those stupid protesters. I need to work."

"I'm sorry, man. It's not right you're losing business because of me."

"Not your fault. You're a good kid." He pointed outside at the crowd. "They're the problem. But there's nothing we can do."

"Maybe there is." I'd been thinking while I inked my client. "Joni, you about ready for a bathroom break?"

"Sure."

While she headed to the restroom, I called my friend Zia Pearson, a member of the Phoenix Gender Alliance who worked for the Lambda Resource Center in Ironwood. She served as a liaison with the Cortes County Sheriff's Office. I wondered if she might have contacts in the Glendale Police Department.

"Hey, Avery, I heard what happened at the Pride Parade. How're you holding up?"

"I'm out of the hospital and back at work. Which is why I'm calling. You got any friends at Glendale PD?"

"Glendale? No. Why? What's up?"

"There's a mob of protesters outside the tattoo studio. We called the cops, but they said that unless the landlord wants them gone, there's nothing they can do."

"And the landlord doesn't want them gone?" Zia asked.

"He's a MAGA Republican, apparently."

"Damn. I'm sorry. Look, I'm with the Sisterhood on a ride down to Organ Pipe Cactus National Monument. You just caught me as we're gassing up near Eloy."

The Athena Sisterhood Motorcycle Club was an all-women's biker group with chapters across the western US. I'd inked several of their members over the years. Officially, they were not an outlaw biker gang. Rumor was a few of them were law enforcement. But I knew from the stories that they weren't afraid to cross the line if it meant protecting friends of the club.

"I can make some calls when I get back to Ironwood if you like. See if I can get you some help. Would that work?"

"I suppose," I replied dejectedly.

"How bad is it?"

"I'm guessing sixty, maybe seventy protesters. About a dozen of them look like members of the Sovereign Sons."

"The Sons? How do you know?" Zia asked.

"Body armor, assault weapons, white-power tattoos. They're harassing anyone who tries to approach the shop. Several of our clients have canceled appointments. And they keep getting louder."

I held my phone toward the front door, where the crowd shouted a string of slurs. "Tranny! Faggot! Groomer! Pervert! Child molester! Rapist!"

"Hear that?" I asked when I put the phone back to my ear.

"Tell you what—I may have a solution. Call ya back in a minute, okay?" Zia asked.

"Yeah."

Joni returned to my station. "Wow! I could hear them all the way from the restroom."

Just as I was getting gloved up to get back to work, my phone rang. "Avery, the Sisters and I will be there in a couple of hours. Can you hold out that long?" Zia asked.

I looked out at the increasingly raucous crowd. The members of the Sovereign Sons, who'd had semiautomatic rifles slung over their backs, now held them in their arms. "If you could make it closer to an hour, that would be great."

"We'll get there as quick as we can."

I got back to work on my client, but the transphobic slurs and shouts of violence had me rattled. It was hard to get into my creative zone with all that going on. Still, there wasn't much I could do. I practiced some of the mind-focusing breathing techniques Bobby had taught me when I was a teenager. They seemed to help, but I still couldn't get into a flow state. The lines I was creating weren't as clean as they should have been. I considered asking Joni to postpone, but I pressed on.

Around noon, the deep rumble of dozens of motorcycles overtook the endless shouts of the rabble. I'd never seen so many bikes in one place. There had to be at least thirty, maybe more. Joni had left, and I didn't have another client scheduled.

"What's that?" Frisco asked, looking out the plate glass window.

"The Athena Sisterhood," I proudly announced. "Come to send those assholes packing."

Bobby held my gaze with a worried expression. "You called in a motorcycle gang?"

"Our clients shouldn't have to risk their lives just to get inked, Appa. If the cops won't help and the landlord won't help, then it's time to bring in someone who can." I approached the front door.

"Avery, do not go out that door," Bobby warned. "We don't need the situation escalating into violence."

"Sorry, Appa. Those douchebags showed up looking for a fight. It's time we fight back."

I pushed open the door just as Zia Pearson reached it. She had long blue braids interspersed with her naturally black ones. Like the other Sisters, she wore a bulletproof vest and leather chaps. Accompanying Zia was a white woman with a pixie cut.

"Avery, I think you may know our VP, Havoc," Zia said.

I shook Havoc's hand. I knew her by her real name, Shea Stevens. "Of course. I inked that Celtic-knot armband on your left biceps. Good to see you again, and thanks for showing up."

"I'd heard about the trouble those neo-Nazi thugs had been causing down here in the Valley," Havoc said. "Soon as Indigo called us, I figured it was time to join the party."

It took me a second to realize that Indigo was Zia's biker nickname.

"My foster dad, Bobby J., doesn't want things to get violent, but our clients are afraid to show up for fear of being harassed or worse. Can the Sisterhood help without bloodshed?"

Havoc shrugged. "We'll do the best we can to de-escalate the situation and get these assholes to move on."

I stood by the door as a dozen members of the Athena Sisterhood rode their motorcycles to form a line between the crowd and the front door. The Sovereign Sons raised their weapons, as did the Sisterhood. Shouts between the two sides grew louder. The women formed a solid line, two deep, from one end of the parking lot to the other, completely blocking off the building from the protesters.

The tension grew so thick I feared the confrontation would erupt into a bloodbath. But though the size of the mob was large, only a dozen of them were neo-Nazi militia. The Athena Sisterhood outnumbered the Sovereign Sons three to one.

A Sister with hair cut in a short bob held a badge high in the air, facing the crowd. "Ladies and gentlemen, I am Trooper Calvin of the Arizona Department of Public Safety. I am ordering you to disperse immediately. Should you refuse, my deputized associates and I will arrest you."

The Sovereign Sons at first did not appear willing to back down and instead shouted louder. The rest of the protesters joined in.

"Biker bitches!"

"Fucking dykes on bikes!"

"You ain't no cop!"

"Get the fuck out of here!"

As one, the Sisterhood advanced toward the militia members. They might have been women, but there was nothing soft or feminine about the way they drove the Sovereign Sons backward step-by-step. I couldn't help but smile.

Just as I was hoping things would be resolved without gunfire and bloodshed, a shot rang out. The unarmed protesters fled, screaming. The Sisters took advantage of the confusion and, in the blink of an eye, disarmed the outnumbered Sovereign Sons.

I scanned the crowd to see if anyone had been hit, but no one appeared injured. *Thank goth for that.* In a matter of minutes, the dozen or so Sovereign Sons lay on their bellies, hands flex-cuffed behind their backs. Their weapons were piled up on the sidewalk.

I started to relax until the *whoop-whoop* of police sirens

caught my attention. Glendale PD patrol cars blocked off the exit. Uniformed officers jumped out, their weapons trained on the Sisterhood, demanding that they get down on the ground.

Smokey once again held up her badge. "Trooper Calvin, Arizona DPS. These are the people you want to arrest." She gestured toward the Sons in their combat gear. "They were harassing innocent civilians entering the businesses and threatening violence to the employees. We had no choice but to alleviate the threat."

Not taking chances, the Glendale PD nevertheless disarmed the Sisterhood and me, since I was standing with them. For thirty minutes, we sat cuffed on the sidewalk in front of Seoul Fire while the Sovereign Sons were cuffed at the other end of the shopping center. I caught Bobby looking out from inside the studio, a mask of concern on his face. A bullet hole marked the wall separating Seoul Fire from La Panaderia Sol next door. Judging from the trajectory of the shot, I guessed the bullet must have come from one of the Sovereign Sons' weapons. If it had hit a foot to the left, someone inside the bakery could have been killed.

Smokey spent several minutes speaking with the police lieutenant. I couldn't hear the conversation, but there was a lot of gesturing and pointing. Eventually, Smokey returned to us, accompanied by three uniformed officers.

"Good news, ladies," she said. "We're free to go."

One of the officers snipped the flex-cuffs holding me. I rubbed my raw wrists, trying to restore feeling to my tingling fingers. I wondered if I'd be able to do more tattoo work for the rest of the day, assuming I could get another client or two to show.

"The bad news," Smokey continued, "is they're letting the Sovereign Sons go as well. But they and the other protesters have to leave and are not allowed to return. Otherwise, they'll be arrested."

"Do the Sisterhood have to leave too?" I asked, fearful of what might happen if they were.

"We explained to the officers that we're here to get new tattoos, so we have a legitimate business reason to be here. The Sovereign Sons and the protesters do not."

I breathed a sigh of relief. "Any tattoos you all want are on me. Thank you so much for helping out."

Once the Sovereign Sons, the other protesters, and the police were gone, I accompanied the Sisters inside and explained to Bobby what had happened, leaving out the part about the bullet embedded in the wall.

"Avery," Bobby said, a stern look on his face. "I'm not happy with how you handled this. Things could've ended very badly. Innocent people could've been killed. You could've been killed."

"I know, Appa, but those armed militia men were ready to storm this place anyway. If the Sisterhood hadn't shown up, things could've gone so much worse. Did the Rebel Alliance sit on their hands when faced with the Death Star—or the second Death Star or the third Death Star?"

Bobby grasped my hand. "No, they did not. I don't know if your actions today were warranted, but you're my daughter, and I love you, and I have your back. Any members of the Athena Sisterhood who want tattoos, they're on the house."

"Thank you." I hugged him, feeling a mix of relief and gratitude.

CHAPTER 43
GOING TO WAR

HAVOC TOOK a seat at my station and asked if I could expand on a back piece she had. I positioned a privacy screen so that she could take off her shirt. An owl, much like the emblem on the back of her vest, extended its wings from shoulder to shoulder just above the band of her bra. She showed me a photograph she'd taken on her phone a year earlier. A line of motorcycles sat parked against the backdrop of a brilliant Arizona sunset over the mountains surrounding Ironwood.

"I'm thinking you could color in the sunset around the owl on my back with the motorcycles below it," she said.

"Photorealism isn't my specialty, and the owl is kind of stylized, but I think I can blend the owl with the sunset and the bikes so that they match."

"Sounds good. Let's do it."

The clash with the Sovereign Sons had rattled me more than I liked. Periodically, I would peek outside the privacy screen to see if they or the other protesters had returned. They hadn't, but I remained paranoid. Also the cuffs had done a number on my wrist, affecting my fine motor skills.

"So, Havoc, how much do you know about the Sovereign

Sons?" I asked as she leaned forward over the back of the chair she was sitting in.

"The Sisterhood's had a few run-ins with them. Why?"

"They were the ones behind the Trans March massacre."

"That doesn't surprise me. They're a bunch of trigger-happy Nazis who see anyone not like them as a threat. I heard the cops arrested one of them at the scene. Another one turned up dead. Third one's still on the loose."

A nervous tremor ran down my spine. They'd found Cameron Shrike's body. "Dead, huh? They know who did it?"

"The first shooter they arrested. Something Byrne. Revoked his bail."

"Wylie Byrne. He's my brother."

"No shit? Wow! Your home life must've been interesting growing up."

"Hadn't seen him since my father kicked me out ten years ago. They arrested Wylie for killing his buddy?" I asked.

"That's what I read. They found a text message from your brother asking to meet behind a building supply company out near Mesa last night. That's where they found this other guy's body. Police think he was tortured before he was killed. Apparently, they had a falling-out. My bet's the dead guy agreed to flip, and your brother found out."

My heart was hammering against my rib cage. I was frankly surprised that my plan to frame my brother for Cameron's death had worked. Now I could only hope that the forensics wouldn't later point to me.

"Did the police confirm the dead guy was the second shooter?" I asked.

"Apparently, the cops matched some of the ballistics from the Pride Parade massacre to an AR-15 they found at the dead guy's house."

"Do the cops know who the third shooter was?"

"Still looking for him, apparently. The media shared a police sketch from witnesses, but I haven't heard a name."

The conversation lagged. My thoughts drifted back to Zoë Hildebrandt. She was alive but undergoing who knew what by people trying to brainwash her into thinking she wasn't trans.

"Have you heard about Zoë Hildebrandt?" I asked Havoc.

"The trans girl who went missing? Yeah. She part of your support group?"

"Yeah, she's a member of the Hatchlings. Her parents are going out of their minds."

"No doubt. I'm raising my niece, and she was kidnapped. There's some really fucked-up people in this world. I hope to God they find Zoë safe."

"Thing is, I know for a fact that her grandfather took her. She's been taken to a conversion therapy camp run by the Sovereign Sons."

"Seriously? How'd you hear this?" Havoc asked.

"I'd rather not say."

"Do the cops know?"

"The cop who was supposed to be looking for her is in on it. She's a member of the Sons."

"Shit. You're sure they have her?" she asked.

"One hundred percent. I just have no idea where this camp is. Somewhere in the mountains near Ironwood."

"I know the Sons have a retreat camp there. Pretty remote, from what I've heard. But I don't know the exact location. Maybe someone needs to pay a visit to the Sons' clubhouse and beat the information out of them."

I chuckled darkly. "I wish I could. But I'm just one person. And I'm still recovering from being shot."

"Hmm… if only there was an organization that hated the Sons, a group with sufficient numbers and firepower that they might be able to get such information out of them."

"You think it's possible?"

"Possible? Yes. Risky? Definitely. Might be better to tell what you know to the cops."

"Except the cops are dirty. At least the one assigned to the case," I said.

"Right. You mentioned that. Well, it's late afternoon on Saturday. In a few hours, you can find them all hanging out at the Iron Eagle. That's their clubhouse."

The name rang a bell. "The Iron Eagle bar? In Mesa?"

Havoc gave me a wary look. "Tell me you haven't been in there."

"Only to use the restroom. But I've been in the Red Mountain Gun Club next to it."

"Both are owned by the Sons. Best to steer clear of them. Unless you're looking for trouble."

"Well, tonight, I'm looking for answers. If that means trouble, I say bring it on. You think the Sisterhood would do this?"

"Me and the other officers would have to put it to a vote, but I'm in. Tell you what—let's take a break. I'll be back in a few."

She got up and signaled to Fuego—the Sisterhood's president—and a few of the other Sisters to follow her. About six of them huddled near the back of the room.

Ten minutes later, Havoc returned. "We'll head out there now before the place gets too packed. I'll let you know what we find out. And if the kid is up at their camp in the mountains, we've got a few members in Ironwood who can be there in no time."

"I'm coming with you," I said.

"Avery, I don't think that's a good idea. Things could get a little rough."

"I can handle rough. Trust me. I survived as a homeless kid on the streets of Phoenix for three years. I know how to fight, and even kill, if I have to."

Havoc looked me over. I wondered if I'd revealed too much. Then she shrugged. "All right. I've got a spare helmet on the back of my bike. You ever ride bitch before?"

"No," I said.

"You're about to learn."

When I called Roz to tell her I wouldn't be home right away, she said, "Babe, what are you thinking, getting in the middle of a gang war?"

"It's not a gang war, sweetie. You hated me trying to find Zoë on my own. Now I've got a few dozen women helping me."

"I know, but…"

"I know you're worried about what could happen. Especially after… last night. But sweetie, if we can get Zoë out of whatever torture camp they're holding her at, we should."

"Avery the avenger. You're the best thing that's ever happened to me. And I need you—now more than ever, with what's happened to my family. I don't want to risk losing you too."

"You won't lose me. Not unless you forget where you put me."

She chuckled. "You dope! I love you."

"I love you too. I'll call you back as soon as we know something."

"Watch your back, don't get shot, and come home safe."

"I will. I promise."

CHAPTER 44
IRON EAGLE

WE REACHED the Iron Eagle bar shortly after sunset. Riding on the back of Havoc's motorcycle was exhilarating. I felt like I was flying as we raced down Grand Avenue to the Loop 202, slipping between lanes when the traffic slowed.

The down side was that the passenger seat was hard and the wound in my thigh was starting to burn. And the day's warmth had faded with the setting sun. My hands felt like icicles. I had a feeling it was going to be a long night.

Already, the parking lot that the bar shared with the gun club was starting to fill up. I'd feared the rumbling thunder of the motorcycles had cost us the advantage of surprise. But once the Sisters had all killed their engines, I heard the rhythmic thump of a bassline and the faint twang of guitars coming from inside the building.

Havoc turned to me after we got off the bike. "How was the ride?"

"Cold."

She pulled an extra bulletproof vest and a pair of gloves from the top case on the back of her bike, where I had stashed my purse. "I don't have an extra jacket, but these might help keep you warm. It's okay if you want to wait here until we can get the location of the camp."

"No way. These fuckers slaughtered my friends, hacked my bank account, and kidnapped Zoë. I'm seeing this to the end."

"Okay, then. Keep your helmet on. It won't stop a bullet, but it'll keep them from seeing your face."

"What about a gun?" I asked.

"You ever used one?"

"Once."

"Unless you really know how to use one, it's best not to. It would be too easy to get yourself into trouble. But the vest and helmet should keep you as safe as the rest of us. Okay?"

"Yeah, okay. Let's just get this done."

We all huddled up near the bikes around Fuego, the MC chapter's president. Like me, the rest of the women had their helmets on and wore Kevlar over their cuts, which I'd learned was what they called their leather biker vests. My pulse raced as the reality of the situation hit me.

"¡Órale, hermanas! Here's the deal," Fuego said to the group. "These *pinche* neo-Nazi *cabrones* are holding a little girl hostage at their camp outside of Ironwood. Our objective is to find out where she is and rescue her. Ideally, without any of us getting shot.

"Savage, Raven, and Hellcat are up there waiting for our call. Once we give them the location, they'll secure the camp until the rest of us get there. These *pendejos* are likely to be armed, but we have superior numbers and the element of surprise. Don't shoot unless you have to. Last thing we want is to leave behind ballistic evidence. If we control the situation properly, we should be okay."

She assigned a group of women to cover the rear entrance. Another few stood guard outside. The rest of us would be going in to rock these fuckers' world.

"Okay, hermanas," Fuego said. "¡*Vamos*! Let's rock their world."

We charged toward the entrance, guns drawn. My heart hammered in my chest, my bullet wound smarting with every stride. But the thought of rescuing Zoë spurred me on.

I felt gravel in the treads of my boots crunch as I walked across the concrete slab floor in the dimly lit bar. The air was thick with the stink of stale beer, cigarette smoke, and pine-scented cleaning products. Nazi and Confederate flags and a neon swastika I hadn't noticed before adorned the wooden walls. A Jason Aldean song played on a jukebox.

One of the Sisters pulled the plug on the jukebox while the rest of us began shouting orders. "Get on the ground! Police! Hands behind your head! Do it now!"

By the time they realized we weren't cops, it was all over. Every one of the dozen or so patrons, as well as the bartender, was face down on the floor.

I pulled a revolver off an old man who'd been sitting at a table with a woman I guessed was his date. I held the gun on them while Havoc frisked them for more weapons.

"Shit!" Havoc held up a detective's shield she'd pulled off the woman.

"You bitches just screwed up big-time," said a familiar female voice.

I looked down to get a better look at the woman. "Hausman. You fucking bitch."

"You know this woman, Tats?" Havoc asked.

I guess I had a nickname now.

"She's the cop who's supposed to be looking for Zoë." I kicked her hard in the ribs with my Doc Martens. "Where the fuck is she, Hausman?"

"You'll never find him." The older man rolled onto his side and glared up at me.

I recognized him from the photo Marilyn had sent me. "You're Colonel Odin, leader of the Sovereign Sons."

"No shit," Havoc remarked. "Guess tonight's our lucky night."

"Real name's Joseph Patterson. He's Zoë's transphobic grandfather. The one who kidnapped her."

"*Zach's* grandfather!" he insisted. "And I didn't kidnap anyone. I'm getting him the help he needs. Away from you child molesters. Fucking men in dresses!"

"The only men in dresses molesting children are Catholic priests, not trans people, you fucking fascist. Zoë was miserable until she was allowed to transition. If you loved her, you'd accept her for who she is."

"Transgenderism is a mental illness. You're all sick."

"Nazism is the real sickness, asshole." I pressed the barrel of his revolver against his temple. "Tell me where she is, or so help me, I will blow your fucking brains out."

"Don't do it, Tats," Havoc warned. "He ain't worth it."

"No, but Zoë is." I looked at Hausman. "What do you think, Detective? Should I splatter his brains all over the floor?"

"You won't do it," Hausman scoffed. "Even with that helmet on, I know who you are. Those tattoo sleeves are a dead giveaway. You're Avery Byrne, that freaky tattoo artist who attacked those people at the library. I'll see that you spend the rest of your life in a men's prison."

"You think I won't shoot him?" I pressed the gun against Patterson's right knee and pulled the trigger. The gunshot echoed in the small bar. Blood and bone splatted across the floor. Patterson started howling.

"Fuck, girl!" Havoc reached for the revolver, but I pushed her away.

"No," I told her. "Someone's going to tell me exactly where she is, or I'm going to keep putting holes in wannabe Hitler here. Now, where the fuck is she?"

From his pitiful screaming, it was clear that Patterson was in too much pain to speak.

When I took aim at his other knee, Hausman cried "Stop! Wait! Don't shoot him again."

I stared at her. "I'm waiting, bitch. Five... four..."

"She's at our compound south of Ironwood," Hausman said with a huff. "Off of Forest Service Road 171 on Red Cedar Lake."

Before I could ask anything else, gunfire erupted outside in the parking lot, followed by a lot of shouting. One of the Sisters who'd been guarding the front ducked inside. "Ladies, we got a problem."

Bullets began flying, shattering the bottles and the mirror behind the bar. One hit the neon swastika on the wall, turning it dark. Another struck Patterson in the chest.

"Everyone! Out the back!" Havoc shouted.

I hurled Patterson's revolver across the room and raced toward the rear door. As I was rounding the bar, I felt a sharp blow in my lower back. My knees buckled, and I hit the floor, gasping for breath and writhing in pain.

"Fuck! Help!"

Arms pulled me to my feet. "Come on! Keep going! Run!"

With Havoc helping me keep my balance, I found the strength to follow the group out the door into the night. My back and my thigh both felt like they were on fire. I collapsed onto the ground.

"You all right, Tats?" Havoc asked.

I stared down at the gravel, gritting my teeth against the pain. "Shot. In back," I managed to say.

Indigo reached under my vest to the focal point of the pain. "You're okay. It didn't penetrate. The vest stopped it."

"Still fucking hurts, don't it?" Havoc said with a chuckle.

"Yeah."

"We gotta get out of here," Fuego said. "Havoc and Indigo, help Avery walk. The rest of us will clear a route to our bikes."

As soon as we came around the side of the building, the air exploded with gunfire. I worried this whole thing had been a mistake. And now I was putting these women at risk as well. *What the fuck was I thinking?*

My ears were ringing when the shooting stopped, but I still managed to hear Havoc shout, "It's clear! Let's go!"

I pushed down the pain into the depths of my mind and forced my legs to keep up with the rest of the women. Havoc climbed onto her bike, and I threw a leg over and gripped her body for dear life. The motorcycles roared to life, and we raced out of the parking lot like rolling thunder. I prayed to the eldritch gods I didn't get shot in the back again.

CHAPTER 45
THE CAMP

THE RIDE UP to Ironwood on the back of Havoc's motorcycle seemed like an endless nightmare. The bitch seat was hard as a rock. The pain in my back and thigh was penetrating my strongest mental walls. More than anything, I wanted to be at home with Roz.

I tried to distract myself by figuring out where we were going. We took a series of freeways from Mesa around the North Valley until we picked up State Route 60, a four-lane divided highway heading northwest through the desert. From then on, I couldn't see much aside from the long line of taillights of the bikes in front of me.

After what felt like an eternity, we turned off the highway onto another road that wound through foothills then twisted through tight mountain turns. Rather than slow down, Havoc leaned the bike hard into each curve. More than once, sparks exploded when the foot pegs scraped the pavement.

I would have enjoyed the thrill ride if I hadn't been in such pain. The air was growing noticeably chillier, and I couldn't help but wonder what would happen if a deer or a family of javelinas crossed the road in front of us. My anxiety and pain level rose when the road we were on became unpaved and riddled with potholes.

Just as the last of my strength was ebbing, we rounded a turn and saw headlights ahead of us. When Havoc slowed to a stop, I saw that they were from two SUVs blocking the narrow road. Two women stood in front, silhouetted by the glare.

"Who are they?" I asked when Havoc killed the engine. Every word formed a cloud of vapor in the chilly air.

"Friends." Havoc put down the bike's side stand, and I immediately slid off. My knees wobbled, forcing me to grab the bike to stay upright.

"You all right?"

"Yeah." I took in a deep cleansing breath and blew out all the pain, or at least, I tried to. "Glad to be off that thing."

"How's your back?"

"Hurts like a motherfucker, but I think I'll live."

With my boots back on terra firma, I started to regain my strength and followed Havoc and the others to the women standing near the trucks.

"Tats, meet my girlfriend, Toni Rios, aka Hellcat." Havoc gestured to a grim-faced Latinx woman I took for a cop.

"Pleasure to meet you, Tats. Sorry about what happened at Phoenix Pride."

"Thanks."

"I'm Savage," said the stocky white woman with a crew-cut, next to Hellcat. "Indigo's wife."

"Savage is an EMT," Havoc added. "In case Zoë needs medical attention."

Hellcat's expression darkened. "Havoc, I think we should contact the sheriff's office. Let them handle this."

"Not a chance." Havoc shook her head. "I know they're your former colleagues, but even with the new sheriff, I don't trust them to protect Zoë or any other trans kids that may be at the Sons' compound."

"That's the thing. Savage, Raven, and I scouted around the camp on foot a little while ago. We saw two men carrying a small body from one of the cabins and taking it off deeper into the woods. They returned thirty minutes later without it. This is a crime scene."

My heart sank. "Was it Zoë?"

"We couldn't tell from a distance. I'm sorry."

The pain in my back, butt, and thigh began to throb once again. I could picture Marilyn's face when I told her Zoë was dead. Still, I clung to the hope that it wasn't her.

"We find Zoë first. Make sure she's safe, assuming that wasn't her they killed. Once she's safe, we can call in the cavalry. So, where is this place?"

"The camp is down the hill about a half mile. No cell signal there, so it's a good thing I brought the sat phone. There are three small cabins and a larger meeting hall. No security cameras, fence, or armed guards, surprisingly. Not much movement either. I have no idea how many people are down there, but there are three pickup trucks and an SUV. My guess is we're facing between five and ten hostiles, maybe more. Likely armed. Raven's still down there with a walkie-talkie and will alert us if she sees anything of interest."

"Okay, gather round, everyone," Fuego said. Three dozen bikers surrounded her. "Our objective is to locate Zoë and any others who are here against their will. We're going to head down on foot. Havoc, Riptide, and Indigo, take the nearest cabin. Rah-Rah, Viper, and Siren, the next. Blitz, Fury, and Rattles, disable their vehicles then hit the farthest cabin. The rest of us will secure the big building. Got it?"

The women nodded.

"I don't know if they heard our bikes, but be prepared for

armed resistance. That said, we're here to rescue at least one child. Possibly others. So don't shoot anyone unless you have to. Understood?"

"But, Prez, they're fucking Nazis," said one woman. "Can't we at least shoot a few of them?"

Fuego shook her head. "Sorry, Riptide. No can do. But feel free to punch as many of them as you like."

That elicited a rumble of laughter from the Sisterhood.

"Once the kids are safely in our custody, we'll call in the sheriff's office to mop up what's left. Okay?"

The others replied that they understood.

Havoc turned to Hellcat. "Check with Raven. See if there's any activity down there."

"Copy that." Hellcat raised her walkie-talkie to her mouth. "Raven, Hellcat. Any movement?"

"Negative, Hellcat. All seems to be quiet here at Stalag 13."

"Roger, Raven. We're on our way."

Havoc turned to me. "You've already taken one for the team. No shame in staying up here with the trucks."

My body wanted nothing more than to take a couple of pain pills and curl up for a nap. But as long as Zoë was in danger, I had to see this through. "I'm going down with the rest of you."

She clapped me on the helmet. "All right, then. Help me and Riptide secure the nearest cabin. Let's go save the girl and rock their world."

I followed Havoc and the others down the hill to a clearing, feeling vulnerable as the only one without a weapon. The sound of three dozen pairs of heavy boots charging toward the camp must have caught someone's attention. Just as we reached the camp, a man in an army utility jacket emerged from the large building.

"Oh shit! We're under assault!" he yelled before disappearing back into the building.

I followed Havoc, Indigo, and Riptide to the nearest cabin, where we found a padlock securing the door from the outside.

"Locked, naturally." Havoc patted down her vest. "Shit, I left my picks at home."

"I got it." I pulled my set from my back pocket. I'd almost forgotten I'd stuck them there. No wonder sitting on the motorcycle seat for so long had started to hurt.

While the other women stood ready with pistols in hand, I set to work with a hook pick and tension wrench. Unlike deadbolts, most padlocks didn't have security pins, so I had the thing open in under a minute. The shank popped, and I removed it from the latch and chucked it into the woods.

I pocketed my picks and opened the cabin door. Havoc rushed in, followed by Riptide and Indigo. I brought up the rear.

The interior of the rough-hewn cabin was illuminated by a weak, flickering bulb, with long, ominous shadows dancing across the wall. The musty air held the scent of pine, sweat, and urine. The floor creaked with each step we took.

Three small bunks with bare mattresses took up the space. A Black teenager lay curled in a fetal position on the nearest one. The other two were empty. Next to the one in the far corner, a white kid with a shaved head sat handcuffed to a metal ring in the wall.

Upon seeing us, both kids wailed in panic.

"Relax, relax," Havoc said, gesturing for the rest of us to lower our weapons. "We're here to rescue you. Does anyone know where Zoë Hildebrandt is?"

"I'm Zoë," whimpered the kid chained to the wall. "Who are you people?"

My heart leapt. I ran to her and pulled off my helmet. "Zoë, it's me. Avery!"

Her eyes widened in recognition. "Avery? What are you doing—"

Automatic gunfire erupted outside in the direction of the main building. The kids again started screaming. I pulled a handcuff key out of my lockpick set and freed Zoë.

"We gotta get out of here," I told Havoc.

Indigo glanced out the door. "Looks like we've got the big building surrounded, but those fuckers aren't giving up without a fight."

A bullet shot through the plywood wall and embedded itself in a two-by-four near my head. A second one hit Riptide. She fell, clutching her side.

Indigo rushed to her. "You're okay. The vest stopped it. But we can't sit here. We have to take cover in the woods."

I turned to the kid who'd been curled up in the bed. "We're taking Zoë home to her parents. You can either come with us, or you can stay here."

"Take me with you," the kid pleaded and hurriedly put on a pair of shoes.

"What's your name?" I asked.

The kid stared at the ground. "My real name's Dante Howard. But I prefer the name Danae."

"Then Danae it is. Did your parents send you here?"

She shook her head. "The youth pastor at my church did. He said he was taking me and a few others camping. But he brought us here."

"What's his name?"

"Reverend James King. He runs the Believers in Christ Church in Glendale."

"I know that place," I replied, shaking my head. "A Black preacher working with Nazis. How pathetic. Do your parents know you're trans?"

"I haven't told them. I was too ashamed."

"Nothing to be ashamed about. But we can deal with that later. Right now, we have to get you to safety. Zoë, where are your shoes?"

"They took them when I refused to say I was a boy." She started to cry. "That's why they chained me to the wall."

"No worries. I'll carry you." I pulled off my Kevlar vest, put it on her, and fit the Velcro straps as tight as I could on her smaller frame. Indigo did the same with Danae.

"Climb onto my back," I told Zoë.

When she did, the spot where the vest had caught the bullet throbbed painfully. But I didn't care. I had Zoë. I just had to get her to safety. Outside, the gunfire continued.

"Let's get out of here!" I shouted. "Hang on!"

I took a big breath, charged out the door, and ran up the hill into the woods. The others followed. Occasionally, bullets zipped past, but I kept running, fueled by pure adrenaline. By the time I collapsed onto a bed of pine needles, the gunfire below had ceased. My lungs burned for air. My heart hammered in my chest.

"I think... we're... safe," I managed. "Anyone hit?"

Indigo sat on a fallen log, catching her breath, with Danae next to her. "We're good. Havoc? Riptide?"

Shea scanned the scene in the clearing below. "Okay."

Riptide gave a thumbs-up, gasping for air.

The camp was a hundred yards below us. I could hear voices shouting but couldn't make out what was being said. From the tone, it sounded as if the Sisters had taken control.

"I think it's safe to go back down now," I said.

"I don't want to go back there." Zoë's voice trembled with fear.

"Don't worry. We're taking you back to your parents. Okay?" *Now for the hard question.* "We saw some men carrying off a body earlier. Any idea who that was?"

Danae and Zoë started crying.

"That was Les Collins," Danae said. "She preferred the name Leslie, though. They kept beating her and using electric shocks. But she wouldn't give in. They killed her."

"Motherfuckers," Riptide said. "We should put a bullet in every single one of them assholes."

"Easy, girl," Havoc chided her. "Don't talk like that with kids present."

"Sorry, VP."

"No worries. Let's head back down there."

CHAPTER 46
DESPERATE ACTS

BY THE TIME we returned to the camp, Fuego and the rest of the Sisterhood had taken the seven members of the Sovereign Sons prisoner and relieved them of their weapons. One member of the Sisterhood had been shot in the arm and was being treated by Savage. Hellcat contacted a friend of hers at the FBI to report the Sons for multiple counts of child kidnapping and abuse and one count of murder.

While we waited for the feds to show up, I managed to find some shoes for Zoë to wear.

"I'm sorry to have caused so much trouble," Zoë said as we waited in one of the Sisterhood's SUVs.

"Trouble? What trouble did you cause?"

"Making all y'all come all the way out here for me. You nearly got killed because of me."

"This isn't on you, Zoë. This is the fault of those men who did these things to you. And your grandfather, who kidnapped you and brought you here."

"But I'm the one that contacted him. I missed him and Meemaw."

"Maybe you did, but that doesn't make what he did your fault. You acted with love, and he acted with hate. Never apologize for being the amazing person you are, Zoë. My foster father once told me that the people who matter won't mind that you're trans. And the people, like your grandfather, who do mind—they don't matter. Your parents love you. They want you home safe."

"Thank you for coming to get me, Avery."

"It's these women you should thank. They're a bunch of badass bikers. And a few of them are trans like you and me."

"I think you're badass. I saw how you fought those protesters at the library all by yourself. I could never be that brave," Zoë said.

"I was an idiot and got myself into trouble. But thank you. And every day you decide to honor your true self, you are being brave."

When the feds arrived, they confiscated everyone's weapons. After Hellcat, who was a retired detective with the Cortes County Sheriff's Office, spoke with them, the feds arrested the Sons. In addition to Zoë and Danae, the Sisterhood rescued five kids from the other cabins.

Emotionally, I was overjoyed with how it had all turned out. Physically, I'd had about all I could take. I hurt all over and was exhausted. Unfortunately, the feds insisted the Sisters and I drive to FBI headquarters in Phoenix to answer questions.

Rather than endure another ride on the back of Havoc's bike, I rode in the van and called Kirsten to let her know that I'd be needing her services yet again. She agreed to meet us there.

I then called Roz after reading a slew of her increasingly frantic texts. "Hey, it's me. I'm okay. Me and the Sisterhood rescued Zoë and six other queer kids. We're on our way back to the Valley now."

"What happened at that bar in Mesa? There was a local news story about a shootout there."

"Yeah, it got a little hairy. But Zoë's safe. I'm safe. One of the Sisters got shot, but I think she's going to be okay. The feds showed up to arrest the Sons for kidnapping, abuse, and murder. They'll probably round up the ones from the bar as well. We're on our way to give our statement to the feds. Then I'll be home. Not sure how long it will take, though."

"You under arrest?"

"No. Kirsten is meeting us there. It should be okay." I hoped, at least.

"I'm so glad. I've been so worried. I've got some good news too."

"Yeah? What?" I asked.

"Mr. Goldstein called from the embassy. They negotiated the release of my mom, my brother, and his wife. They're en route to Jerusalem and plan to fly home in the next day or so."

"I'm so glad your family's safe."

"Yeah, me too. Unfortunately, Hamas still has a lot of hostages. I have no idea when they'll be released. Meanwhile, the IDF continues to slaughter innocent Palestinians. This is so *farkakte*. Poor Torch. His family members are all dead because of this."

"I know."

I wanted to say something more profound and comforting. But I thought of what my foster mother, Melissa, used to tell me: "The world is a fucked-up place filled with a lot of cruel people, Avery. It has been for a long time. It probably always will be. All we can do is help people whenever and however we can."

Melissa was dead now, too, killed by a terrorist's bomb. Which was why I didn't feel a lot of guilt about killing a neo-Nazi like Cameron and shooting Zoë's grandfather. Payback was due.

"I also have news about Danielle," Roz said more somberly. "She's dead."

"What? How?"

"The police reported she hanged herself. I didn't want to believe it, but they found a lot of old scars on her thighs. Apparently, she was a cutter."

"Fuck!" The guilt over what she'd done, coupled with the prospect of spending years in a men's prison, must have been too much for her.

"I also learned who her father was," Roz continued.

"Who?"

"Sergeant Troy Rivers of *The River of Truth*."

"Are you fucking kidding me? He's her father? No wonder he could pay back the scholarship fund. He really had her over a barrel."

"Pretty messed up, huh?" Roz asked.

"Totally. How'd you find this out?"

"I found a way to reactivate the SkipTrakkr account."

"My partner in crime," I said with a smile.

"You know that Sovereign Sons motto that you-know-who spewed the other night?"

She meant Cameron. "I remember. What about it?"

"I'd seen it somewhere, but I couldn't remember where. Then I watched the episode of *The River of Truth* with Danielle. That motto is printed on the background of Sergeant Rivers's videos."

"No shit. So he's a member of the SS," I said.

"Apparently."

"Motherfucker. Well, try to get some sleep, sweetie. I'll be along eventually."

"Be safe, babe."

When we arrived at the FBI headquarters, we were escorted into a large meeting room and told not to talk. There was a video surveillance camera in the corner of the room, so most of us just tried our best to get some sleep on the carpeted floor or sitting in a chair against the wooden table in the middle of the room. An agent took Zoë out to be with her family.

"Avery Byrne?" a woman in a rumpled suit called from the meeting room's doorway.

I pulled myself to my feet. Every muscle ached. "That's me."

"Special Agent Velasco. Please follow me."

I trailed her down a corridor into a smaller room with a square table and three chairs. Kirsten was already sitting at one of them.

"Would you like a cup of coffee or a soda?" Velasco asked.

"No thanks. Let's just get this over with."

"Very well. I'll give you some time to speak with your attorney, and then we can get on with the interview."

"Sorry to get you up again," I told Kirsten.

"Not a problem. I was planning to call you tomorrow anyway. The county attorney has dropped the charges against you for the incident at the library."

"Just in time for the feds to charge me with trying to save some trans kids."

She put a hand on mine. "I don't think that's going to happen. They've already interviewed several members of the Sisterhood. None of you are being charged. The FBI had already been investigating the Sovereign Sons for a number of related crimes. Why don't you tell me what happened?"

I gave her the rundown, and she made some suggestions about what to say and not say. She also warned me that unlike with the cops, lying to the feds was a felony. When in doubt, I should keep my mouth shut. We then called in Agent Velasco.

"So, what can you tell me, Ms. Byrne?"

"I'd been looking for Zoë Hildebrandt since she disappeared, because Detective Hausman didn't seem to have a clue. Said Zoë was a chronic runaway and that she'd turn up. But I knew that was bullshit from talking to Zoë's friends. And it turns out that bitch Hausman was in on it from the start. I saw her meeting with my brother's lawyer outside the gun club and found her at the Son's bar this evening."

"What happened at the bar?"

This was where things got tricky from a legal standpoint. "We walked in. I spotted Hausman having drinks with Joe Patterson, Zoë's estranged grandfather. I questioned them, and Patterson told me where Zoë had been taken."

"He told you where she was? Just like that?"

"We knew they were violent and armed, so we managed to disarm them before things could get out of control. Also, Hausman and Patterson knew they were facing kidnapping charges. Maybe they were hoping they'd get a lesser sentence if they gave her up."

"I'm told that things did turn violent. Patterson is in critical from multiple gunshot wounds. Were you armed?" Velasco asked.

"I don't own a firearm."

"Did you borrow one from one of the bikers?"

"No, I did not."

"Did you shoot Joseph Patterson?"

"Agent Velasco," Kirsten interrupted. "As you may recall, Ms. Byrne risked her life to stop the shooters during the Pride Festival massacre. And while still recovering from her injuries, she did everything in her power to rescue a girl kidnapped by her own grandfather. And the fact that Detective Hausman, a sworn officer with the Peoria Police Department and a detective with their Special Victims Unit, conspired with Patterson... it boggles the mind that you would insinuate that my client had anything to do with him getting shot."

"Ms. Pasternak, listen—"

"No, Agent Velasco, you listen. The transgender community in Arizona has been repeatedly and violently attacked over the past few years. And rather than protect them, law enforcement and the Maricopa County Attorney's Office have been complicit in their persecution."

Go, Kirsten, I thought.

"Ms. Byrne and the Athena Sisterhood, a few of whom are sworn officers themselves, went to the Iron Eagle to peaceably ask questions of the Sovereign Sons criminal organization. This after a confrontation earlier that day in which members of the Sons threatened and shot at Ms. Byrne's place of work."

I pulled up my shirt and showed Velasco my back. "The Sovereign Sons shot me tonight. I'd be dead if I hadn't been wearing a vest. They also shot me at the Pride Festival massacre and murdered many of my friends."

"Ms. Byrne, I..."

"Don't 'Ms. Byrne' me. You want to know who shot Patterson? Look at the Sovereign Sons. Look at Detective Hausman. I suspect she shot Patterson because he told me where Zoë and the other kids were being held. These people are monsters, Agent Velasco. They murdered one of those kids up at their Nazi conversion therapy camp. They'll do anything to protect their secrets, including murdering their own."

I couldn't tell how much Velasco was buying, but I wasn't going to confess to shooting Patterson. And considering that he was facing a whole slew of felonies, he didn't have a leg to stand on. Well, maybe one leg, but not two anymore.

"What happened after you left the bar?"

"We followed the directions Patterson gave us to the Sovereign Sons camp, where we rescued several kids who had been kidnapped and tortured. We're the good guys in all of this."

I expected another slew of questions, but to my surprise,

Agent Velasco said, "Okay, that'll be all for now. Thank you for your assistance. We've been monitoring the Sovereign Sons for a while but were not aware they were murdering and abusing children."

"What's going to happen to the kids we rescued?"

"They'll be returned to their families."

"What about the ones with family members who put them there to be tortured?"

Her face was unreadable. "That will be up to the Department of Child Safety. But if the parents were responsible for putting them in harm's way, the children may be temporarily placed in a foster situation until their safety can be guaranteed."

"Okay." I sighed. "Can I go home now?"

"Yes, but we may have more questions at a later time."

"Then I'll be sure to make up some more answers."

Kirsten shot me a look that said, *What the fuck?*

"Just kidding. I'm cold. I'm hungry. And I'm beyond exhausted. I'm calling an Uber."

CHAPTER 47
THE MAN, THE MYTH, THE ASSHOLE

I FELL ASLEEP the moment my head hit the pillow, Roz's arms around me. I woke around noon when Roz's phone rang. From her joyful tears, I could tell it was her mother calling. She walked into another part of the apartment so as not to disturb me, but by that time, I was already awake.

I had a text message from Marilyn Hildebrandt thanking me for Zoë's safe return and apologizing for not believing my suspicions about Zoë's grandfather. I replied that I understood—that until now, she'd had no reason to distrust cops, and the important thing was that Zoë was home. I went through the list of clients whose appointments I'd missed while recovering from my injuries. Most of them had rescheduled, though I still had the next few days clear.

Detective Rutherford called to let me know that two of the SWAT officers had been indicted by a grand jury for manslaughter. Though there was no guarantee of a conviction, I thanked her for her diligence.

I had lingering questions about all that had happened. I still didn't know who had hacked into my bank account. And I hadn't heard back from Detective Valentine about the death threats I'd received. And I would probably never know whether Danielle killed herself or if she had "help." But what disturbed me more was that her father was Sergeant Rivers.

Danielle hadn't had a chance once the scholarship was revoked. For a girl her age to suddenly face such debt and the threat of legal action would be terrifying. Saying no to such a devil's bargain would have been difficult, even if saying yes to it meant betraying herself and those she loved. Not only had Rivers screwed over his own daughter, but he was also the mouthpiece of the Sovereign Sons, spewing their toxic ideology on his talk show and getting quoted in both the mainstream media and the right-wing echo chambers. I was all for freedom of speech, but his transphobic lies and vitriol fueled the ongoing violence against my community. It was time to shut him up.

I considered tracking him down and putting a bullet in his brain. But that would only make him a martyr. I'd rather have had his rabid fans turn on him like starving dogs smelling fresh meat. It was time to start digging.

Now that Roz had figured out how to hack the Skip-Trakkr app, I could run a full background on Rivers. I also enlisted the help of one of Roz's friends, an IT security consultant and part-time hacker named Becca Alvarez, who could access some of the more protected information I was seeking.

Meanwhile, I did a little research on my own. After locating Rivers's recording studio in downtown Phoenix, I donned a blond wig, put on one of my less goth outfits, and borrowed Roz's spy tools and inconspicuous SUV to do some more surveillance. I managed to find the coffee shop where he bought his three-shot vanilla lattes. Standing behind him in line, I cloned his phone. For two days, I ate, drank, and breathed Sergeant Rivers.

I knew Rivers and his staff concocted conspiracy stories

about trans people with elaborate but phony evidence, but even so, I was shocked by how much time and effort they put into it. His team of writers and researchers weren't the idiots I had expected. Every story they fabricated was crafted for maximum shock value. I could track when each new fake revelation appeared on *The River of Truth* then was later repeated word for word on every other right-wing network. Eventually, the lies and clickbait quotes showed up as headlines on mainstream media to garner more clicks and ad revenue because outrage attracted more eyeballs than actual journalism.

That was just the tip of the iceberg when it came to Sergeant Troy Rivers. I had expected a fat-cat right-wing celeb with influential friends. But what I found shocked even me, with my jaded attitude. And I suspected it might upset Rivers's most devoted fans, particularly military veterans.

But what to do with all I had learned? I considered giving it to *Phoenix Living,* the city's weekly alternative newspaper. An exposé on Rivers would be just up their alley. But what would that accomplish? His fans probably didn't read *Phoenix Living.* For that matter, I'd have bet that a sizable portion of his fans didn't read, period.

I needed to turn Rivers's own influence against him, to find where he was most vulnerable and exploit it. And then it occurred to me. It was time to face the man directly.

I explained my plan to Roz.

"You're joking, right?"

"I'm not," I insisted.

"You want to be a guest on his show?"

"Yep."

"Ave, I think you're obsessed with this man. You've barely slept the last couple of nights. You can't go on his show. He'd eat you alive. And what makes you think he'd even have you?"

"He had Danielle on."

"She was his daughter, and at the time, she had temporarily detransitioned."

"And she was just a regular member of Phoenix Gender Alliance. What would be a better get than for the vice chair to come forth, claiming to have detransitioned and spilling all the dirt on the Alliance. Stuff even Danielle didn't know."

"What dirt?" Roz asked.

"That's the thing. Obviously, there is no dirt. But he doesn't know that. I know how guys like him operate. It's all about ratings and clicks. Since this whole campaign against trans people ramped up a few years ago, his ratings have skyrocketed. Most of his shows are focused on how trans people are supposedly grooming young children, coercing them to go on HRT and get genital surgery. If he thinks he's got someone from the inside who will prove his absurd conspiracies true, he won't be able to resist."

She thought about it for a moment. "I suppose that's better than outright shooting the man."

"There'd be a certain amount of satisfaction in that too," I said with a smirk. "But once I reveal him for the fraud he is, on his own show no less, I think his own disillusioned fans may take care of that for us."

"You sure you want to pretend to be detransitioned? I mean, won't that trigger your gender dysphoria?"

"Big-time. But if it will shut him down, it will be worth it."

"Well, all right, then. Whatever I can do, I'm in."

"Thanks, babe. I'm thinking I might need some additional help," I said.

"Not the Athena Sisterhood again. You might be able to talk yourself onto the show, but I doubt he'd let any of them on."

"Actually I was thinking of Theo Carter, Julio Vega, and Marcus Reid."

"From Phoenix Gender Alliance?"

"Yep, but I doubt Rivers or his staff would clock any of them. All three guys are very buff. I could say they were my bodyguards, that since I resigned from the group, I needed protection."

"I don't understand. Why do you need them?" she asked.

I told her what I planned. And she smiled. "I like it."

I called Julio, Marcus, and Theo and explained the situation and even promised to pay them for their time. Julio couldn't get out of work. But Theo and Marcus agreed to show up once I'd been confirmed as a guest.

CHAPTER 48
SETTING THE TRAP

IN MY RESEARCH ON RIVERS, I'd acquired a list of his entire staff, including his scheduler, Natalie Stern. I called her to get the ball rolling.

"River of Truth Media, this is Natalie. How can I help you?"

I dropped my voice into a male register. "My name's Avery Byrne, the acting chair of the Phoenix Gender Alliance."

"I know who you are."

"But what you don't know is that I go by Andy now." It hurt to say those words. "After seeing Sergeant Rivers's interview with Danny Kirkpatrick, it got me thinking. The last several years of my life have been a lie. I finally came to my senses. I can see through all the brainwashing and mind control and perversions. All thanks to Sergeant Rivers."

"Wow. I'm sure Sergeant Rivers will be happy to hear that, Mr. Byrne."

"I'd like to share this with him personally. He might be interested to know that I just resigned as acting chair of the Phoenix Gender Alliance. I have a lot of information on them he'd be interested in hearing and sharing on his show. I know he's shared a lot, even what his son Danny shared when he was on. God rest his soul. But Danny wasn't one of the officers and doesn't know the organization's dirtiest, most heartbreaking secrets. Solid facts, not rumor or speculation."

"I can certainly talk him to see if he would be interested in having you on. We're booked through the end of the year. If he wants you on, I could probably slot you in in January."

"What I've got can't wait. Children's lives are in peril. I tried to tell the cops, but they wouldn't listen. I heard the feds have arrested dozens of members of the Sovereign Sons. They don't understand what these radicalized trans freaks are doing to these kids. My own brother, Wylie, has taken one for the team for his part at their pathetic Pride parade."

The words I was saying left me feeling nauseous. But I had to be convincing.

"Fair enough. Let me talk to Sergeant Rivers and get back to you."

I gave her my number and ended the call then ran to the bathroom and threw up my breakfast.

"You okay?" Roz was by my side, holding my hair.

When the heaving stopped, I said, "I don't know how I'm going to pull this off."

"I have to say, you were convincing. You even had me worried you'd lost your mind and gone over to the dark side."

"I know who I am. But pretending I'm not, saying these awful lies…"

"You only have to get on the show. And you won't be alone. You'll have me and the guys with you."

A very long and nerve-racking hour later, my phone rang. The caller ID said *River of Truth*.

"Hello?" I answered in my male voice.

"Mr. Byrne, this is Sergeant Troy Rivers."

My insides turned into a hurricane. One part of me was

fist pumping and mouthing, "Yeah!" But a deeper, more emotional part was absolutely terrified. I took a breath, trying to embody the character I was playing. The male me. The fake me. The me I would rather die than become again.

"Nat says you're Wylie's brother."

"That's right. We've been estranged the past few years because... well, frankly, I lost my way. Got swept up in this, whatever you want to call it."

"Transgender derangement syndrome?" Rivers suggested.

"I couldn't have said it better myself. But, Sergeant Rivers, you saved me. I started listening to your show when Danny was on it. I'm sorry about what happened to him. My deepest condolences."

"Thank you, son."

"If it's any consolation, him being on your show opened my eyes. He may have lost his life, but he saved mine. And for the first time, it started to sink in. I started to see through the lies and deceptions that I'd been telling myself for so long. I'm not a woman. I never was. I just got lost along the way."

"And you were the acting chair of the Phoenix Trans-sexual Alliance?"

I didn't bother to correct him on the name. "Yes, sir, I was. I ran the Hatchlings youth group. And I hate to admit I was complicit in so many of the harms we committed, especially to the younger members."

"You were the one who started the fight at the library, when members of our River of Truth Nation tried to take a stand against the grooming and abuse of the children in your organization. That was you, right?"

A little voice in the back of my head told me to be careful how I answered. "I did get into a physical altercation with the people there. I'm truly sorry. As you said, I wasn't in my right mind. But you helped me see God's light. My hope is to stop any more children from being mutilated. I know all of the Alliance's dirty secrets. Will you help me spread the truth?"

There was a long pause, and I wondered if I'd over-played my hand.

"Andy, we would love to have you on the show and help expose these groomers for what they are. How does tomorrow work for you?"

"That would be great," I said.

"Wonderful. I can send you the link to join me via Zoom."

Shit. I hadn't counted on not being in the same room.

"Sergeant, while all this fancy new technology is great. I would love nothing more than to be able to shake your hand in person. I believe your studio's here in Phoenix."

"Well, Andy, if that's what you'd prefer, I would be honored to have you as a live guest." He gave me directions.

"Could I ask one more favor, Sergeant? Since coming to my senses and disavowing the Alliance, I've had a lot of threats on my life. It's gotten so frightening that I've had to hire a few bodyguards."

"I'm so sorry to hear that. But frankly, I'm not surprised. What's the favor?"

"Would you mind if my bodyguards accompany me to the studio? They don't have to come into the recording booth. But just having them close by will make me feel safer. Safe enough to divulge the group's darkest secrets."

"Absolutely. I'll let my staff know to expect them."

"Thank you, Sergeant. I'm looking forward to speaking with you and letting the truth be told."

CHAPTER 49
BOY DRAG

MARCUS STOPPED by the apartment that afternoon with a box of items to help me get into character and look the part. He was a white guy about my height, with a buzz cut and an athletic build that looked believable as a fake bodyguard.

"Thanks for your help with this," I said when I led him to our bedroom.

"If it helps bring that scumbag down, I'm all for it. And to see you in boy drag, well, that would be the cherry on top," he added with a chuckle. "I'm sorry. This isn't going to be too triggering for you, is it?"

I caught a sympathetic glance from Roz. "It was really weird when I was talking to Rivers, pretending to be the old, fake me. Cranked my dysphoria up to eleven, to be honest. But if we can expose Rivers for the fraud he is and save transgender lives, I'm willing to endure a little discomfort."

Roz put an arm over my shoulder. "You'll have Marcus, Theo, and me by your side, so you won't be alone."

"That's right," Marcus added. "You're a real hero, Ave."

There was that word again. Hero. *Do heroes kill unarmed*

men in cold blood, frame their own brothers for the murder, and shoot old men in the knee? Do they illegally clone people's phones and download background reports? Probably not. But if he wanted to call me a hero, well, I'd let him.

Marcus opened the box he'd brought. "Why don't we start by finding a binder that will fit?"

An hour later, we'd decided on a binder to hide my breasts along with a men's dress shirt and slacks for me to wear. The shoes he'd brought were a little tight, but I figured I could manage. The real issue, it turned out, was my hair.

Marcus didn't have a male-styled wig. And I loved my black Bettie bangs and long hair.

"Babe, I hate to say this, but if you're going to pull this off, you may have to cut it."

The thought curled my stomach. "What about that wig shop down on Thomas Road next to the *carnicería*?"

Roz shrugged. "We can give it a try."

The three of us piled into her SUV and drove to Wigs by Stella. Unfortunately, when we got there, we found it had closed for the day.

"Shit. Now what?" I asked.

"I hate to say it, girl," Marcus said, an apologetic look in his eyes, "but my advice is to cut it. We passed a barber shop a block from here."

It seemed stupid that I would have such a physical reaction to a simple haircut. It was fucking hair, after all. It grew back. But the thought of stepping into a barber shop had me questioning this whole ridiculous plan. Maybe I should just turn over what I'd learned to *Phoenix Living* after all.

"My friend Sue's a hairdresser," Roz said. "Her shop's not far from here. Maybe she can give you a haircut that is androgynous enough that it will pass muster with those jerks at the studio, but then afterward, you can restyle into something more goth-punk."

At that point, I didn't have a lot of options. Either I forgot about this ridiculous plan or got the chop. "Okay, call her. See if she can squeeze me in."

At seven o'clock, Sue the hairdresser turned me around in the chair to look at my reflection. Try as I might, I couldn't stop the tears. The male version of myself stared back at me. All my worst childhood memories rushed into my mind, even if I knew intellectually this was all a ruse to expose Rivers.

Sue gave me a side hug. "Don't worry, girl," she said in a sweet Costa Rican accent. "It will grow back again. So many female actors have shaved their heads for a role—Charlize Theron, Demi Moore, Millie Bobby Brown, just to name a few. You still have most of your hair."

"But it looks so…"

"Boyish? I know. But that's the goal. Come back afterward, and I'll modify it so it looks more femme. Okay?"

"I know I'm acting stupid," I said, wiping my face.

"Not stupid," Roz assured me. "You fought hard to live as your true self. This isn't a setback. This is you braving your dysphoria to take down a predator."

I took in a deep breath, inhaling all the love from the people around me—Roz, Marcus, and even my new friend, Sue. It helped.

"Thank you all. I couldn't do this without you."

The next morning, I considered taking a pill to ease my nerves and help with residual pain in my back where the bullet had hit my vest and left a bruise the size of a grapefruit. But I decided it was better to keep my wits sharp, and I settled for a couple of ibuprofen instead.

I spent an hour getting ready in the bathroom. I refused to let Roz see me until I was done.

When I stepped out, she gasped. "Holy shit! It's still you but definitely a guy version of you. Gender is so weird."

"You think I'll pass?"

"Definitely. I mean, the story is you transitioned for ten years and only recently switched back. So the feminine softness of your face is totally believable. And if you start to freak out, just think about what these fuckers did to Zoë and the others. You're going in as a spy to take them down. It's just a role."

"I keep telling myself that," I said.

Marcus and Theo met us in the parking lot of the studio shortly before nine.

"Fuck me," Theo said, doing a double take. "I hardly recognize you, Avery."

"It's Andy now. At least until we get this interview going." I handed him a USB drive and told him and Marcus the game plan. "The video file named 'dirtysecrets.mov' is the only thing on here."

"I'll make sure they play it when you give the signal."

The four of us marched into the River of Truth lobby. I gave the receptionist my deadname, and she directed us to a small waiting room. In the broadcast biz, it would be called a green room, but the walls were a sickly beige, not green. A half dozen chairs surrounded a small table in the middle, covered with a Bible and a stack of religious and gun-nut magazines. *Praise Jesus and pass the ammunition.*

We weren't there long before Sergeant Troy Rivers walked in. I stood, my pulse quickening.

"Andy?" Rivers extended his hand.

The name was a cue, and I dropped my voice. "Pleasure to meet you, Sergeant. Thank you for giving me the opportunity to tell my story."

"Well, as the name implies, we are about spreading the truth to all who have ears to hear. My producer, Ethan Crane, will be in the control booth. He'll play our intro, and then we'll jump right into the interview. Okay?"

"Sounds good." I introduced Theo, Marcus, and Roz then added, "I brought some video interviews with some of my former associates that I think your viewers and listeners will find revelatory. Theo has the video file on a USB drive."

"Well, I'm excited to see them. Normally, I would prefer to preview them prior to airing to help me prep questions, but in light of the circumstances, I say let's trust in the Lord. Speaking of which, shall we pray?"

I so wanted to say, "Hell no!" But I reminded myself that I was playing a role.

"Certainly."

The five of us huddled up. "Dear Lord Jesus, I thank you for bringing these young people here today and ask that their message of truth reach the hearts of each of my listeners and viewers. Open their hearts and minds so that your river of truth flows through them. In your precious name we pray, Amen."

The rest of us echoed "Amen," and we followed Rivers into the control room. A scrawny guy with wire-rimmed glasses sat in front of a large control panel with three video screens and an array of knobs and switches.

"Ethan, meet my guest Andy Byrne."

I shook his hand, which was as clammy as a dead fish.

"Pleasure to meet you, Andy. I'm looking forward to hearing what you have to share," he said.

"Thanks."

"Ethan, Andy's friends will hang out here with you during the show. Her friend Theo has a thumb drive with a video file that we'll play. Andy says it will be quite the revelation."

"You got it, boss."

"Excellent." Rivers checked his watch. "Two minutes to showtime. Let's do this thing."

I followed him into the soundproof recording booth. A large plate glass window separated the booth from the control room. Rivers gave me a set of headphones, and we each sat on a stool in front of a mic.

My pulse was racing, and I had to take some deep breaths to steady my nerves. Rivers gave me a smile as the show's intro played. *Keep smiling, asshole,* I thought.

CHAPTER 50
SHOWTIME

"HELLO, patriots, and welcome to today's episode of *The River of Truth*. As always, I'm your host, Sergeant Troy Rivers. Retired Special Forces. Congressional Medal of Honor winner. Veteran of both Iraq and Afghanistan. Recipient of the Purple Heart and the Silver Star. And having proudly served my country and fought for freedom, I'm here now, fighting for truth, even as our country is assaulted by the woke mafia who want to take away your rights to life, liberty, and the pursuit of happiness.

"Today, I have with me a very special guest. And when I tell you who he is, you may wonder if Old Sarge has lost his marbles. But trust me, dear listeners, I have not. Many of you may know that I recently lost my son Danny."

His voice choked with emotion, and I, too, felt a heaviness in my heart.

"Danny was a good kid who fell in with a bad crowd. I'll admit he was always a bit sensitive—his mother's fault if I'm being honest. And it made him susceptible to the twisted perversions of the Phoenix Transsexual Alliance. They preyed upon him at a time when he was just a teen and while his mother and I were having marital issues. They groomed him and brainwashed him into thinking he was a girl and that he'd find happiness if he took hormones and mutilated his body."

I felt my anger rise at Rivers's mischaracterizations, but I tried to play along.

"But did he find happiness? No. He found only lies and deception. And when his life fell apart—as it was bound to do, by God's grace—he came to the people who he knew in his heart loved him. Like the prodigal son, I welcomed him back without judgment. I knew what a twisted, perverted world we lived in. We helped him out financially and provided him with the proper Christian counseling he most desperately needed. And he came on this very show to speak his truth."

I grew increasingly uncomfortable sitting on the stool. I wanted nothing more than to run screaming from this place. But when I spotted Roz, stone-faced in the control room, I remembered that I wasn't alone.

"Sadly, the radical transsexuals hated my son for revealing their lies and deceptions. And so they mounted a witch hunt against him, accusing him of making a bogus 911 call. The shame of being falsely accused drove my son to attempt suicide. My guest today saved him and helped him get medical attention. But sadly, it was not enough. He was arrested, and then alone in his cell, away from the people who loved and supported him, he took his own life.

"But thanks to my guest today, my son's voice will continue to be heard. Because my guest is none other than Andy Byrne, until recently the chairman of the Phoenix Transsexual Alliance. Andy has at last come to his senses. And he is here today to expose this evil Alliance for the child abusers they are. Welcome to the show, Andy."

"Thank you." The words came out too feminine. I dropped my voice. "Thank you, Sergeant Rivers."

He laughed. "Bad habits are hard to break. But don't

worry. We're all here to support you and hear what you have to say. Why don't we start with a little of your background. What kind of home environment did you have when you grew up?"

Since confirming the interview, I had spent time going over how I would answer Rivers's questions. "Well, to be honest, Sergeant, not a good one. My dad was abusive to my mom, me, and my little brother."

"So, not a Godly man," he replied.

"No, definitely not."

"And not a very good role model of what a husband and father should be. No wonder you got your wires crossed. Where you ever sexually molested?"

"Not that I can recall."

"Yeah, well, sometimes we can repress such memories. But the damage can still be there. Them homosexuals do like to prey on little kids."

I wanted to punch him in his fat face and say, "No we don't." But again, I held back and stuck to the role.

"Needless to say, growing up in such a godless, dare I say dysfunctional environment, it's understandable that you were confused about being a boy. Who would want to be an abuser like their old man? So, what happened?"

"My father kicked me out of the house when I was thirteen. And I transitioned on the street."

"Just so my viewers and listeners understand, what do you mean when you say 'transitioned'?"

"I started taking black market hormones. Started wearing makeup. Just living as a girl."

"No surprise. The streets are no place for a kid. Did you work as a hooker?"

"Yeah." A lie.

"Let's cut to today. You're in your early twenties now. And until recently, you were living as a woman, working at a sleazy tattoo parlor. And worst of all, you were the chairman of the Phoenix Transsexual Alliance, an organization that targets young children, convinces them that they're transsexual, and encourages them to take hormones and mutilate their young, growing bodies. Is that correct?"

Controlling my temper became more difficult with every hateful, deceitful word out of his mouth. It was time to rock his world.

"You know, Sergeant, just me saying what this organization does really won't do it justice. Honestly, I don't think your viewers would believe me. But I brought a video of some interviews that frankly will shock your fans. Can we play that?"

"Absolutely! Folks, I have not had a chance to preview what we're about to see, but I have a feeling we're about to be shocked and amazed. Ethan, go ahead and play it."

As soon as Rivers gave the cue, Ethan started the recording. I could see it playing on a small monitor on the floor in the recording booth. At the same time, Marcus stepped to the door separating the two rooms.

"Hi, everyone. My name is Avery Byrne. I am a transgender woman. What I'm about to share with you may shock you. But I swear it is the absolute truth."

The video cut to me on a Zoom call that I had recorded. On half of the screen was a stern-faced man in a US Army dress uniform.

"Please introduce yourself."

"I am Colonel Gabriel Hawkins of the US Army Seventy-Fifth Ranger Regiment."

"Are you familiar with Sergeant Troy Rivers?"

"I do not know the man personally, but I do know of him," Hawkins said.

"What the hell is this?" Rivers blurted, anger coloring his face.

"It's the truth! That's what your show's all about isn't it, Sergeant?"

"Stop the video!" he shouted at his producer on the other side of the glass.

However, Theo had pushed poor Ethan to the corner of the room. Roz now sat at the control panel. Meanwhile, Marcus had wedged a chair against the door separating the two rooms.

"Did Troy Rivers ever serve in the Seventy-Fifth Ranger Regiment?" I asked Colonel Hawkins as the video continued to play.

"I have checked our records, and there is no evidence that he served in this unit or in any unit of the United States Army. There have been a number of people named Troy Rivers who have served, but I am fairly certain that the man who hosts the *River of Truth* talk show isn't one of them."

Rivers tried to exit the recording booth, but the door wouldn't open. He pounded on it and yelled, "Open this door, or so help me I will have you people arrested!"

"So, did the man claiming to be Sergeant Troy Rivers ever receive a Congressional Medal of Honor or a Purple Heart or anything?"

"No, ma'am, he did not," Hawkins said.

"He's not even a sergeant?"

"Not in this man's army."

"Is there a name for what he's done?"

"It's called stolen valor. It's a disgrace. And if he's used it for fraudulent purposes, it is a federal crime."

Rivers turned on me, looking like an enraged bull. "You have them open this door or, so help me, I will kill you."

He looked like he meant it. But now that the jig was up, I was no longer upset. No longer afraid. I was Avery the avenger.

"You lied to me!" he spat.

"You lie every damned day. Worse, you're responsible for the deaths of dozens of people, including your daughter Danielle."

"Danny killed himself."

"With your help. Turns out you're on the Quinn Fund board of directors. You pressured them to revoke Danielle's scholarship, threatening her with legal action. Then you swooped in with an offer she couldn't refuse. But she couldn't live with the guilt of what you drove her to do, much less the thought of spending years in a men's prison. She and so many others are dead because of you."

The video had switched to a different interview. I pointed to the monitor. "Hey, look! Isn't that your ex-wife?"

"Why does he call himself Sergeant?" the video showed me asking the woman on the screen.

"It's not a rank. It was the name his parents gave him. Like Sargent Shriver or Major Garrett. Or Judge Reinhold."

"So this whole thing about him being an army ranger—"

"It's a lie. The man is a compulsive liar," his ex-wife said.

"But he set up a fund to raise money for homeless vets. Is that a lie too?"

She nodded, wiping tears with a crumpled tissue. "The last year we were married, I helped him set up the fund. The whole thing was a scam. Not a penny he raised went to provide housing to homeless vets or to pay for their physical therapy. It went to him to fund his private army."

"What army? The US Army?"

"No, the Sovereign Sons. They are a racist, misogynist neo-Nazi militia. The worst people imaginable. They're violent and hateful, and many are convicted criminals. But he sends them out to do his dirty work."

Rivers screamed with rage. "It's a lie! It's a lie! Don't believe that fat, ugly bitch!"

"Your listeners can't hear you," I told him. "All they hear is the video. You're done."

"You're going to regret this, you perverted freak!"

"Maybe. But I'm taking you down with me. The feds have taken control of the Sons' camp up near Ironwood and the bar and gun club in Mesa. They'll be coming for you next. They'll get you on multiple counts of wire fraud, kidnapping, and murder. *The River of Truth* is nothing but a fetid, dried-up swamp."

He swung at me. I dodged and drove the heel of my palm into his nose, followed by a knee to the groin. When he fell, I kicked him in the ribs for good measure. "That's for Danielle."

Marcus and Theo rushed in, but I didn't need rescuing. Rivers was down for the count in more ways than one.

CHAPTER 51
REMEMBRANCE

OFFICERS from the Phoenix Police showed up after about twenty minutes. Rivers naturally tried to accuse us of kidnapping him and holding him against his will. He demanded the officers arrest us at once and drag our sorry asses to jail.

But his producer, poor little old Ethan, told a different story. He said that the door between the recording booth and the control room had been sticking a lot lately. He also concurred with our story that he, being shocked by the contents of the interviews, chose to let them play over the air despite Rivers's demands to cut the feed and stop the video.

Not that I blamed poor Ethan. Marcus had let him know that we had him on video sleeping with an underage girl at a strip club known as the Pussy Palace. Technically, the girl he slept with wasn't underage. She was a youthful-looking friend of mine who worked at the club and had reached out to me when she'd heard through the grapevine what I was planning to do.

We met Roz's family at the airport the following morning. The embassy in Jerusalem had taken a few days to issue new passports. As soon as they walked past the security gate, Roz rushed to meet them. I was so happy for her to have them home. And I was a little bit jealous. They were a normal family. Loving, teasing, encouraging. Something I hadn't had growing up. At least, not until I met Bobby and Melissa when I was sixteen.

"Hey, you!" Roz called to me. "Get your ass over here! You're family too."

Am I? I supposed I was in a way. Grafted in. A shiksa in a beautiful Jewish family. As I joined in the group hug and met her brother and his family for the first time, I thought about Torch and the loved ones he would never see again.

A week later was Halloween, the celebration of a new year for a semi-Pagan goth like me. I was at Seoul Fire bright and early. I was still sore from the past week's adventures, but I was healing. And Sue had done her magic on my hair to make it more feminine, with the help of some product. I decided to keep the sides shaved for a while. Everyone at the studio was shocked to see the new do. And naturally, Bobby immediately escorted me to the back room for a father-daughter talk.

"How are you doing, kiddo?" he asked after giving me a hug.

"Honestly, I feel good, Appa."

"Really?" He sounded skeptical.

"Zoë is safe. My brother and the rest of the Sovereign Sons are behind bars, including Sergeant Rivers. One of the Pride Festival shooters is dead. The third one has been identified and arrested. And there are no more protesters outside the studio."

"That's good to hear. I saw on the news that two Phoenix police officers have been arrested for shooting your friend Sophia and her boyfriend."

"Yeah, Detective Rutherford called me about that. Question is, will they be convicted?" I said.

"We can only wait and see. Oh, and your mother called."

"Who?"

"Your mother, Jacqueline. She called the main studio number. I think she would like to get to know you. The real you."

"That woman is not my mother."

"My beautiful daughter." He placed a hand on my arm. His dark eyes touched a place in my heart only he could reach. "Melissa and I were so blessed to be for you what she could not. We are truly family, you and I. But she, too, is family. She gave birth to you. She raised you. And yes, I know, she failed to protect you from your father's abuse. She made many mistakes and has much to atone for. But I encourage you to consider giving her that chance."

"I liked it better when I could just hate her for being a lousy mother," I said.

"Yes, hate can be difficult to give up. But forgiveness brings healing and peace. You have had such a troubled life, especially for one so young. I can't think of anyone who needs healing and peace more. So will you return her call?"

"I'll consider it."

"I watched the video you made. The whole thing, not just the little bit that was shown on the Sergeant Rivers show. I was impressed. You are so very smart. Perhaps you should give another thought to going to college."

"Appa, please. We've been over this. What can college give me that I don't already have? I have a career that I enjoy and make a good living at with people I love and respect. And I'm sure I'll come to respect Dakota too. Assuming they don't steal all my clients."

"They are a very nice person. I think you'll come to love them the way you love Frisco, Butcher, and me."

"I could never love someone the way I love you, Appa.

You saved me."

"You were worth saving."

We hugged.

"When is your first client?" he asked.

I glanced at my watch, but before I could answer, Dakota poked their head through the door. "Hey, Avery. Your client's here."

"Go make some magic, kiddo."

That night, Roz and I hosted the Hatchlings Halloween party in the community room at our apartment complex. One of the great things about living in a queer-friendly complex was that no one was going to boot us out for being trans.

I was dressed as a black cat, complete with tail and whiskers. Roz was the legendary pirate Anne Bonny. Bobby came dressed as a Jedi, naturally. And Jinx Ballou showed up in a Wonder Woman costume that looked better than the one in the movies.

The kids came dressed up as fairies, princesses, super-heroes, zombies, and all sorts of characters. And to every-one's delight, I had convinced Damaged Souls to provide the musical entertainment.

A few weeks later, the Phoenix Gender Alliance and hundreds of members of the Valley's LGBTQ+ community and allies gathered outside the Valley Church of Hope for a candlelight vigil honoring the Transgender Day of Remembrance.

Standing with me were Roz and her mother, brother, and sister-in-law as well as Bobby J., Dana, Frisco, Butcher, and Dakota. I spotted Zoë and her parents in the crowd along with Theo, Marcus, Kimi, Chupa, and the rest of the guys from Damaged Souls.

But the biggest surprise was that my birth mother, Jacqueline Byrne, had shown up. We each held an unlit candle and a long list of names.

Reverend Aisha, the church's pastor, lit his candle. "This past year has been especially challenging for the transgender community and for those of us who love them. The violence during the Trans March highlighted how dangerous it can be to live as one's true self. Trans women of color continue to be the ones who suffer the worst of it.

"But so long as we stand strong, arm in arm, hand in hand, heart to heart, we will overcome. Because light will always overcome darkness. And love will always conquer hate. Together, we can open hearts, change minds, and transform the world. In the words of Reverend Martin Luther King Jr., 'We shall overcome because the arc of the moral universe is long, but it bends toward justice.'"

I wasn't a religious person, but something about Reverend Aisha's words struck me.

"And so tonight, we honor those we have lost over the past year, starting with Jasmine Washington." Reverend Aisha lit the candle of the woman standing next to him.

When the glow lit up her face, I recognized her as Detective Rutherford. "Jacob Williamson." She lit the candle of the next person, who was her brother, Chris.

"London Price." Chris lit Jinx Ballou's candle.

"Lisa Love," Jinx said.

"Dominic Dupree," Colleen Kirkpatrick, Danielle's mother, said when her candle was lit.

Sophia said, "Luis Ángel Díaz Castro."

I lost track of the number of names, but by the end, we were all sobbing. I hated that we lived in a world that treated us like vermin, a world where our younger members could be deprived of life-affirming medical care, a world where kids could be tortured, our books could be banned, and the very words *transgender* and *gay* could be forbidden from being spoken in a school.

Avery the avenger couldn't change such a world. Even exposing Rivers for the liar and hypocrite he was wouldn't be enough. There would always be more talking heads, more mass shootings, more dirty cops, and more hatred than all the love in the world could extinguish.

My mother caught my eye and put an arm around me in the increasing glow of the candlelight. "Cashay B. Henderson," she said, reading the next name on the list.

"Maria Fer," I followed.

I looked out on the sea of faces in the flickering glow of candlelight and realized I couldn't stop all the violence against our community. No one could. But maybe Reverend Aisha was right. Together, we might make a difference.

Melissa had once told me, "Every time we choose compassion over cruelty, speak truth to power, and stand up for the vulnerable and the oppressed, we make the world a little brighter and safer for us all."

Is Avery the avenger making the world brighter? I didn't know. But it was certainly safer. Cameron Shrike would never murder another trans person. Zoë was once again home with her family. And Sergeant Troy Rivers had been exposed for the fraud he was and now faced years in prison, as did Joseph Patterson, Detective Hausman, Wylie, and the other members of the Sovereign Sons. I could sleep better knowing that.

∾

ENJOY A BONUS SHORT STORY

Did you enjoy *A Plague of Grackles*? Would you like a free bonus story? No need to subscribe. No strings attached. Just click the link below to read.

https://dharmakelleher.com/pages/a-plague-of-grackles-bonus-content

AUTHOR'S NOTE

I came out as transgender thirty years ago in the suburbs of Atlanta. I'd known I was a girl since I was five but didn't have the vocabulary to explain why someone with a boy's body would feel like a girl.

No one had groomed me. I'd never been sexually abused. It was simply how my brain was wired. And the gender dysphoria that began in childhood only grew worse when I reached puberty. My body was changing in all the wrong ways.

In college, I thought I might be gay even though I was attracted to women. It wasn't until transgender model Caroline Cossey posed nude in a men's magazine that I realized what I was and decided to transition.

I lost everything—my marriage, my home, my family, my friends, my church, and my job. My mother called me an abomination. Atlanta Gender Explorations, a support group started by Dallas Denny, saved my life. There, I found the love, acceptance, and support I needed.

In the 1990s and early 2000s, life for most transgender people improved. More and more people recognized that we weren't crazy or perverted or a threat to women or children.

We were simply different. We just wanted to live our lives in bodies that fit our gender identity.

We appeared on magazine covers and as characters in TV shows played by trans actors. The world was finally starting to see us as we were. That's not to say things were easy. And trans people, especially trans women of color, were still murdered at appalling rates.

Then fascism raised its ugly head. The heady days of the Obama administration gave way to the vitriol and violence of Trump and his MAGA movement. States began once again banning trans kids from athletics and restrooms that matched their gender identities. They banned our books and passed laws banning gender-affirming care, despite overwhelming evidence of how it saves lives.

And rather than taking a stand against this kind of fascism, the mainstream media gave it a greater voice. They now publish clickbait stories that spread the outrageous transphobic claims of the right, often uncontested by the truth. Even the *New York Times* and *Newsweek* publish articles that are nothing more than misinformation and hate because outrage generates clicks to sell ads.

The names listed in the Trans Day of Remembrance chapter were actual transgender people murdered in 2023. You can find the complete list at *https://glaad.org/tdor-memoriam/*. Note that this list does not include people who took their own lives because of relentless harassment, violence, and anti-trans legislation.

As much as I would rather write about topics other than the fight for transgender civil rights, I cannot remain silent when so many transgender people are dying. We are being denied the most basic of civil rights. And writing these books is the best way I know how to fight.

While I was writing the first draft of this novel, the war in Gaza broke out. And because I set the story in October

2023, with one major character Jewish and another Palestinian American, I felt the need to recognize it.

My great-grandmother, Virginia Gottlieb, was Jewish, as was my ex-husband, my best friend in college, and many of my friends now. I love the Jewish people and believe that Israel has a right to exist.

At the same time, I also have friends who are Palestinian. One friend, a professional photographer with no connections to Hamas, had her home blown up by the Israeli army. They killed her family members.

Both Israelis and Palestinians deserve to live in freedom, safety, and peace. While Israel has a right to exist, the occupation by Israel of the Palestinian territories is wrong. The illegal settlements in Palestinian territories are wrong. The Hamas terrorist attacks on Israeli civilians are wrong. Hamas taking Israelis hostage is wrong. And murdering innocent civilians is wrong, Israeli and Palestinian alike.

I don't know what the solution is. There is no magic formula for creating peace when so many people in this world are filled with hate and prone to violence—when so many have abandoned responsibility, compassion, and integrity for greed, power, and cruelty. So many of the institutions that were once bulwarks against tyranny have become corrupted and are now used as tools of fascism.

All too often, the people with the power to stop the decay of democracy have abdicated their responsibility. Rather than hold men like Trump, Netanyahu, and Putin accountable for their criminal behavior, they choose to line their pockets, oppress the vulnerable, and support the rich white patriarchy.

If each of us who cares for our fellow person can attempt to educate ourselves to the truth, speak out against the lies, act with compassion for those in need, protect the vulnerable, vote against fascism and patriarchy, and stop supporting people and institutions who foment hate, cruelty, and violence —and without lowering ourselves to that level—then we can make this a brighter, safer, and more loving world for us all.

Transphobia and homophobia must end.

Antisemitism and Islamophobia must end.

The denial of reproductive rights must end.

Racism must end.

Hatred and cruelty toward immigrants must end.

Corruption and propaganda must end.

We can no longer sit on the sidelines.

We must act with compassion.

We must embrace diversity.

We must embrace rigorous honesty and integrity.

We must hold ourselves and our leaders accountable.

Let's make a world where people are free and safe and where they can make a livable wage with affordable housing and medical care, clean air, and water. It starts with love.

Will you join me?

With love,

Dharma Kelleher

ENJOY A FREE E-BOOK

Download a free copy of *Blood and Fire*, a Jinx Ballou novel, by subscribing to Dharma Kelleher's Readers Club at dharmakelleher.com/subscribe.

Join now to receive special offers, exclusive behind-the-scenes details, cover reveals, new release announcements, and to **get your free e-book**.

You can unsubscribe at any time.

ABOUT THE AUTHOR

Dharma Kelleher writes crime thrillers where queer women kick ass. As the most prolific transgender author in her genre, she entertains readers with action-packed stories and a diverse cast of characters, while exploring themes of justice, trauma, community, and moral conflict. Learn more about Dharma and her work at https://dharmakelleher.com.

ACKNOWLEDGEMENTS

Even in the world of self-publishing, bringing forth a new book into the world is always a team effort.

Let me start by thanking every member of the transgender community. It is not easy for us to live as our true selves. It takes courage, persistence, and deep level of self-trust. But it also takes the generosity of community to reach out and lift each other up. We are stronger together.

For their brilliant editing skills, I want to thank my editors at Red Adept Editing.

Last, but certainly not least, I want to thank all my loyal fans, especially those who buy direct from my website. Together, we are making the world a better, safer place for us all. Hugs!